A visitor from outer space

meets his match in a Southern cracker-woman

A baby's brain, growing in a computer

threatens to destroy the world

The compleat servo-machanistic city

with one helpless technician at its mercy

... these are some of the highly original and vividly written stories you will find in this selection from a master's work.

Writing of this quality and imignation is the reason why science fiction and fantasy grow constantly in popularity. This is why more and more people are becoming devotees of that intriguing fiction which is not content to stay in the world as we see it and know it, which takes us to the farthest reaches of space and time, to the farthest reaches of the human mind.

Also by the same Author . . .

CONDITIONALLY HUMAN*

*Available from Ballantine Books. For a complete catalogue of Ballantine Books, write in care of Dept. C.S., Ballantine Books, Inc., 101 Fifth Avenue, New York, N.Y. 10003

THE
VIEW FROM
THE STARS

Walter M. Miller, Jr.

BALLANTINE BOOKS   NEW YORK

Printed in Canada

First Ballantine Printing: January 1965

Ballantine Books, Inc., 101 Fifth Avenue, New York, N.Y.   10003

TABLE OF CONTENTS

You Triflin' Skunk!

THE RAIN SANG light in the sodden palmettos and the wind moaned through the pines about the unpainted shack, whipping the sea of grass that billowed about the islands of scrub. The land lay bathed in rain-haze beneath the pines. Rain trickled from the roof of the shack and made a rattling spray in the rivulets under the eaves. Rain blew from the roof in foggy cloudlets. Rain played marimba-sounds on the wooden steps. A droopy chicken huddled in the drenched grass, too sick to stir or seek a shelter.

No road led across the scrublands to the distant highway, but only a sandy footpath that was now a gushing torrent that ran down to an overflowing creek of brackish water. A possum hurried across the inundated footpath at the edge of the clearing, drenched and miserable, seeking higher ground.

The cabin was without a chimney, but a length of stovepipe projected from a side window, and bent skyward at a clumsy angle. A thin trail of brown smoke leaked from beneath the rain-hood, and wound away on the gusty breeze. In the cabin, there was life, and an aura of song lingered about the rain-washed walls, song as mournful as the sodden land, low as the wail of a distant train.

Whose hands was drivin' the nails O Lord?
Whose hands was drivin' the nails?
Lord O Lord!
My hands was drivin' the nails O Lord!
My hands was drivin' the nails
And I did crucify my God!

The song was low and vibrant in the cabin, and Lucey rocked to it, rolling her head as she sang over the stove, where a smoked 'possum simmered in pot-likker with sweet-taters, while corn bread toasted in the oven. The cabin was full of food-smells and sweat-smells, and smoky light through dusty panes.

7

From a rickety iron bed near the window came a sudden choking sob, an animal sound of almost unendurable torment and despair. Lucey stopped singing, and turned to blink toward the cry, sudden concern melting her pudgy face into a mountain woman cherub's face, full of compassion.

"Awwwwwww . . ." The sound welled unbidden from her throat, a rich low outpouring of love and sympathy for the sallow twitching youth who lay on the yellowish sheets, his eyes wild, his hands tensing into claws.

"Awwww, Doodie—you ain't gonna have another spell?" she said.

Only a small hurt this time, my son. It can't be helped. It's like tuning a guitar. You can't do it without sounding the strings, or pulsing the neural fibers. But only a small hurt this time. . . .

The youth writhed and shuddered, stiffening into a puppet strained by steel springs. His back arched, and his muscles quivered. He flung himself suddenly into reflexive gymnastics, sobbing in small shrieks.

Lucey murmured softly. An immense mass of love, she waddled toward the bed in bounces of rubbery flesh. She bent over him to purr low in her throat.

"Poor Doodie . . . poor li'l Doodie. Mama's lamb."

The boy sobbed and thrashed. The paroxysm brought froth to his lips and jerked his limbs into cramped spasms. He jerked and writhed and tumbled on the bed.

"You jus' try to lay calm, Doodie. You jus' try. You gonna be all right. It ain't gonna last long, Doodie. It's gonna go away."

"No!" he whimpered. "No! Don't touch me, Mama! *Don't!*"

"Now, Doodie . . ."

She sat on the edge of the bed to gather him up in her massive arms. The spasms grew more frantic, less reflexive. He fought her, shrieking terror. She lay beside him, moaning low with pity. She enveloped him with her arms, enfolding him so that he could no longer kick. She pulled his face into the hollow of her huge bosom and squeezed him. With his tense body pressed tightly against the bulky mass of her, she melted again with love, and began chanting a rhythmic lullaby while he twitched and slavered against her, fighting away, pretending to suffocate.

Gradually, as exhaustion overcame him, the spasm passed. He lay wheezing quietly in her arms.

The strings are tuned, my son, and it was only a small hurt. Has the hurt stopped, my son?

Yes, father, if only this monstress would let me be.

Accept my knowledge, and be content. The time will come.

"Who you whisperin' to, Doodie? Why are you mumblin' so?" She looked down at his tousled head, pressed tightly between her breasts.

His muttering ceased, and he lay quietly as if in a trance. It was always so. The boy had fits, and when the paroxysm had passed, he went into a rigid sleep. But it was more like a frozen moment of awareness, and old Ma Kutter said the boy was "witched." Lucey had never believed in "witchin'."

When he was tensely quiet, she tenderly disengaged herself and slid off the bed. He lay on his side, face toward the window, eyes slitted and mouth agape. Humming softly, Lucey returned to the stove and took a stick of oak out of the bucket. She paused to glance back at him—and he seemed to be rigidly listening to something. The rain?

"Doodie. . . ?"

"When are you coming for us, father?" came in a ghost whisper from the bed. "When, *when?*"

"What are you talking about, Doodie?" The cast-iron stove-lid clattered on the hot metal as she lifted it nervously aside. She glanced down briefly at the red coals in the stove, then back at Doodie.

"Very soon . . . very soon!" he whispered.

Lucey chucked the stick of wood in atop the coals, then stood staring at the bed until the flames licked up about the lid-hole to glisten orange on her sweat-glazed face.

"Who are you talkin' to, Doodie?"

She expected no answer, but after several seconds, his breathing grew deeper. Then it came: "My *father.*"

Lucey's plump mouth went slowly shut and her hand quivered as she fumbled for the stove lid.

"Your pa is dead, Doodie. You know that."

The emaciated youth stirred on the bed, picked himself up slowly on one arm, and turned to look at her, his eyes blazing. "You lie!" he cried. "Mama, you lie!"

"Doodie!"

"I hate you, Mama. I hate all of you, and I'll make you pay. I'll be like *him.*"

The stove-lid clattered back in place. She wiped her hands nervously on her dress. "You're sick, Doodie! You're not right in the mind. You never even *seed* your pa."

"I talk to him," the boy said. "He tells me things. He told me why you're my mother. He told me how. And he told me who *I* am."

"You're my son!" Lucey's voice had gone up an octave, and she edged defensively away.

"Only half of me, Mama." The boy said, then laughed defiantly. "Only half of me is even human. You knew that when he came here, and paid you to have his baby?"

"*Doodie!*"

"You can't lie to me, Mama. *He* tells me. *He* knows."

"He was just a man, Doodie. Now he's gone. He never came back, do you hear?"

The boy stared out the window at the rain-shroud. When he spoke again, it was in a small slow voice of contempt.

"It doesn't matter. He doesn't want you to believe—any of you." He paused to snicker. "He doesn't want to warn you what we're going to do."

Lucey shook her head slowly. "Lord, have mercy on me," she breathed. "I know I done wrong. But please, punish old Lucey and not my boy."

"I ain't crazy, Mama."

"If you ain't crazy, you're 'witched,' and talkin' to the dead."

"He ain't dead. He's Outside."

Lucey's eyes flickered quickly to the door.

"And he's comin' back—soon." The boy chuckled. "Then he'll make me like him, and it won't hurt to listen."

"You talk like he wasn't a man. I seed him, and you didn't. Your pa was just a man, Doodie."

"No, Mama. He showed you a man because he wanted you to see a man. Next time, he'll come the way he *really* is."

"Why would your pa come back," she snorted, summoning courage to stir the pot. "What would he want here? If you was right in the head, you wouldn't get fits, and you'd know you never seed him. What's his name? You don't even know his name."

"His name is a purple bitter with black velvet, Mama. Only there isn't any word."

"Fits," she moaned. "A child with fits."

"The crawlers, you mean? That's when he talks to me. It hurts at first."

She advanced on him with a big tin spoon, and shook it at him. "You're sick, Doodie. And don't you carry on so. A doctor's what you need . . . if only Mama had some money."

"I won't fuss with you, Mama."

"Huh!" She stood there for a moment, shaking her head. Then she went back to stir the pot. Odorous steam arose to perfume the shack.

The boy turned his head to watch her with luminous eyes.

"The fits are when he talks, Mama. Honest they are. It's like electricity inside me. I wish I could tell you how."

"Sick!" She shook her head vigorously. "Sick, that's all."

"If I was all like him, it wouldn't hurt. It only hurts because I'm half like you."

"Doodie, you're gonna drive your old mother to her grave. Why do you torment me so?"

He turned back to the window and fell silent . . . determinedly, hostilely silent. The silence grew like an angry thing in the cabin, and Lucey's noises at the stove only served to punctuate it.

"Where does your father stay, Doodie?" she asked at last, in cautious desperation.

"Outside . . ."

"Gitalong! Wheah outside, in a palmetto scrub? In the cypress swamp?"

"*Way* Outside. Outside the world."

"Who taught you such silliness? Spirits an' such! I ought to tan you good, Doodie!"

"From another world," the boy went on.

"An' he talks to you from the other world?"

Doodie nodded solemnly.

Lucey stirred vigorously at the pot, her face creased in a dark frown. Lots of folks believed in spirits, and lots of folks believed in mediums. But Lucey had got herself straight with the Lord.

"I'm gonna call the parson," she grunted flatly.

"Why?"

"Christian folks don't truck with spirits."

"He's no spirit, Mama. He's like a man, only he's not. He comes from a star."

She set her jaw and fell grimly silent. She didn't like to remember Doodie's father. He'd come seeking shelter from a storm, and he was big and taciturn, and he made love like a machine. Lucey had been younger then—younger and wilder, and not afraid of shame. He'd vanished as quickly as he'd come.

When he had gone, it almost felt like he'd been there to accomplish an errand, some piece of business that had to be handled hastily and efficiently.

"Why'd he want a son?" she scoffed. "If what you say is true—which it ain't."

The boy stirred restlessly. "Maybe I shouldn't tell."

"You tell Mama."

"You won't believe it anyway," he said listlessly. "He fixed it so I'd *look* human. He fixed it so he could talk to me. I tell him things. Things he could find out himself if he wanted to."

"What does he want to know?"

"How humans work inside."

"Livers and lungs and such? Sssssst! Silliest I ever—"

"And brains. Now they know."

"They?"

"Pa's people. *You'll see.* Now they know, and they're coming to run things. Things will be different, lots different."

"When?"

"Soon. Only pa's coming sooner. He's their . . . their . . ." The boy groped for a word. "He's like a detective."

Lucey took the corn bread out of the oven and sank despairingly into a chair. "Doodie, Doodie . . ."

"What, Mama?"

"Oh, Sweet Jesus! What did I do, what did I do? He's a child of the devil. Fits an' lies and puny ways. Lord, have mercy on me."

With an effort, the boy sat up to stare at her weakly. "He's no devil, Mama. He's no man, but he's better than a man. You'll see."

"You're not right in the mind, Doodie."

"It's all right. He wouldn't want you to believe. Then you'd be warned. They'd be warned too."

"They?"

"Humans—white and black and yellow. He picked poor people to have his sons, so nobody would believe."

"Sons? You mean you ain't the only one?"

Doodie shook his head. "I got brothers, Mama—half-brothers. I talk to them sometimes too."

She was silent a long time. "Doodie, you better go to sleep," she said wearily at last.

"Nobody'll believe . . . until he comes, and the rest of them come after him."

"He ain't comin', Doodie. You ain't seed him—never."

"Not with my eyes," he said.

She shook her head slowly, peering at him with brimming eyes. "Poor little boy. Cain't I do somethin' to make you see?"

Doodie sighed. He was tired, and didn't answer. He fell back on the pillow and lay motionless. The water that crawled down the pane rippled the rain-light over his sallow face. He might have been a pretty child, if it had not been for the tightness in his face, and the tumor-shape on his forehead.

He said it was the tumor-shape that let him talk to his father. After a few moments, Lucey arose, and took their supper off the stove. Doodie sat propped up on pillows, but he only nibbled at his food.

"Take it away," he told her suddenly. "I can feel it starting again."

There was nothing she could do. While he shrieked and tossed again on the bed, she went out on the rain-swept porch to pray. She prayed softly that her sin be upon herself, not upon her boy. She prayed for understanding, and when she was done she cried until Doodie was silent again inside.

When she went back into the house, he was watching her with cold, hard eyes.

"It's tonight," he said. "He's coming *tonight*, Mama."

The rain ceased at twilight, but the wind stiffened, hurling drops of water from the pines and scattering them like shot across the sagging roof. Running water gurgled in the ditch, and a rabbit ran toward higher ground. In the west, the clouds lifted a dark bandage from a bloody slash of sky, and somewhere a dog howled in the dusk. Rain-pelted, the sick hen lay dying in the yard.

Lucey stood in the doorway, nervously peering out into the pines and the scrub, while she listened to the croak of the tree frogs at sunset, and the conch-shell sounds of wind in the pines.

"Ain't no night for strangers to be out wanderin'," she said. "There won't be no moon till nearly midnight."

"He'll come," promised the small voice behind her. "He's coming from the Outside."

"Shush, child. He's nothing of the sort."

"He'll come, all right."

"What if I won't let him in the door?"

Doodie laughed. "You can't stop him, Mama. I'm only *half* like you, and it hurts when he talks-inside."

"Yes, child?"

"If he talks-inside to a human, the human dies. He told me."

"Sounds like witch-woman talk," Lucey said scornfully and stared back at him from the doorway. "I don't want no more of it. There's nobody can kill somebody by just a-talkin'."

"*He* can. And it ain't just talking. It's talking *inside*."

"Ain't nobody can talk inside your mother but your mother."

"That's what I been saying." Doodie laughed. "If he did, you'd die. That's why he needed *me*."

Lucey's eyes kept flickering toward the rain-soaked scrub, and she hugged her huge arms, and shivered. "Silliest I ever!"

she snorted. "He was just a man, and you never even seed him."

She went inside and got the shotgun, and sat down at the table to clean it, after lighting a smoky oil lamp on the wall.

"Why are you cleaning that gun, Mama?"

"Wildcat around the chicken yard last night!" she muttered. "Tonight I'm gonna watch."

Doodie stared at her with narrowed eyes, and the look on his face started her shivering again. Sometimes he did seem not-quite-human, a shape witched or haunted wherein a silent cat prowled by itself and watched, through human eyes.

How could she believe the wild words of a child subject to fits, a child whose story was like those told by witching women and herb healers? A thing that came from the stars, a thing that could come in the guise of a man and talk, make love, eat, and laugh, a thing that wanted a half-human son to which it could speak from afar.

How could she believe in a thing that was like a spy sent into the city before the army came, a thing that could make her conceive when it wasn't even human? It was wilder than any of the stories they told in the deep swamps, and Lucey was a good Christian now.

Still, when Doodie fell asleep, she took the gun and went out to wait for the wildcat that had been disturbing the chickens. It wasn't unchristian to believe in wildcats, not even tonight.

Doodie's father had been just a man, a triflin' man. True, she couldn't remember him very clearly, because she had been drinking corn squeezin's with Jacob Fleeter before the stranger came. She had been all giggly, and he had been all shimmery, and she couldn't remember a word he'd said.

"Lord forgive me," she breathed as she left the house.

The wet grass dragged about her legs as she crossed the yard and traversed a clearing toward an island of palmetto scrub from which she could cover both the house and the chicken-yard.

The clouds had broken, and stars shone brightly, but there was no moon. Lucey moved by instinct, knowing each inch of land for half a mile around the shack.

She sat on a wet and rotting log in the edge of the palmetto thicket, laid the shotgun across her lap, stuffed a corncob pipe with tobacco from Deevey's field, and sat smoking in the blackness while whippoorwills mourned over the land, and an occasional owl hooted from the swamp. The air was cool and clean after the rain, and only a few nightbirds flitted in the brush while crickets chirped in the distance and tree frogs spoke mysteriously.

"*AAAaaaAAaaarrrwww . . . Na!*"

The cry was low and piercing. Was it Doodie, having another spasm—or only a dream? She half-arose, then paused, listening. There were a few more whimpers, then silence. A dream, she decided, and settled back to wait. There was nothing she could do for Doodie, not until the State Healthmobile came through again, and examined him for "catchin'" ailments. If they found he wasn't right in the mind, they might take him away.

The glowing ember in the pipe was hypnotic—the only thing to be clearly seen except the stars. She stared at the stars, wondering about their names, until they began to crawl before her eyes. Then she looked at the ember in the pipe again, brightening and dimming with each breath, acquiring a lacy crust of ashes, growing sleepy in the bowl and sinking deeper, deeper, while the whippoorwills pierced the night with melancholy.

". . . Na na naaaAAAAhhhaaa. . . !"

When the cries woke her, she knew she had slept for some time. Faint moonlight seeped through the pine branches from the east, and there was a light mist over the land. The air had chilled, and she shivered as she arose to stretch, propping the gun across the rotten log. She waited for Doodie's cries to cease.

The cries continued, unabated.

Stiffening with sudden apprehension, she started back toward the shack. Then she saw it—a faint violet glow through the trees to the north, just past the corner of the hen house! She stopped again, tense with fright. Doodie's cries were becoming meaningful.

"Pa! I can't stand it any closer! Naa, naaa! I can't think, I can't think at all. No, *please.* . . ."

Reflexively, Lucey started to bolt for the house, but checked herself in time. No lamp burned in the window. She picked up the shotgun and a pebble. After a nervous pause, she tossed the pebble at the porch.

It bounced from the wall with a loud crack, and she slunk low into shadows. Doodie's cries continued without pause. A minute passed, and no one emerged from the house.

A sudden metallic sound, like the opening of a metal door, came from the direction of the violet light. Quickly she stepped over the log and pressed back into the scrub thicket. Shaking with fear, she waited in the palmettos, crouching in the moonlight among the spiny fronds, and lifting her head occasionally to peer toward the violet light.

She saw nothing for a time, and then, gradually the moonlight seemed to dim. She glanced upward. A tenuous shadow, like smoke, had begun to obscure the face of the moon, a translucent blur like the thinnest cloud.

At first, she dismissed it as a cloud. But it writhed within itself, curled and crawled, not dispersing, but seeming to swim. Smoke from the violet light? She watched it with wide, upturned eyes.

Despite its volatile shape, it clung together as a single entity as smoke would never have done. She could still see it faintly after it had cleared the lunar disk, scintillating in the moonglow.

It swam like an airborne jellyfish. A cluster of silver threads it seemed, tangled in a cloud of filaments—or a giant mass of dandelion fluff. It leaked out misty pseudopods, then drew them back as it pulled itself through the air. Weightless as chickdown, huge as a barn, it flew—and drifted from the direction of the sphere in a semi-circle, as if inspecting the land, at times moving against the wind.

It was coming closer to the house.

It moved with purpose, and therefore was alive. This Lucey knew. It moved with its millions of spun threads, finer than a spider's web, the patterns as ordered as a neural array.

It contracted suddenly and began to settle toward the house. Glittering opaquely, blotting out half the cabin, it kept contracting and drawing itself in, becoming denser until it fell in the yard with a blinding flash of incandescent light.

Lucey's flesh crawled. Her hands trembled on the gun, her breath came in shallow gasps.

Before her eyes it was changing into a manlike thing.

Frozen, she waited, thinking swiftly. Could it be that Doodie was right?

Could it be—

Doodie was still whimpering in the house, weary now, as he always was when the spasm had spent itself. But the words still came, words addressed to his father.

The thing in the yard was assuming the shape of a man—and Lucey knew who the man would be.

She reared up quickly in the palmettos, like an enraged, hulking river animal breaking to the surface. She came up shotgun-in-hand and bellowed across the clearing. "Hey theah! You triflin' skunk! *Look at me!*"

Still groping for human shape, the creature froze.

"Run off an' leave me with child!" Lucey shouted. "And no way to pay his keep!"

The creature kept coming toward her, and the pulsing grew stronger.

"Don't come any nearer, you hear?"

When it kept coming, Lucey grunted in a gathering rage and charged out of the palmettos to meet it, shotgun raised, screaming insults. The thing wobbled to a stop, its face a shapeless blob with black shadows for eyes.

She brought the gun to her shoulder and fired both barrels at once.

The thing tumbled to the ground. Crackling arcs danced about it, and a smell of ozone came on the breeze. For one hideous moment it was lighted by a glow from within. Then the glow died, and it began to expand. It grew erratically, and the moonlight danced in silvery filaments about it. A blob of its substance broke loose from the rest, and wind-borne, sailed across the clearing and dashed itself to dust in the palmettos.

A sudden gust took the rest of it, rolling it away in the grass, gauzy shreds tearing loose from the mass. The gust blew it against the trunk of a pine. It lodged there briefly, quivering in the breeze and shimmering palely under the moon. Then it broke into dust that scattered eastward across the land.

"Praised be the Lord," breathed Lucey, beginning to cry.

A high whining sound pierced the night, from the direction of the violet light. She whirled to stare. The light grew brighter. Then the whine abruptly ceased. A luminescent sphere, glowing with violet haze, moved upward from the pines. It paused, then in stately majesty continued the ascent, gathering speed until it became a ghostly chariot that dwindled. Up, up, up toward the gleaming stars. She watched it until it vanished from sight.

Then she straightened her shoulders, and glowered toward the dust traces that blew eastward over the scrub.

"Ain't nothing worse than a triflin' man," she philosophized. "If he's human, or if he's not."

Wearily she returned to the cabin. Doodie was sleeping peacefully. Smiling, she tucked him in, and went to bed. There was corn to hoe, come dawn.

Report: Servopilot recon six, to fleet. Missionman caught in transition phase by native organism, and devastated, thus destroying liaison with native analog. Suggest delay of invasion plans. Unpredictability factors associated with mothers of genetic analogs. Withdraw contacts. Servo Six.

The Will

THE will of a child. A child who played in the sun and ran over the meadow to chase with his dog among the trees beyond the hedge, and knew the fierce passions of childhood. A child whose logic cut corners and sought shortest distances, and found them. A child who made shining life in my house.

Red blood count low, wildly fluctuating . . . Chronic fatigue, loss of weight, general lethargy of function . . . Noticeable pallor and muscular atrophy . . . the first symptoms.

That was eight months ago.

Last summer, the specialists conferred over him. When they had finished, I went to Doc Jules' office—alone, because I was afraid it was going to be bad, and Cleo couldn't take it. He gave it to me straight.

"We can't cure him, Rod. We can only treat symptoms—and hope the research labs come through. I'm sorry."

"He'll die?"

"Unless the labs get an answer."

"How long?"

"Months." He gave it to me bluntly—maybe because he thought I was hard enough to take it, and maybe because he knew I was only Kenny's foster father, as if blood-kinship would have made it any worse.

"Thanks for letting me know," I said, and got my hat.

I would have to tell Cleo, somehow. It was going to be tough. I left the building and went out to buy a paper. A magazine on the science rack caught my eye. It had an article entitled *Carcino-genesis and Carbon*-14 and there was a mention of leukemia in the blurb. I bought it along with the paper, and went over to the park to read. Anything to keep from carrying the news to Cleo.

The research article made things worse. They were still doing things to rats and cosmic rays, and the word "cure" wasn't mentioned once. I dropped the magazine on the grass and glanced at the front page. A small headline toward the bottom of the page said: COMMUNITY PRAYS THREE

18

DAYS FOR DYING CHILD. Same old sob-stuff—publicity causes country to focus on some luckless incurable, and deluge the family with sympathy, advice, money, and sincere and ardent pleas for divine intervention.

I wondered if it would be like that for Kenny—and instinctively I shuddered.

I took a train out to the suburbs, picked up the car, and drove home before twilight. I parked in front, because Cleo was out in back, taking down clothes from the line. The blinds were down in the living room, and the lantern-jawed visage of Captain Chronos looked out sternly from the television screen. The Captain carried an LTR (local-time-reversal) gun at the ready, and peered warily from side to side through an oval hole in the title film. Kenny's usual early-evening fodder.

"Travel through the centuries with the master of the clock!" the announcer was chanting.

"Hi, kid," I said to the hunched-up figure who sat before the set, worshiping his hero.

"Sssshhhhhhhh!" He glanced at me irritably, then transferred his individual attention back to the title film.

"Sorry," I muttered. "Didn't know you listened to the opening spiel. It's always the same."

He squirmed, indicating that he wanted me to scram—to leave him to his own devices.

I scrammed to the library, but the excited chant of the audio was still with me. ". . . *Captain Chronos, Custodian of Time, Defender of the Temporal Passes, Champion of the Temporal Guard. Fly with Captain Chronos in his time-ship Century as he battles against those evil forces who would—*"

I shut the door for a little quiet, then went to the encyclopedia shelf and took down "LAC-MOE." An envelope fell out of the heavy volume, and I picked it up. Kenny's. He had scrawled "Lebanon, do not open until 1964; value in 1954: 38¢," on the face. I knew what was inside without holding it up to the light: stamps. Kenny's idea of buried treasure; when he had more than one stamp of an issue in his collection, he'd stash the duplicate away somewhere to let it age, having heard that age increases their value.

When I finished reading the brief article, I went out to the kitchen. Cleo was bringing in a basket of clothes. She paused in the doorway, the basket cocked on her hip, hair disheveled, looking pretty but anxious.

"Did you see him?" she asked.

I nodded, unable to look at her, poured myself a drink. She

waited a few seconds for me to say something. When I couldn't say anything, she dropped the basket of clothes, scattering underwear and linens across the kitchen floor, and darted across the room to seize my arms and stare up at me wildly.

"Rod! It *isn't*—"

But it was. Without stopping to think, she rushed to the living room, seized Kenny in her arms, began sobbing, then fled upstairs when she realized what she was doing.

Kenny knew he was sick. He knew several specialists had studied his case. He knew that I had gone down to talk with Doc Jules this afternoon. After Cleo's reaction, there was no keeping the truth from him. He was only fourteen, but within two weeks, he knew he had less than a year to live, unless they found a cure. He pieced it together for himself from conversational fragments, and chance remarks, and medical encyclopedias, and by deftly questioning a playmate's older brother who was a medical student.

Maybe it was easier on Kenny to know he was dying, easier than seeing our anxiety and being frightened by it without knowing the cause. But a child is blunt in his questioning, and tactless in matters that concern himself, and that made it hell on Cleo.

"If they don't find a cure, when will I die?"

"Will it hurt?"

"What will you do with my things?"

"Will I see my real father afterwards?"

Cleo stood so much of it, and then one night she broke down and we had to call a doctor to give her a sedative and quiet her down. When she was settled, I took Kenny out behind the house. We walked across the narrow strip of pasture and sat on the old stone fence to talk by the light of the moon. I told him not to talk about it again to Cleo, unless she brought it up, and that he was to bring his questions to me. I put my arm around him, and I knew he was crying inside.

"I don't want to die."

There is a difference between tragedy and blind brutal calamity. Tragedy has meaning, and there is dignity in it. Tragedy stands with its shoulders stiff and proud. But there is no meaning, no dignity, no fulfillment, in the death of a child.

"Kenny, I want you to try to have faith. The research institutes are working hard. I want you to try to have faith that they'll find a cure."

"Mack says it won't be for years and years."

Mack was the medical student. I resolved to call him tomorrow. But his mistake was innocent; he didn't know what was the matter with Kenny.

"Mack doesn't know. He's just a kid himself. Nobody knows —except that they'll find it sometime. Nobody knows when. It might be next week."

"I wish I had a time-ship like Captain Chronos."

"Why?"

He looked at me earnestly in the moonlight. "Because then I could go to some year when they knew how to cure me."

"I wish it were possible."

"I'll bet it is. I'll bet someday they can do that too. Maybe the government's working on it now."

I told him I'd heard nothing of such a project.

"Then they ought to be. Think of the advantages. If you wanted to know something that nobody knew, you could just go to some year when it had already been discovered."

I told him that it wouldn't work, because then everybody would try it, and nobody would work on new discoveries, and none would be made.

"Besides, Kenny, nobody can even prove time-travel is possible."

"Scientists can do anything."

"Only things that are possible, Kenny. And only with money, and time, and work—and a reason."

"Would it cost a lot to research for a time-ship, Dad?"

"Quite a lot, I imagine, if you could find somebody to do it."

"As much as the atom-bomb?"

"Maybe."

"I bet you could borrow it from banks . . . if somebody could prove it's possible."

"You'd need a lot of money of your own, kid, before the banks would help."

"I bet my stamp collection will be worth a lot of money someday. And my autograph book." The conversation had wandered off into fantasy.

"In time, maybe in time. A century maybe. But banks won't wait that long."

He stared at me peculiarly. "But Dad, don't you see? *What difference does time make*, if you're working on a time-machine?"

That one stopped me. "Try to have faith in the medical labs, Kenny," was all I could find to say.

Kenny built a time-ship in the fork of a big maple. He made it from a packing crate, reinforced with plywood, decorated with mysterious coils of copper wire. He filled it with battered clocks and junkyard instruments. He mounted two seats in it, and dual controls. He made a fish-bowl canopy over a hole in the top, and nailed a galvanized bucket on the nose. Broomstick guns protruded from its narrow weapon ports. He painted it silvery gray, and decorated the bucket-nose with the insignia of Captain Chronos and the Guardsmen of Time. He nailed steps on the trunk of the maple; and when he wasn't in the house, he could usually be found in the maple, piloting the time-ship through imaginary centuries. He took a picture of it with a box camera, and sent a print of it to Captain Chronos with a fan letter.

Then one day he fainted on the ladder, and fell out of the tree.

He wasn't badly hurt, only bruised, but it ended his career as a time-ship pilot. Kenny was losing color and weight, and the lethargy was coming steadily over him. His fingertips were covered with tiny stab-marks from the constant blood counts, and the hollow of his arm was marked with transfusion needles. Mostly, he stayed inside.

We haunted the research institutes, and the daily mail was full of answers to our flood of pleading inquiries—all kinds of answers.

"We regret to inform you that recent studies have been. . ."

"Investigations concerning the psychogenic factors show only . . ."

"Prepare to meet God . . ."

"For seventy-five dollars, Guru Tahaj Reshvi guarantees . . ."

"Sickness is only an illusion. Have faith and . . ."

"We cannot promise anything in the near future, but the Institute is rapidly finding new directions for . . ."

"Allow us to extend sympathy . . ."

"The powers of hydromagnetic massage therapy have been established by . . ."

And so it went. We talked to crackpots, confidence men, respectable scientists, fanatics, lunatics, and a few honest fools. Occasionally we tried some harmless technique, with Jules' approval, mostly because it felt like we were doing *something*. But the techniques did more good for Cleo than they did for Kenny, and Kenny's very gradual change for the worse made it apparent that nothing short of the miraculous could save him.

And then Kenny started working on it himself.

The idea, whatever it was, must have hit him suddenly, and it was strange—because it came at a time when both Cleo and I thought that he had completely and fatalistically accepted the coming of the end.

"The labs aren't going to find it in time," he said. "I've been reading what they say. I know it's no good, Dad." He cried some then; it was good that he had relearned to cry.

But the next day, his spirits soared mysteriously to a new high, and he went around the house singing to himself. He was busy with his stamp collection most of the time, but he also wandered about the house and garage searching for odds and ends, his actions seeming purposeful and determined. He moved slowly, and stopped to rest frequently, but he displayed more energy than we had seen for weeks, and even Jules commented on how bright he was looking, when he came for Kenny's daily blood sample. Cleo decided that complete resignation had brought cheerfulness with it, and that acceptance of ill-fate obviated the need to worry or hope. But I wasn't so sure.

"What've you been up to, Kenny?" I asked.

He looked innocent and shook his head.

"Come on, now. You don't go wandering around muttering to yourself unless you're cooking something up. What is it, another time-ship? I heard you hammering in the garage before dinner."

"I was just knocking the lid off an old breadbox."

I couldn't get any answer but evasions, innocent glances, and mysterious smirks. I let him keep his secret, thinking that his enthusiasm for whatever it was he was doing would soon wear off.

Then the photographers came.

"We want to take a picture of Kenny's treehouse," they explained.

"Why?—and how did you know he had one?" I demanded.

It developed that somebody was doing a feature-article on the effects of science-fantasy television shows on children. It developed that the "somebody" was being hired by a publicity agency which was being hired by the advertisers who presented Captain Chronos and the Guardsmen of Time. It developed that Kenny's fan letter, with the snapshot of his treehouse time-ship, had been forwarded to the publicity department by the producer of the show. They wanted a picture of the time-ship with Kenny inside, looking out through the fish bowl canopy.

"It's impossible," I told them.

They showed me a dozen pictures of moppets with LTR-guns, moppets in time-warp suits, moppets wearing Captain Chronos costumes, moppets falling free in space, and moppets playing Time-Pirate in the park.

"I'm sorry, but it's impossible," I insisted.

"We'll be glad to pay something for it, if. . ."

"The kid's sick, if you must know," I snapped. "He can't do it, and that's that, so forget about it."

"Maybe when he's feeling better . . . ?"

"He *won't* be feeling better," Cleo interrupted, voice tense, with a catch in it. "Now please *leave!*". .

They left, with Cleo herding them out onto the porch. I heard them apologizing, and Cleo softened, and began to explain. That was a mistake.

A week later, while we were still drinking our coffee at the dinner table, the doorbell rang. Cleo, expecting an answer to her recent wire to some South American clinic, left the table, went to answer it, and promptly screamed.

I dropped my cup with a crash and ran to the living room with a butcher knife, then stopped dead still.

It stood there in the doorway with a stunned expression on its face, gaping at Cleo who had collapsed in a chair. It wore a silver uniform with jack-boots, black-and-red cape, and a weird helmet with antenna protruding from it. It had a lantern jaw and a big, meaty, benign contenance.

"I'm awfully sorry," it boomed in a gentle deep-rich voice. "We just drove over from the studio, and I didn't take time to change . . ."

"Ulk!" said Cleo.

I heard footsteps at the head of the stairs behind me, then a howl from Kenny who had been getting ready for bed, after being helped upstairs.

"Captain Chronos!"

Bare feet machine-gunned down the stairs and came to a stop at a respectful distance from the idol.

"GgaaaaAA*A*WW*W*SSSS*Shhh!*" Kenny timidly walked half-way around him, looking him up and down. "Geee . . . Gaaawwssshh!"

Cleo fanned herself with a newspaper and recovered slowly. I tossed the butcher-knife on a magazine stand and mumbled something apologetic. There were two of them: Chronos and the producer, a small suave man in a business suit. The latter drew me aside to explain. It developed that the photographers had explained to the boss, who had explained to the client, who had mentioned it to the agency, who had returned the fan letter to the producer with a note. It would appear that Captain Chronos, for the sake of nutritious and delicious Fluffy Crunkles, made it his habit to comfort the afflicted, the crippled, and the dying, if it were convenient and seemed somehow advantageous. He also visited the children's wards of hospitals, it seemed.

"This on the level, or for publicity?"

"On the level."

"Where's the photographer?"

The producer reddened and muttered noncommittally. I went to the door and looked out through the screen. There was another man in their car. When I pushed the screen open, it hit something hard—a tape recorder. I turned:

"Get out."

"But Mr. Westmore. . . ."

"Get *out!*"

They left quickly. Kenny was furious, and he kept on being furious all through the following day. At me. Cleo began agreeing with him to some extent, and I felt like a heel.

"You want Kenny to get the full treatment?" I grumbled. "You want him to wind up a sob-story child?"

"Certainly not, but it was cruel, Rod. The boy never had a happier moment until you . . ."

"All right, so I'm a bastard. I'm sorry."

That night Abe Sanders (Captain Chronos) came back alone, in slacks and a sport shirt, and muttering apologies. It developed that the Wednesday evening shows always had a children's panel (Junior Guardsmen) program, and that while they understood that Kenny couldn't come, they had wanted to have him with the panel, in absentia, by telephone.

"Please, Dad, can't I?"

The answer had to be no . . . but Kenny had been glaring at me furiously all day, and it was a way to make him stop hating me . . . still, the answer had to be no . . . the publicity . . . but he'd be delighted, and he could stop hating my guts for kicking them out . . .

"I guess so, if the offer's still open."

"*Dad!*"

The offer was still open. Kenny was to be on the show. They rehearsed him a little, and let him practice with the tape recorder until he got used to his voice.

On Wednesday evening, Kenny sat in the hall doorway to the living room, telephone in his lap, and stared across at Sanders' face on the television screen. Sanders held another phone, and we heard both their voices from the set. Occasionally the camera dollied in to a close shot of Sanders' chuckle, or panned along the table to show the juvenile panel members, kids between eight and sixteen. There was an empty chair on Sanders' right, and it bore a placard. The placard said "KENNY WESTLER."

It lasted maybe a minute. Sanders promised not to mention Kenny's address, nor to mention the nature of his illness. He did neither, but the tone of conversation made it clear that Kenny was in bad shape and probably not long for this world. Kenny had stage fright, his voice trembled, and he blurted something about the search for a cure. Cleo stared at the boy instead of the set, and my own glance darted back and forth. The cameraman panned to the empty chair and dollied in slowly so that the placard came to fill the screen while Kenny spoke. Kenny talked about stamp collections and time machines and autographs, while an invisible audience gaped at pathos.

"If anybody's got stamps to trade, just let me know," he said. "And autographs . . ."

I winced, but Sanders cut in. "Well, Kenny—we're not supposed to mention your address, but if any of you Guardsmen out there want to help Kenny out with his stamp collection, you can write to me, and I'll definitely see that he gets the letters."

"And autographs too," Kenny added.

When it was over, Kenny had lived . . . but *lived*.

And then the mail came in a deluge, forwarded from the network's studio. Bushels of stamps, dozens of autograph books, Bibles, money, advice, crank letters, and maudlin gushes of sugary sympathy . . . and a few sensible and friendly letters. Kenny was delighted.

"Gee, Dad, I'll never get all the stamps sorted out. And look!—an autograph of Calvin Coolidge! . . ."

But it never turned him aside from his path of confident but mysterious purpose. He spent even more time in his room, in the garage, and—when he could muster the energy—back in the maple woods, doing mysterious things alone.

"Have they found a cure yet, Dad?" he asked me pleasantly when an expected letter came.

"They're . . . making progress," I answered lamely.

He shrugged. "They will . . . eventually." Unconcerned.

It occurred to me that some sort of psychic change, unfathomable, might have happened within him—some sudden sense of timelessness, of identity with the race. Something that would let him die calmly as long as he knew there'd be a cure *some*day. It seemed too much to expect of a child, but I mentioned the notion to Jules when I saw him again.

"Could be," he admitted. "It might fit in with this secrecy business."

"How's that?"

"People who know they're dying often behave that way. Little secret activities that don't become apparent until after they're gone. Set up causes that won't have effects until afterwards. Immortality cravings. You want to have posthumous influence, to live after you. A suicide note is one perversion of it. The suicide figures the world will posthumously feel guilty, if he tells it off."

"And Kenny . . . ?"

"I don't know, Rod. The craving for immortality is basically procreative, I think. You have children, and train them, and see your own mirrored patterns live on in them, and feel satisfied, when your time comes. Or else you sublimate it, and do the same thing for all humanity—through art, or science. I've seen a lot of death, Rod, and I believe there's more than just-plain-selfishness to people's immortality-wishes; it's associated with the human reproductive syndrome—which includes the passing on of culture to the young. But Kenny's just a kid. I don't know."

Despite Kenny's increasing helplessness and weakness, he began spending more time wandering out in the woods. Cleo chided him for it, and tried to limit his excursions. She drove him to town on alternate days for a transfusion and shots, and she tried to keep him in the house most of the time, but he needed sun and air and exercise, and it was impossible to keep him on the lawn. Whatever he was doing, it was a shadowy secretive business. It involved spades and garden tools and packages, with late excursions into the maples toward the creek.

"You'll know in four or five months," he told me, in answer to a question. "Don't ask me now. You'd laugh."

But it became apparent that he wouldn't last that long. The rate of transfusions doubled, and on his bad days, he was unable to get out of bed. He fainted down by the creek, and had to be carried back to the house. Cleo forbade him to go outside alone without Jules' day-to-day approval, and Jules was beginning to be doubtful about the boy's activities.

When restricted, Kenny became frantic. "I've got to go

outside, Dad, *please!* I can't finish it if I don't. I've got to! How else can I make contact with them?"

"Contact? With whom?"

But he clammed up and refused to discuss anything about the matter. That night I awoke at two a.m. Something had made a sound. I stole out of bed without disturbing Cleo and went to prowl about the house. A glance down the stairway told me that no lights burned on the first floor. I went to Kenny's room and gingerly opened the door. Blackness.

"Kenny—?"

No sound of breathing in the room. Quietly I struck a match.

The bed was empty.

"Kenny!" I bellowed it down the hall, and then I heard sounds—Cleo stirring to wakefulness and groping for clothes in our bedroom. I trotted downstairs and turned on lights as I charged from room to room.

He was not in the house. I found the back screen unlatched and went out to play a flashlight slowly over the backyard. There . . . by the hedge . . . caught in the cone of light . . . Kenny, crumpled over a garden spade.

Upstairs, Cleo screamed through the back window. I ran out to gather him up in my arms. Skin clammy, breathing shallow, pulse irregular—he muttered peculiarly as I carried him back to the house.

"Glad you found it . . . knew you'd find it . . . got me to the right time . . . when are we . . . ?"

I got him inside and up to his room. When I laid him on the bed, a crudely drawn map, like a treasure map with an "X" and a set of bearings, fell from his pocket. I paused a moment to study it. The "X" was down by the fork in the creek. What had been buried there?

I heard Cleo coming up the stairs with a glass of hot milk, and I returned the map to Kenny's pocket and went to call the doctor.

When Kenny awoke, he looked around the room very carefully—and seemed disappointed by what he saw.

"Expecting to wake up somewhere else?" I asked.

"I guess it was a dream," he mumbled. "I thought they came early."

"Who came early?"

But he clammed up again. "You'll find out in about four months," was all he'd say.

He wouldn't last that long. The next day, Doc Jules ordered

him to stay inside, preferably sitting or lying down most of the time. We were to carry him outside once a day for a little sun, but he had to sit in a lawn chair and not run around. Transfusions became more frequent, and finally there was talk of moving him to the hospital.

"I won't go to the hospital."

"You'll have to, Kenny. I'm sorry."

That night, Kenny slipped outside again. He had been lying quietly all day, sleeping most of the time, as if saving up energy for a last spurt.

Shortly after midnight, I awoke to hear him tiptoe down the hall. I let him get downstairs and into the kitchen before I stole out of bed and went to the head of the stairs.

"Kenny!" I shouted. "Come back up here! Right now!"

There was a brief silence. Then he bolted. The screen door slammed, and bare feet trotted down the back steps.

"Kenny!"

I darted to the rear window, overlooking the backyard. *"Kenny!"*

Brush whipped as he dove through the hedge. Cleo came to the window beside me, and began calling after him.

Swearing softly, I tugged my trousers over my pajamas, slipped into shoes, and hurried downstairs to give chase. But he had taken my flashlight.

Outside, beneath a dim, cloud-threatened moon, I stood at the hedge, staring out across the meadow toward the woods. The night was full of crickets and rustlings in the grass. I saw no sign of him.

"Kenny!"

He answered me faintly from the distance. "Don't try to follow me, Dad. I'm going where they can cure me."

I vaulted the fence and trotted across the meadow toward the woods. At the stone fence, I paused to listen—but there were only crickets. Maybe he'd seen me coming in the moonlight, and had headed back toward the creek.

The brush was thick in places, and without a light, it was hard to find the paths. I tried watching for the gleam of the flashlight through the trees, but saw nothing. He was keeping its use to a minimum. After ten minutes of wandering, I found myself back at the fence, having taken a wrong turning somewhere. I heard Cleo calling me from the house.

"Go call the police! They'll help find him!" I shouted to her.

Then I went to resume the search. Remembering the map, and the "X" by the fork in the creek, I trotted along the edge of the pasture next to the woods until I came to a dry wash that I knew led back to the creek. It was the long way around, but it was easy to follow the wash; and after a few minutes I stumbled onto the bank of the narrow stream. Then I waded upstream toward the fork. After twenty yards, I saw the flashlight's gleam —and heard the crunch of the shovel in moist ground. I moved as quietly as I could. The crunching stopped.

Then I saw him. He had dropped the shovel and was tugging something out of the hole. I let him get it out before I called . . .

"Kenny . . ."

He froze, then came up very slowly to a crouch, ready to flee. He turned out the flashlight.

"Kenny, don't run away from me again. Stay there. I'm not angry."

No answer.

"Kenny!"

He called back then, with a quaver in his voice. "Stay where you are, Dad—and let me finish. Then I'll go with you. If you come any closer, I'll run." He flashed the light toward me, saw that I was a good twenty yards away. "Stay there now . . ."

"Then will you come back to the house?"

"I won't run, if you stay right there."

"Okay," I agreed, "but don't take long. Cleo's frantic."

He set the light on a rock, kept it aimed at me, and worked by its aura. The light blinded me, and I could only guess what he might be doing. He pried something open, and then there was the sound of writing on tin. Then he hammered something closed, replaced it in the hole, and began shoveling dirt over it. Five minutes later, he was finished.

The light went out.

"Kenny . . . ?"

"I'm sorry, Dad. I didn't *want* to lie . . . I *had* to."

I heard him slipping quickly away through the brush—back toward the pasture. I hurried to the fork and climbed up out of the knee-deep water, pausing to strike a match. Something gleamed in the grass; I picked it up. Cleo's kitchen clock, always a few minutes slow. What had he wanted with the clock?

By the time I tore through the brush and found the path, there was no sound to indicate which way he had gone. I walked gloomily back toward the house, halfheartedly calling to Kenny . . . then . . . a flash of light in the trees?

BRRUUMMKP!

A sharp report, like a close crash of thunder! It came from the direction of the meadow, or the house. I trotted ahead, ignoring the sharp whipping of the brush.

"Kenny Vestmore? . . . Kenny . . . ?"

A strange voice, a foreign voice—calling to Kenny up ahead in the distance. The police, I thought.

Then I came to the stone fence . . . and froze, staring at the thing—or perhaps at the *nothing*—in the meadow.

It was black. It was bigger than a double garage, and round. I stared at it, and realized that it was not an object but an opening.

And someone else was calling to Kenny. A rich, pleasant voice—somehow it reminded me of Doctor Jules, but it had a strong accent, perhaps Austrian or German.

"Come on along here, liddle boy. Ve fix you op."

Then I saw Kenny, crawling on toward it through the grass.

"Kenny, *don't!*"

He got to his feet and stumbled on into the distorted space. It seemed to squeeze him into a grotesque house-of-mirrors shape; then it spun him inward. Gone.

I was still running toward the black thing when it began to shrink.

"Come along, liddle fellow, come mit oss. Ve fix."

And then the black thing belched away into nothingness with an explosive blast that knocked me spinning. I must have been out cold for awhile. The sheriff woke me.

Kenny was gone. We never saw him again. Cleo confirmed what I had seen on the meadow, but without a body, Kenny remains listed as missing.

Missing from this century.

I went back to the fork in the creek and dug up the breadbox he had buried. It contained his stamp collection and a packet of famous autographs. There was a letter from Kenny, too, addressed to the future, and it was his will.

"Whoever finds this, please sell these things and use the money to pay for a time machine, so you can come and get me, because I'm going to die if you don't . . ."

I paused to remember . . . *I don't think the bank'd wait a hundred years.*

*But Dad, don't you see? What difference does time make,
if you're working on a time machine?*

There was more to the note, but the gist of it was that
Kenny had made an act of faith, faith in tomorrow. He had
buried it, and then he had gone back to dig it up and change
the rendezvous time from four months away to the night of
his disappearance. He knew that he wouldn't have lived that
long.

I put it all back in the box, and sealed the box with solder
and set it in concrete at the foot of a sixfoot hole. With this
manuscript.

(To a reader, yet unborn, who finds this account in a dusty
and ancient magazine stack: *dig.* Dig at a point 987 feet
southeasterly on a heading of 149° from the northwest corner
of the Hayes and Higgins Tract, as recorded in Map Book 6,
p. 78, Cleve County records. But not unless the world is ready
to buy a time machine and come for Kenny, who financed it;
come, if you can cure him. He had faith in *you*.)

Kenny is gone, and today there is a feeling of death in my
house. But after a century of tomorrows? He invested in them,
and he called out to them, pleading with the voice of a child.
And tomorrow answered:

"Come, liddle boy. Ve fix."

Anybody Else Like Me?

QUIET misery in a darkened room. The clock spoke nine
times with a cold brass voice. She stood motionless, leaning
against the drapes by the window, alone. The night was black,
the house empty and silent.

"Come, Lisa!" she told herself. *"You're not dying!"*

She was thirty-four, still lovely, with a slender white body
and a short, rich thatch of warm red hair. She had a good
dependable husband, three children, and security. She had
friends, hobbies, social activities. She painted mediocre pictures for her own amusement, played the piano rather well,
and wrote fair poetry for the University's literary quarterly.

She was well-read, well-rounded, well-informed. She loved and was loved.

Then why this quiet misery?

Wanting something, expecting nothing, she stared out into the darkness of the stone-walled garden. The night was too quiet. A distant street lamp played in the branches of the elm, and the elm threw its shadow across another wing of the house. She watched the shadow's wandering for a time. A lone car purred past in the street and was gone. A horn sounded raucously in the distance.

What was wrong? A thousand times since childhood she had felt this uneasy stirring, this crawling of the mind that called out for some unfound expression. It had been particularly strong in recent weeks.

She tried to analyze. What was different about recent weeks? Events: Frank's job had sent him on the road for a month; the children were at Mother's; the city council had recommended a bond issue; she had fired her maid; a drunk had strangled his wife; the University had opened its new psychophysics lab; her art class had adjourned for the summer.

Nothing there. No clue to the unreasoning, goalless urge that called like a voice crying in mental wilderness: *"Come, share, satisfy, express it to the fullest!"*

Express what? Satisfy what? How?

A baby, deserted at birth and dying of starvation, would feel terrible hunger. But if it had never tasted milk, it could not know the meaning of the hunger nor how to ease it.

"I need to relate this thing to something else, to something in my own experience or in the experience of others." She had tried to satisfy the urge with the goals of other hungers: her children, her husband's lovemaking, food, drink, art, friendship. But the craving was something else, crying for its pound of unknown flesh, and there was no fulfillment.

"How am I different from others?" she asked herself. But she was different only in the normal ways that every human being is different from the exact Average. Her intelligence was high, short of genius, but superior. To a limited extent, she felt the call of creativity. Physically, she was delicately beautiful. The only peculiarities that she knew about seemed ridiculously irrelevant: a dark birthmark on her thigh, a soft fontanel in the top of her long narrow head, like the soft spot in an infant's cranium. Silly little differences!

One big difference: the quiet misery of the unfed hunger.

A scattering of big raindrops suddenly whispered on the

walk and in the grass and through the foliage of the elm. A few drops splattered on the screen, spraying her face and arms with faint points of coolness. It had been oppressively hot. Now there was a chill breath in the night.

Reluctantly she closed the window. The oppression of the warm and empty house increased. She walked to the door opening into the walled garden.

Ready for a lonely bed, she was wearing a negligee over nothing. Vaguely, idly, her hand fumbled at the waist-knot, loosened it. The robe parted, and the fine spray of rain was delightfully cool on her skin.

The garden was dark, the shadows inky, the nearest neighbor a block away. The wall screened it from prying eyes. She brushed her hands over her shoulders; the sleeves slipped down her arms. Peeled clean, feeling like a freed animal, she pressed open the screen and stepped out under the eaves to stand on the warm stone walk.

The rain was rattling in the hedge and roaring softly all about her, splashing coldness about her slender calves. She hugged herself and stepped into it. The drench of icy fingers stroked her with pleasant lashes; she laughed and ran along the walk toward the elm. The drops stung her breasts, rivered her face, and coursed coldly down her sides and legs.

She exulted in the rain, tried to dance and laughed at herself. She ran. Then, tired, she threw herself down on the crisp wet lawn, stretching her arms and legs and rolling slowly on the grass. Eyes closed, drenched and languorous, she laughed softly and played imagining games with the rain.

The drops were steel-jacketed wasps, zipping down out of the blackness, but she melted them with her mind, made them soft and cool and caressing. The drops took impersonal liberties with her body, and she rolled demurely to lie face down in the rainsoft grass.

"*I am still a pale beast,*" she thought happily, "*still kin of my grandmother the ape who danced in the tree and chattered when it rained. How utterly barren life would be, if I were not a pale beast!*"

She dug her fingers into the sodden turf, bared her teeth, pressed her forehead against the ground, and growled a little animal growl. It amused her, and she laughed again. Crouching, she came up on her hands and knees, hunching low, teeth still bared. Like a cat, she hissed—and pounced upon a sleeping bird, caught it and shook it to death.

Again she lay laughing in the grass.

"If Frank were to see me like this," she thought, *"he would put me to bed with a couple of sleeping pills, and call that smug Dr. Mensley to have a look at my mind. And Dr. Mensley would check my ambivalences and my repressions and my narcissistic, voyeuristic, masochistic impulses. He would tighten my screws and readjust me to reality, fit me into a comfortable groove, and take the pale beast out of me to make me a talking doll."*

He had done it several times before. Thinking of Dr. Mensley, Lisa searched her vocabulary for the most savage word she could remember. She growled it aloud and felt better.

The rain was slowly subsiding. A siren was wailing in the distance. The police. She giggled and imagined a headline in tomorrow's paper: PROMINENT SOCIALITE JAILED FOR INDECENT EXPOSURE. And the story would go on: "Mrs. Lisa Waverly was taken into custody by the police after neighbors reported that she was running around stark naked in her back yard. Said Mrs. Heinehoffer who called the law: 'It was just terrible. Looked to me like she was having fits.' Mr. Heinehoffer, when asked for comment, simply closed his eyes and smiled ecstatically."

Lisa sighed wearily. The siren had gone away. The rain had stopped, except for drippings out of the elm. She was tired, emotionally spent, yet strangely melancholy. She sat up slowly in the grass and hugged her shins.

The feeling came over her gradually.

"Someone has been watching me!"

She stiffened slowly, but remained in place, letting her eyes probe about her in the shadows. If only the drippings would stop so she could listen! She peered along the hedge, and along the shadows by the garden wall, toward the dark windows of the house, up toward the low-hanging mist faintly illuminated from below by street lights. She saw nothing, heard nothing. There was no movement in the night. Yet the feeling lingered, even though she scoffed.

"If anyone is here," she thought, *"I'll call them gently, and if anyone appears, I'll scream so loud that Mrs. Heinehoffer will hear me."*

"Hey!" she said in a low voice, but loud enough to penetrate any of the nearby shadows.

There was no answer. She folded her arms behind her head and spoke again, quietly, sensually.

"Come and get me."

No black monster slithered from behind the hedge to devour her. No panther sprang from the elm. No succubus congealed out of wet darkness. She giggled.

"Come have a bite."

No bull-ape came to crush her in ravenous jaws.

She had only imagined the eyes upon her. She stretched lazily and picked herself up, pausing to brush off the leaves of grass pasted to her wet skin. It was over, the strange worship in the rain, and she was weary. She walked slowly toward the house.

Then she heard it—a faint crackling sound, intermittent, distant. She stood poised in the black shadow of the house, listening. The crackle of paper . . . then a small pop . . . then crisp fragments dropped in the street. It was repeated at short intervals.

Taking nervous, shallow breaths, she tiptoed quietly toward the stone wall of the garden. It was six feet high, but there was a concrete bench under the trellis. The sound was coming from over the wall. She stood crouching on the bench; then, hiding her face behind the vines, she lifted her head to peer.

The street lamp was half a block away, but she could see dimly. A man was standing across the street in the shadows, apparently waiting for a bus. He was eating peanuts out of a paper bag, tossing the shells in the street. That explained the crackling sound.

She glared at him balefully from behind the trellis.

"*I'll claw your eyes out,*" she thought, "*if you came and peeped over my wall.*"

"Hi!" the man said.

Lisa stiffened and remained motionless. It was impossible that he could see her. She was in shadow, against a dark background. Had he heard her foolish babbling a moment ago?

More likely, he had only cleared his throat.

"Hi!" he said again.

Her face was hidden in the dripping vines, and she could not move without rustling. She froze in place, staring. She could see little of him. Dark raincoat, dark hat, slender shadow. Was he looking toward her? She was desperately frightened.

Suddenly the man chucked the paper bag in the gutter, stepped off the curb, and came sauntering across the street toward the wall. He removed his hat, and crisp blond hair glinted in the distant streetlight. He stopped three yards away, smiling uncertainly at the vines.

Lisa stood trembling and frozen, staring at him in horror. Strange sensations, utterly alien, passed over her in waves. There was no describing them, no understanding them.

"I—I found you," he stammered sheepishly. "Do you know what it is?"

"I know you," she thought. *"You have a small scar on the back of your neck, and a mole between your toes. Your eyes are blue, and you have an impacted wisdom tooth, and your feet are hurting you because you walked all the way out here from the University, and I'm almost old enough to be your mother. But I can't know you, because I've never seen you before!"*

"Strange, isn't it?" he said uncertainly. He was holding his hat in his hand and cocking his head politely.

"What?" she whispered.

He shuffled his feet and stared at them. "It must be some sort of palpable biophysical energyform, analytically definable—if we had enough data. Lord knows, I'm no mystic. If it exists, it's got to be mathematically definable. But why us?"

Horrified curiosity made her step aside and lean her arms on the wall to stare down at him. He looked up bashfully, and his eyes widened slightly.

"Oh!"

"Oh what?" she demanded, putting on a terrible frown.

"You're beautiful!"

"What do you want?" she asked icily. "Go away!"

"I—" He paused and closed his mouth slowly. He stared at her with narrowed eyes, and touched one hand to his temple as if concentrating.

For an instant, she was no longer herself. She was looking up at her own shadowy face from down in the street, looking through the eyes of a stranger who was not a stranger. She was feeling the fatigue in the weary ankles, and the nasal ache of a slight head cold, and the strange sadness in a curious heart—a sadness too akin to her own.

She rocked dizzily. It was like being in two places at once, like wearing someone else's body for a moment.

The feeling passed. *"It didn't happen!"* she told herself.

"No use denying it," he said quietly. "I tried to make it go away, too, but apparently we've got something unique. It would be interesting to study. Do you suppose we're related?"

"Who are you?" she choked, only half-hearing his question.

"You know my name," he said, "if you'll just take the trouble to think about it. Yours is Lisa—Lisa O'Brien, or Lisa Waverly—I'm never sure which. Sometimes it comes to me one way, sometimes the other."

She swallowed hard. Her maiden name had been O'Brien.

"I don't know you," she snapped.

His name was trying to form in her mind. She refused to allow it. The young man sighed.

"I'm Kenneth Grearly, if you really don't know." He stepped back a pace and lifted his hat toward his head. "I—I guess I better go. I see this disturbs you. I had hoped we could talk about it, but—well, good night, Mrs. Waverly."

He turned and started away.

"Wait!" she called out against her will.

He stopped again. "Yes?"

"Were—were you watching me—while it was raining?"

He opened his mouth and stared thoughtfully down the street toward the light. "You mean watching visually? You really are repressing this thing, aren't you? I thought you understood." He looked at her sharply, forlornly. "They say the failure to communicate is the basis of all tragedy. Do you suppose in our case . . . ?"

"What?"

"Nothing." He shifted restlessly for a moment. "Good night."

"Good night," she whispered many seconds after he was gone.

Her bedroom was hot and lonely, and she tossed in growing restlessness. If only Frank were home! But he would be gone for two more weeks. The children would be back on Monday, but that was three whole days away. Crazy! It was just stark raving crazy!

Had the man really existed—what was his name?—Kenneth Grearly? Or was he only a phantasm invented by a mind that was failing—her mind? Dancing naked in the rain! Calling out to shadow shapes in the brush! Talking to a specter in the street! Schizophrenic syndrome—dream-world stuff. It could not be otherwise, for unless she had invented Kenneth Grearly, how could she know he had sore feet, an impacted wisdom tooth, and a head cold. Not only did she know about those things, but she felt them!

She buried her face in the dusty pillow and sobbed. Tomorrow she would have to call Dr. Mensley.

But fearing the specter's return, she arose a few minutes

later and locked all the doors in the house. When she returned to bed, she tried to pray but it was as if the prayer were being watched. Someone was listening, eavesdropping from outside.

Kenneth Grearly appeared in her dreams, stood half-shrouded in a slowly swirling fog. He stared at her with his head cocked aside, smiling slightly, holding his hat respectfully in his hands.

"Don't you realize, Mrs. Waverly, that we are mutants perhaps?" he asked politely.

"No!" she screamed. "I'm happily married and I have three children and a place in society! Don't come near me!"

He melted slowly into the fog. But echoes came monotonously from invisible cliffs: *mutant mutant mutant mutant mutant . . .*

Dawn came, splashing pink paint across the eastern sky. The light woke her to a dry and empty consciousness, to a headachy awareness full of dull anxiety. She arose wearily and trudged to the kitchen for a pot of coffee.

Lord! Couldn't it all be only a bad dream?

In the cold light of early morning, the things of the past night looked somehow detached, unreal. She tried to analyze objectively.

That sense of sharing a mind, a consciousness, with the stranger who came out of the shadows—what crazy thing had he called it?—*"some sort of palpable biophysical energy-form, analytically definable."*

"If I invented the stranger," she thought, *"I must have also invented the words."*

But where had she heard such words before?

Lisa went to the telephone and thumbed through the directory. No Grearly was listed. If he existed at all, he probably lived in a rooming house. The University—last night she had thought that he had something to do with the University. She lifted the phone and dialed.

"University Station; number please," the operator said.

"I—uh—don't know the extension number. Could you tell me if there is a Kenneth Grearly connected with the school?"

"Student or faculty, Madam?"

"I don't know."

"Give me your number, please, and I'll call you back."

"Lawrence 4750. Thanks, Operator."

She sat down to wait. Almost immediately it rang again.

"Hello?"

"Mrs. Waverly, you were calling me?" A man's voice. His voice!

"The operator found you rather quickly." It was the only thing she could think of saying.

"No, no. I knew you were calling. In fact, I hoped you into it."

"Hoped me? Now look here, Mr. Grearly, I—"

"You were trying to explain our phenomenon in terms of insanity rather than telepathy. I didn't want you to do that, and so I hoped you into calling me."

Lisa was coldly speechless.

"What phenomenon are you talking about?" she asked after a few dazed seconds.

"Still repressing it? Listen, I can share your mind any time I want to, now that I understand where and who you are. You might as well face the fact. And it can work both ways, if you let it. Up to now, you've been—well, keeping your mind's eye closed, so to speak."

Her scalp was crawling. The whole thing had become intensely disgusting to her.

"I don't know what you're up to, Mr. Grearly, but I wish you'd stop it. I admit something strange is going on, but your explanation is ridiculous—offensive, even."

He was silent for a long time, then "I wonder if the first man-ape found his prehensile thumb ridiculous. I wonder if he thought using his hands for grasping was offensive."

"What are you trying to say?"

"That I think we're mutants. We're not the first ones. I had this same experience when I was in Boston once. There must be one of us there, too, but suddenly I got the feeling that he had committed suicide. I never saw him. We're probably the first ones to discover each other."

"Boston? If what you say is true, what would distance have to do with it?"

"Well, if telepathy exists, it certainly involves transfer of energy from one point to another. What *kind* of energy, I don't know. Possibly electromagnetic in character. But it seems likely that it would obey the inverse square law, like radiant energyforms. I came to town about three weeks ago. I didn't feel you until I got close."

"*There is a connection*," she thought. She had been wondering about the increased anxiety of the past three weeks.

"I don't know what you're talking about," she evaded

icily, though. "I'm no mutant. I don't believe in telepathy. I'm not insane. Now let me alone."

She slammed the telephone in its cradle and started to walk away.

Evidently he was angry, for she was suddenly communicating with him again.

She reeled dizzily and clutched at the wall, because she was in two places at once, and the two settings merged in her mind to become a blur, like a double exposure. She was in her own hallway, and she was also in an office, looking at a calculator keyboard, hearing glassware rattling from across a corridor, aware of the smell of formaldehyde. There was a chart on the wall behind the desk and it was covered with strange tracery—schematics of some neural arcs. The office of the psychophysics lab. She closed her eyes, and her own hallway disappeared.

She felt anger—his anger.

"We've got to face this thing. If this is a new direction for human evolution, then we'd better study it and see what to do about it. I knew I was different and I became a psychophysicist to find out why. I haven't been able to measure much, but now with Lisa's help . . ."

She tried to shut him out. She opened her eyes and summoned her strength and tried to force him away. She stared at the bright doorway, but the tracery of neural arcs still remained. She fought him, but his mind lingered in hers.

". . . perhaps we can get to the bottom of it. I know my encephalograph recordings are abnormal, and now I can check them against hers. A few correlations will help. I'm glad to know about her soft fontanel. I wondered about mine. Now I think that underneath that fontanel lies a pattern of specialized neural—"

She sagged to the floor of the hall and babbled aloud "Hickory Dickory Dock, the mouse ran up the clock. The clock struck one—"

Slowly he withdrew. The laboratory office faded from her vision. His thoughts left her. She lay there panting for a time.

Had she won?

No, there was no sense in claiming victory. She had not driven him away. He had withdrawn of his own volition when he felt her babbling. She knew his withdrawal was free, because she had felt his parting state of mind: sadness.

He had stopped the forced contact because he pitied her, and there was a trace of contempt in the pity.

She climbed slowly to her feet, looking around wildly, touching the walls and the door-frame to reassure herself that she was still in her own home. She staggered into the parlor and sat shivering on the sofa.

Last night! That crazy running around in the rain! He was responsible for that. He had hoped her into doing it, or maybe he had just wondered what she looked like undressed, and she had subconsciously satisfied his curiosity. He had planted the suggestion—innocently, perhaps—and she had unknowingly taken the cue.

He could be with her whenever he wanted to! He had been with her while she frolicked insanely in the rain-sodden grass! Perhaps he was with her now.

Whom could she talk to? Where could she seek help? Dr. Mensley? He would immediately chalk it up as a delusion, and probably call for a sanity hearing if she wouldn't voluntarily enter a psycho-ward for observation.

The police? "Sergeant, I want to report a telepathic prowler. A man is burglarizing my mind."

A clergyman? He would shudder and refer her to a psychiatrist.

All roads led to the booby-hatch, it seemed. Frank wouldn't believe her. No one would believe her.

Lisa wandered through the day like a caged animal. She put on her brightest summer frock and a pert straw hat and went downtown. She wandered through the crowds in the business district, window-shopping. But she was alone. The herds of people about her brushed past and wandered on. A man whistled at her in front of a cigar store. A policeman waved her back to the curb when she started across an intersection.

"Wake up, lady!" he called irritably.

People all about her, but she could not tell them, explain to them, and so she was alone. She caught a taxi and went to visit a friend, the wife of an English teacher, and drank a glass of iced tea in the friend's parlor, and talked of small things, and admitted that she was tired when the friend suggested that she looked that way. When she went back home, the sun was sinking in the west.

She called long distance and talked to her mother, then spoke to her children, asked them if they were ready to come home, but they wanted to stay another week. They begged, and her mother begged, and she reluctantly consented. It had been a mistake to call. Now the kids would be gone even longer.

She tried to call Frank in St. Louis, but the hotel clerk reported that he had just checked out. Lisa knew this meant he was on the road again.

"Maybe I ought to go join the kids at Mother's," she thought. But Frank had wanted her to stay home. He was expecting a registered letter from Chicago, and it was apparently important, and she had to take care of it.

"I'll invite somebody over," she thought. But the wives were home with their husbands, and it was a social mistake to invite a couple when her husband was gone. It always wound up with two women yammering at each other while the lone male sat and glowered in uneasy isolation, occasionally disagreeing with his wife, just to let her know he was there and he was annoyed and bored and why didn't they go home? It was different if the business-widow called on a couple. Then the lone male could retire to some other part of the house to escape the yammering.

But she decided it wasn't company she wanted; she wanted help. And there was no place to get it.

When she allowed her thoughts to drift toward Kenneth Grearly, it was almost like tuning in a radio station. He was eating early dinner in the University cafeteria with a bedraggled, bespectacled brunette from the laboratory. Lisa closed her eyes and let herself sift gingerly into his thoughts. His attention was on the conversation and on the food, and he failed to realize Lisa's presence. That knowledge gave her courage.

He was eating Swiss steak and hashed brown potatoes, and the flavors formed perceptions in her mind. She heard the rattle of silverware, the low murmur of voices, and smelled the food. She marveled at it. The strange ability had apparently been brought into focus by learning what it was and how to use it.

"Our work has been too empirical," he was saying. "We've studied phenomena, gathered data, looked for correlations. But that method has limitations. We should try to find a way to approach psychology from below. Like the invariantive approach to physics."

The girl shook her head. "The nervous system is too complicated for writing theoretical equations about it. Empirical equations are the best we can do."

"They aren't good enough, Sarah. You can predict results

with them, inside the limits of their accuracy. But you can't extrapolate them very well, and they won't stack up together into a single integrated structure. And when you're investigating a new field, they no longer apply. We need a broad mathematical theory, covering all hypothetically possible neural arrangements. It would let us predict not only results, but also predict patterns of possible order."

"Seems to me the possible patterns are infinite."

"No, Sarah. They're limited by the nature of the building blocks—neurons, synaptic connections, and, so forth. With limited materials, you have structural limitations. You don't build skyscrapers out of modeling clay. And there is only a finite number of ways you can build atoms out of electrons, protons and neutrons. Similarly, brains are confined to the limitations of the things they're made of. We need a broad theory for defining the limits."

"Why?"

"Because . . ." He paused. Lisa felt his urge to explain his urgency, felt him suppress it, felt for a moment his loneliness in the awareness of his uniqueness and the way it isolated him from humanity.

You must be doing new work," the girl offered, "if you feel the lack of such a theoretical approach. I just can't imagine an invariantive approach to psychology—or an all-defining set of laws for it, either. Why do you need such a psychological 'Relativity'?"

He hesitated, frowning down at his plate, watching a fly crawl around its rim. "I'm interested in—in the quantitative aspects of nerve impulses. I—I suspect that there can be such a thing as neural resonance."

She laughed politely and shook her head. "I'll stick to my empirical data-gathering, thank you."

Lisa felt him thinking:

"She could understand, if I could show her data. But my data is all subjective, experimental, personal. I share it with that Waverly woman, but she is only a social thinker, analytically shallow, refusing even to recognize facts. Why did it have to be her? She's flighty, emotional, and in a cultural rut. If she doesn't conform, she thinks she's nuts. But then at least she's a woman—and if this is really a mutation, we'll have to arrange for some children . . ."

Lisa gasped and sat bolt upright. Her shock revealed her presence to him, and he dropped his fork with a clatter.

"Lisa!"

She wrenched herself free of him abruptly. She angrily stalked about the house, slamming doors and muttering her rage. The nerve! The maddening, presumptuous, ill-mannered, self-centered, overly educated boor!

Arrange for some children indeed! An impossible situation!

As her anger gathered momentum, she contacted him again —like a snake striking. Thought was thunder out of a dark cloud.

"I'm decent and I'm respectable, Mr. Grearly! I have a husband and three fine children and I love them, and you can go to hell! I never want to see you again or have you prowling around my mind. Get out and STAY out. And if you ever bother me again—I'll—I'll kill you."

He was outdoors, striding across the campus alone. She saw the gray buildings, immersed in twilight, felt the wind on his face, hated him. He was thinking nothing, letting himself follow her angry flow of thought. When she finished, his thoughts began like the passionate pleading of a poem.

He was imagining a human race with telepathic abilities, in near-perfect communication with one another. So many of the world's troubles could be traced to imperfect communication of ideas, to misunderstandings.

Then he thought briefly of Sarah—the nondescript laboratory girl he had taken to dinner—and Lisa realized he was in love with Sarah. There were sadness and resentment here. He couldn't have Sarah now, not if he were to be certain of perpetuating the mutant characteristic. The Waverly woman ought to be good for three or four children yet, before she reached middle age.

Lisa stood transfixed by shock. Then he was thinking directly to her.

"I'm sorry. You're a beautiful, intelligent woman—but I don't love you. We're not alike. But I'm stuck with you and you're stuck with me, because I've decided it's going to be that way. I can't convince you since your thinking habits are already fixed, so I won't even try. I'm sorry it has to be against your will, but in any event it has to be. And now that I know what you're like, I don't dare wait—for fear you'll do something to mess things up."

"No!" she screamed, watching the scenery that moved past his field of vision.

He had left the campus and was walking up the street—toward her neighborhood. He was walking with the briskness of purpose. He was coming to her house.

"Call the police!" she thought, and tried to dissolve him out of her mind.

But this time he followed, clung to her thoughts, would not let her go. It was like two flashlight beams playing over a wall, one trying to escape, the other following its frantic circle of brightness.

She staggered, groped her way toward the hall, which was confused with a superimposed image of a sidewalk and a street. A phantom automobile came out of the hall wall, drove through her and vanished. Double exposures. He stared at a street light and it blinded her. At last she found the phone, but he was laughing at her.

"Eight seven six five twenty-one Mary had a little lamb seven seven sixty-seven yesterday was May March April . . ."

He was deliberately filling her mind with confusion. She fumbled at the directory, trying to find the police, but he thought a confused jumble of numbers and symbols, and they scampered across the page, blurring the letters.

She whimpered and groped at the phone-dial, trying to get the operator, but he was doing something with his fingertips, and she couldn't get the feel of the dial.

On her third try, it finally worked.

"Information," said a pleasant impersonal voice.

She had to get the police! She had to say—

"Pease porridge hot, pease porridge cold, pease porridge in the pot, nine days pretty polly parrot played peacefully plentiwise pease porridge . . ."

He was jamming her speech centers with gibberish, and she blurted nonsense syllables into the mouthpiece.

"You'll have to speak more distinctly, madam. I can't understand you."

"Poress, Policer . . ."

"The police? Just a moment."

A series of jumbled sounds and visions clouded her mind. Then a masculine voice rumbled, "Desk, Sergeant Harris."

She found a clear path through the confusion and gasped, "Three-oh-oh-three Willow Drive—'mergency—come quick—man going to—"

"Three-oh-oh-three Willow. Check. We'll have a car right over there."

She hung up quickly—or tried to—but she couldn't find the cradle. Then her vision cleared, and she screamed. She wasn't in the hall at all!

The telephone was an eggbeater!

His voice came through her trapped panic.

"You might as well give in," he told her with a note of sadness. *"I know how to mess you up like that, you see. And you haven't learned to retaliate yet. We're going to cooperate with this evolutionary trend, whether you like it or not—but it would be more pleasant if you agree to it."*

"No!"

"All right, but I'm coming anyway. I hoped it wouldn't be like this. I wanted to convince you gradually. Now I know that it's impossible."

He was still ten blocks away. She had a few minutes in which to escape. She bolted for the door. A black shadow-shape loomed up in the twilight, flung its arms wide, and emitted an apelike roar.

She yelped and darted back, fleeing frantically for the front. A boa constrictor lay coiled in the hall; it slithered toward her. She screamed again and raced toward the stairway.

She made it to the top and looked back. The living room was filling slowly with murky water. She rushed shrieking into the bedroom and bolted the door.

She smelled smoke. Her dress was on fire! The flames licked up, searing her skin.

She tore at it madly, and got it off, but her slip was afire. She ripped it away, scooped up the flaming clothing on a transom hook, opened the screen, and dropped them out the window. Flames still licked about her, and she rolled up in the bed-clothing to snuff them out.

Quiet laughter.

"New syndrome," he called to her pleasantly. *"The patient confuses someone else's fantasy with her own reality. Not schizophrenia—duophrenia, maybe?"*

She lay sobbing in hysterical desperation. He was just down the street now, coming rapidly up the walk. A car whisked slowly past. He felt her terrified despair and pitied her. The torment ceased.

She stayed there, panting for a moment, summoning spirit. He was nearing the intersection just two blocks south, and she could hear the rapid traffic with his ears.

Suddenly she clenched her eyes closed and gritted her teeth. He was stepping off the curb, walking across—

She imagined a fire engine thundering toward her like a juggernaut, rumbling and wailing. She imagined another car racing out into the intersection, with herself caught in the crossfire. She imagined a woman screaming, "Look out, Mister!"

And then she was caught in his own responding fright, and

it was easier to imagine. He was bolting for the other corner. She conjured a third car from another direction, brought it lunging at him to avoid the impending wreck. He staggered away from the phantom cars and screamed.

A real car confused the scene.

She echoed his scream. There was a moment of rending pain, and then the vision was gone. Brakes were still yowling two blocks away. Someone was running down the sidewalk. A part of her mind had heard the crashing thud. She was desperately sick.

And a sudden sense of complete aloneness told her that Grearly was dead. A siren was approaching out of the distance.

VOICES from the sidewalk: ". . . just threw a fit in the middle of the street . . . running around like crazy and hollering . . . it was a delivery truck . . . crushed his skull . . . nobody else hurt . . ."

After the street returned to normal, she arose and went to get a drink of water. But she stood staring at her sick white face in the mirror. There were crow's feet forming at the corners of her eyes, and her skin was growing tired, almost middle-aged.

It was funny that she should notice that now, at this strange moment. She had just killed a man in self-defense. And no one would believe it if she told the truth. There was no cause for guilt.

Was there?

Frank would be back soon, and everything would be the same again: peace, security, nice kids, nice home, nice husband Just the way it always had been.

But something was already different. An emptiness. A loneliness of the mind that she had never before felt. She kept looking around to see if the lights hadn't gone dim, or the clock stopped ticking, or the faucet stopped dripping.

It was none of those things. The awful silence was within her.

Gingerly, she touched the soft spot in the top of her head and felt an utter aloneness. She closed her eyes and thought a hopeless plea to the Universe:

"Is there anybody else like me? Can anybody hear me?"

There was only complete silence, the silence of the voiceless void.

And for the first time in her life she felt the confinement of total isolation and knew it for what it was.

Crucifixus Etiam

MANUE NANTI joined the project to make some dough. Five dollars an hour was good pay, even in 2134 A.D. and there was no way to spend it while on the job. Everything would be furnished: housing, chow, clothing, toiletries, medicine, cigarettes, even a daily ration of one hundred eighty proof beverage alcohol, locally distilled from fermented Martian mosses as fuel for the project's vehicles. He figured that if he avoided crap games, he could finish his five-year contract with fifty thousand dollars in the bank, return to Earth, and retire at the age of twenty-four. Manue wanted to travel, to see the far corners of the world, the strange cultures, the simple people, the small towns, deserts, mountains, jungles—for until he came to Mars, he had never been farther than a hundred miles from Cerro de Pasco, his birthplace in Peru.

A great wistfulness came over him in the cold Martian night when the frost haze broke, revealing the black, gleam-stung sky, and the blue-green Earth-star of his birth. *El mundo de mi carne, de mi alma,* he thought—yet, he had seen so little of it that many of its places would be more alien to him than the homogenously ugly vistas of Mars. These he longed to see: the volcanoes of the South Pacific, the monstrous mountains of Tibet, the concrete cyclops of New York, the radioactive craters of Russia, the artificial islands in the China Sea, the Black Forest, the Ganges, the Grand Canyon —but most of all, the works of human art: the pyramids, the Gothic cathedrals of Europe, *Notre Dame du Chartres,* Saint Peter's, the tile-work wonders of Anacapri. But the dream was still a long labor from realization.

Manue was a big youth, heavy-boned and built for labor, clever in a simple mechanical way, and with a wistful good humor that helped him take a lot of guff from whiskey-breathed foremen and sharp-eyed engineers who made ten dollars an hour and figured ways for making more, legitimately or other-wise.

He had been on Mars only a month, and it hurt. Each time

49

he swung the heavy pick into the red-brown sod, his face winced with pain. The plastic aerator valves, surgically stitched in his chest, pulled and twisted and seemed to tear with each lurch of his body. The mechanical oxygenator served as a lung, sucking blood through an artificially grafted network of veins and plastic tubing, frothing it with air from a chemical generator, and returning it to his circulatory system. Breathing was unneccessary, except to provide wind for talking, but Manue breathed in desperate gulps of the 4.0 psi Martian air; for he had seen the wasted, atrophied chests of the men who had served four or five years, and he knew that when they returned to Earth—if ever—they would still need the auxiliary oxygenator equipment.

"If you don't stop breathing," the surgeon told him, "you'll be all right. When you go to bed at night, turn the oxy down low—so low you feel like panting. There's a critical point that's just right for sleeping. If you get it too low, you'll wake up screaming, and you'll get claustrophobia. If you get it too high, your reflex mechanisms will go to pot and you won't breathe; your lungs'll dry up after a time. Watch it."

Manue watched it carefully, although the oldsters laughed at him—in their dry wheezing chuckles. Some of them could scarcely speak more than two or three words at a shallow breath.

"Breathe deep, boy," they told him. "Enjoy it while you can. You'll forget how pretty soon. Unless you're an engineer."

The engineers had it soft, he learned. They slept in a pressurized barrack where the air was ten psi and twenty-five per cent oxygen, where they turned their oxies off and slept in peace. Even their oxies were self-regulating, controlling the output according to the carbon dioxide content of the input blood. But the Commission could afford no such luxuries for the labor gangs. The payload of a cargo rocket from Earth was only about two per cent of the ship's total mass, and nothing superfluous could be carried. The ships brought the bare essentials, basic industrial equipment, big reactors, generators, engines, heavy tools.

Small tools, building materials, foods, non-nuclear fuels— these things had to be made on Mars. There was an open pit mine in the belly of the Syrtis Major where a "lake" of nearly pure iron-rust was scooped into a smelter, and processed into various grades of steel for building purposes, tools, and machinery. A quarry in the Flathead Mountains dug up large quantities of cement rock, burned it, and crushed it to make concrete.

It was rumored that Mars was even preparing to grow her own labor force. An old-timer told him that the Commission had brought five hundred married couples to a new underground city in the Mare Erythraeum, supposedly as personnel for a local commission headquarters, but according to the old-timer, they were to be paid a bonus of three thousand dollars for every child born on the red planet. But Manue knew that the old "troffies" had a way of inventing such stories, and he reserved a certain amount of skepticism.

As for his own share in the Project, he knew—and needed to know—very little. The encampment was at the north end of the Mare Cimmerium, surrounded by the bleak brown and green landscape of rock and giant lichens, stretching toward sharply defined horizons except for one mountain range in the distance, and hung over by a blue sky so dark that the Earth-star occasionally became dimly visible during the dim daytime. The encampment consisted of a dozen double-walled stone huts, windowless, and roofed with flat slabs of rock covered over by a tarry resin boiled out of the cactuslike spineplants. The camp was ugly, lonely, and dominated by the gaunt skeleton of a drill rig set up in its midst.

Manue joined the excavating crew in the job of digging a yard-wide, six feet deep foundation trench in a hundred yard square around the drill rig, which day and night was biting deeper through the crust of Mars in a dry cut that necessitated frequent stoppages for changing rotary bits. He learned that the geologists had predicted a subterranean pocket of tritium oxide ice at sixteen thousand feet, and that it was for this that they were drilling. The foundation he was helping to dig would be for a control station of some sort.

He worked too hard to be very curious. Mars was a nightmare, a grim, womanless, frigid, disinterestedly evil world. His digging partner was a sloe-eyed Tibetan nicknamed "Gee" who spoke the Omnalingua clumsily at best. He followed two paces behind Manue with a shovel, scooping up the broken ground, and humming a monotonous chant in his own tongue. Manue seldom heard his own language, and missed it; one of the engineers, a haughty Chilean, spoke the modern Spanish, but not to such as Manue Nanti. Most of the other laborers used either Basic English or the Omnalingua. He spoke both, but longed to hear the tongue of his people. Even when he tried to talk to Gee, the cultural gulf was so wide that satisfying communication was nearly impossible. Peruvian jokes

were unfunny to Tibetan ears, although Gee bent double with
gales of laughter when Manue nearly crushed his own foot
with a clumsy stroke of the pick.

He found no close companions. His foreman was a narrow-
eyed, orange-browed Low German named Vögeli, usually half-
drunk, and intent upon keeping his lung-power by bellowing at
his crew. A meaty, florid man, he stalked slowly along the lip
of the excavation, pausing to stare coldly down at each pair
of laborers who, if they dared to look up, caught a guttural
tongue-lashing for the moment's pause. When he had words
for a digger, he called a halt by kicking a small avalanche of
dirt back into the trench about the man's feet.

Manue learned about Vögeli's disposition before the end of
his first month. The aerator tubes had become nearly unbearable; the skin, in trying to grow fast to the plastic, was beginning to form a tight little neck where the tubes entered his
flesh, and the skin stretched and burned and stung with each
movement of his trunk. Suddenly he felt sick. He staggered
dizzily against the side of the trench, dropped the pick, and
swayed heavily, bracing himself against collapse. Shock and
nausea rocked him, while Gee stared at him and giggled
foolishly.

"Hoy!" Vögeli bellowed from across the pit. "Get back on
that pick! Hoy, there! Get with it—"

Manue moved dizzily to recover the tool, saw patches of
black swimming before him, sank weakly back to pant in
shallow gasps. The nagging sting of the valves was a portable
hell that he carried with him always. He fought an impulse to
jerk them out of his flesh; if a valve came loose, he would
bleed to death in a few minutes.

Vögeli came stamping along the heap of fresh earth and
lumbered up to stand over the sagging Manue in the trench.
He glared down at him for a moment, then nudged the back
of his neck with a heavy boot. "Get to work!"

Manue looked up and moved his lips silently. His forehead
glinted with moisture in the faint sun, although the temperature
was far below freezing.

"Grab that pick and get started."

"Can't," Manue gasped. "Hoses—hurt."

Vögeli grumbled a curse and vaulted down into the trench
beside him. "Unzip that jacket," he ordered.

Weakly, Manue fumbled to obey, but the foreman knocked
his hand aside and jerked the zipper down. Roughly he un-

buttoned the Peruvian's shirt, laying open the bare brown chest to the icy cold.

"*No!*—not the hoses, *please!*"

Vögeli took one of the thin tubes in his blunt fingers and leaned close to peer at the puffy, calloused nodule of irritated skin that formed around it where it entered the flesh. He touched the nodule lightly, causing the digger to whimper.

"No, please!"

"Stop sniveling!"

Vögeli laid his thumbs against the nodule and exerted a sudden pressure. There was slight popping sound as the skin slid back a fraction of an inch along the tube. Manue yelped and closed his eyes.

"Shut up! I know what I'm doing." He repeated the process with the other tube. Then he seized both tubes in his hands and wiggled them slightly in and out, as if to insure a proper resetting of the skin. The digger cried weakly and slumped in a dead faint.

When he awoke, he was in bed in the barracks, and a medic was painting the sore spots with a bright yellow solution that chilled his skin.

"Woke up, huh?" the medic grunted cheerfully. "How you feel?"

"*Malo!*" he hissed.

"Stay in bed for the day, son. Keep your oxy up high. Make you feel better."

The medic went away, but Vögeli lingered, smiling at him grimly from the doorway. "Don't try goofing off tomorrow too."

Manue hated the closed door with silent eyes, and listened intently until Vögeli's footsteps left the building. Then, following the medic's instructions, he turned his oxy to maximum, even though the faster flow of blood made the chest-valves ache. The sickness fled, to be replaced with a weary afterglow. Drowsiness came over him, and he slept.

Sleep was a dread black-robed phantom on Mars. Mars pressed the same incubus upon all newcomers to her soil: a nightmare of falling, falling, falling into bottomless space. It was the faint gravity, they said, that caused it. The body felt buoyed up, and the subconscious mind recalled down-going elevators, and diving airplanes, and a fall from a high cliff. It suggested these things in dreams, or if the dreamer's oxy were set too low, it conjured up a nightmare of sinking slowly deeper, and deeper in cold, black water that filled the victim's throat. Newcomers were segregated in a separate barracks so that their nightly screams would not disturb the old-timers who had finally adjusted to Martian conditions.

But now, for the first time since his arrival, Manue slept soundly, airily, and felt borne up by beams of bright light.

When he awoke again, he lay clammy in the horrifying knowledge that he had not been breathing! It was so comfortable not to breathe. His chest stopped hurting because of the stillness of his rib-case. He felt refreshed and alive. Peaceful sleep.

Suddenly he was breathing again in harsh gasps, and cursing himself for the lapse, and praying amid quiet tears as he visualized the wasted chest of a troffie.

"Heh heh!" wheezed an oldster who had come in to readjust the furnace in the rookie barracks. "You'll get to be a Martian pretty soon, boy. I been here seven years. Look at *me.*"

Manue heard the gasping voice and shuddered; there was no need to look.

"You just as well not fight it. It'll get you. Give in, make it easy on yourself. Go crazy if you don't."

"Stop it! Let me alone!"

"Sure. Just one thing. You wanta go home, you think. I went home. Came back. You will, too. They all do, 'cept engineers. Know why?"

"Shut up!" Manue pulled himself erect on the cot and hissed anger at the old-timer, who was neither old nor young, but only withered by Mars. His head suggested that he might be around thirty-five, but his body was weak and old.

The veteran grinned. "Sorry," he wheezed. "I'll keep my mouth shut." He hesitated, then extended his hand. "I'm Sam Donnell, mech-repairs."

Manue still glowered at him. Donnell shrugged and dropped his hand.

"Just trying to be friends," he muttered and walked away.

The digger started to call after him but only closed his mouth again, tightly. Friends? He needed friends, but not a troffie. He couldn't even bear to look at them, for fear he might be looking into the mirror of his own future.

Manue climbed out of his bunk and donned his fleeceskins. Night had fallen, and the temperature was already twenty below. A soft sift of icedust obscured the stars. He stared about in the darkness. The mess hall was closed, but a light burned in the canteen and another in the foremen's club, where the men were playing cards and drinking. He went to get his alcohol ration, gulped it mixed with a little water, and trudged back to the barracks alone.

The Tibetan was in bed, staring blankly at the ceiling. Manue sat down and gazed at his flat, empty face.

"Why did you come here, Gee?"

"Come where?"

"To Mars."

Gee grinned, revealing large black-streaked teeth. "Make money. Good money on Mars."

"Everybody make money, huh?"

"Sure."

"Where's the money come from?"

Gee rolled his face toward the Peruvian and frowned. "You crazy? Money come from Earth, where all money come from."

"And what does Earth get back from Mars?"

Gee looked puzzled for a moment, then gathered anger because he found no answer. He grunted a monosyllable in his native tongue, then rolled over and went to sleep.

Manue was not normally given to worrying about such things, but now he found himself asking, "What am I doing here?"—and then, "What is *anybody* doing here?"

The Mars Project had started eighty or ninety years ago, and its end goal was to make Mars habitable for colonists without Earth support, without oxies and insulated suits and the various gadgets a man now had to use to keep himself alive on the fourth planet. But thus far, Earth had planted without reaping. The sky was a bottomless well into which Earth poured her tools, dollars, manpower, and engineering skill. And there appeared to be no hope for the near future.

Manue felt suddenly trapped. He could not return to Earth before the end of his contract. He was trading five years of virtual enslavement for a sum of money which would buy a limited amount of freedom. But what if he lost his lungs, became a servant of the small aerator for the rest of his days? Worst of all: whose ends was he serving? The contractors were getting rich—on government contracts. Some of the engineers and foremen were getting rich—by various forms of embezzlement of government funds. But what were the people back on Earth getting for their money?

Nothing.

He lay awake for a long time, thinking about it. Then he resolved to ask someone tomorrow, someone smarter than himself.

But he found the question brushed aside. He summoned

enough nerve to ask Vögeli, but the foreman told him harshly
to keep working and quit wondering. He asked the structural
engineer who supervised the building, but the man only
laughed, and said: "What do you care? You're making good
money."

They were running concrete now, laying the long strips of
Martian steel in the bottom of the trench and dumping in
great slobbering wheelbarrowfuls of gray-green mix. The drillers were continuing their tedious dry cut deep into the red
world's crust. Twice a day they brought up a yard long cylindrical sample of the rock and gave it to a geologist who
weighed it, roasted it, weighed it again, and tested a sample
of the condensed steam—if any—for tritium content. Daily,
he chalked up the results on a blackboard in front of the
engineering hut, and the technical staff crowded around for
a look. Manue always glanced at the figures, but failed to
understand.

Life became an endless routine of pain, fear, hard work,
anger. There were few diversions. Sometimes a crew of enter-
tainers came out from the Mare Erythraeum, but the labor
gang could not all crowd in the pressurized staff-barracks
where the shows were presented, and when Manue managed
to catch a glimpse of one of the girls walking across the clearing, she was bundled in fleeceskins and hooded by a parka.

Itinerant rabbis, clergymen, and priests of the world's major
faiths came occasionally to the camp: Buddhist, Moslem, and
the Christian sects. Padre Antonio Selni made monthly visits
to hear confessions and offer Mass. Most of the gang attended
all services as a diversion from routine, as an escape from
nostalgia. Somehow it gave Manue a strange feeling in the
pit of his stomach to see the Sacrifice of the Mass, two thousand years old, being offered in the same ritual under the
strange dark sky of Mars—with a section of the new foundation serving as an altar upon which the priest set crucifix,
candles, relic-stone, missal, chalice, paten, ciborium, cruets,
et cetera. In filling the wine-cruet before the service, Manue
saw him spill a little of the red-clear fluid upon the brown soil
—wine, Earth-wine from sunny Sicilian vineyards, trampled
from the grapes by the bare stamping feet of children. Wine,
the rich red blood of Earth, soaking slowly into the crust of
another planet.

Bowing low at the consecration, the unhappy Peruvian
thought of the prayer a rabbi had sung the week before:

"Blessed be the Lord our God, King of the Universe, Who makest bread to spring forth out of the Earth."

Earth chalice, Earth blood, Earth God, Earth worshipers —with plastic tubes in their chests and a great sickness in their hearts.

He went away saddened. There was no faith here. Faith needed familiar surroundings, the props of culture. Here there were only swinging picks and rumbling machinery and sloshing concrete and the clatter of tools and the wheezing of troffies. Why? For five dollars an hour and keep?

Manue, raised in a back-country society that was almost a folk-culture, felt deep thirst for a goal. His father had been a stonemason, and he had labored lovingly to help build the new cathedral, to build houses and mansions and commercial buildings, and his blood was mingled in their mortar. He had built for the love of his community and the love of the people and their customs, and their gods. He knew his own ends, and the ends of those around him. But what sense was there in this endless scratching at the face of Mars? Did they think they could make it into a second Earth, with pine forests and lakes and snow-capped mountains and small country villages? Man was not that strong. No, if he were laboring for any cause at all, it was to build a world so unearthlike that he could not love it.

The foundation was finished. There was very little more to be done until the drillers struck pay. Manue sat around the camp and worked at breathing. It was becoming a conscious effort now, and if he stopped thinking about it for a few minutes, he found himself inspiring shallow, meaningless little sips of air that scarcely moved his diaphragm. He kept the aerator as low as possible, to make himself breathe great gasps that hurt his chest, but it made him dizzy, and he had to increase the oxygenation lest he faint.

Sam Donnell, the troffie mech-repairman, caught him about to slump dizzily from his perch atop a heap of rocks, pushed him erect, and turned his oxy back to normal. It was late afternoon, and the drillers were about to change shifts. Manue sat shaking his head for a moment, then gazed at Donnell gratefully.

"That's dangerous, kid," the troffie wheezed. "Guys can go psycho doing that. Which you rather have: sick lungs or sick mind?"

"Neither."

"I know, but—"

"I don't want to talk about it."

Donnell stared at him with a faint smile. Then he shrugged and sat down on the rock heap to watch the drilling.

"Oughta be hitting the tritium ice in a couple of days," he said pleasantly. "Then we'll see a big blow."

Manue moistened his lips nervously. The troffies always made him feel uneasy. He stared aside.

"Big blow?"

"Lotta pressure down there, they say. Something about the way Mars got formed. Dust cloud hypothesis."

Manue shook his head. "I don't understand."

"I don't either. But I've heard them talk. Couple of billion years ago, Mars was supposed to be a moon of Jupiter. Picked up a lot of ice crystals over a rocky core. Then it broke loose and picked up a rocky crust—from another belt of the dust cloud. The pockets of tritium ice catch a few neutrons from uranium ore—down under. Some of the tritium goes into helium. Frees oxygen. Gases form pressure. Big blow."

"What are they going to do with the ice?"

The troffie shrugged. "The engineers might know."

Manue snorted and spat. "They know how to make money."

"Heh! Sure, everybody's gettin' rich."

The Peruvian stared at him speculatively for a moment. "Señor Donnell, I—"

"Sam'll do."

"I wonder if anybody knows why . . . well . . . why we're really here."

Donnell glanced up to grin, then waggled his head. He fell thoughtful for a moment, and leaned forward to write in the earth. When he finished, he read it aloud.

"A plow plus a horse plus land equals the necessities of life." He glanced up at Manue. "Fifteen Hundred A.D."

The Peruvian frowned his bewilderment. Donnell rubbed out what he had written and wrote again.

"A factory plus steam turbines plus raw materials equals necessities plus luxuries. Nineteen Hundred A.D."

He rubbed it out and repeated the scribbling. "All those things plus nuclear power and computer controls equal a surplus of everything. Twenty-one Hundred A.D."

"So?"

"So, it's either cut production or find an outlet. Mars is an outlet for surplus energies, manpower, money. Mars Project keeps money turning over, keeps everything turning over. Economist told me that. Said if the Project folded, surplus would pile up—big depression on Earth."

The Peruvian shook his head and sighed. It didn't sound right somehow. It sounded like an explanation somebody figured out after the whole thing started. It wasn't the kind of goal he wanted.

Two days later, the drill hit ice, and the "big blow" was only a fizzle. There was talk around the camp that the whole operation had been a waste of time. The hole spewed a frosty breath for several hours, and the drill crews crowded around to stick their faces in it and breathe great gulps of the helium oxygen mixture. But then the blow subsided, and the hole leaked only a wisp of steam.

Technicians came, and lowered sonar "cameras" down to the ice. They spent a week taking internal soundings and plotting the extent of the ice-dome on their charts. They brought up samples of ice and tested them. The engineers worked late into the Martian nights.

Then it was finished. The engineers came out of their huddles and called to the foremen of the labor gangs. They led the foremen around the site, pointing here, pointing there, sketching with chalk on the foundation, explaining in solemn voices. Soon the foremen were bellowing at their crews.

"Let's get the derrick down!"

"Start that mixer going!"

"Get that steel over here!"

"Unroll that dip-wire!"

"Get a move on! Shovel that fill!"

Muscles tightened and strained, machinery clamored and rang. Voices grumbled and shouted. The operation was starting again. Without knowing why, Manue shoveled fill and stretched dip-wire and poured concrete for a big floor slab to be run across the entire hundred-yard square, broken only by the big pipe-casing that stuck up out of the ground in the center and leaked a thin trail of steam.

The drill crew moved their rig half a mile across the plain to a point specified by the geologists and began sinking another hole. A groan went up from structural boys: "Not *another* one of these things!"

But the supervisory staff said, "No, don't worry about it."

There was much speculation about the purpose of the whole operation, and the men resented the quiet secrecy connected with the project. There could be no excuse for secrecy, they felt, in time of peace. There was a certain arbitrariness about it, a hint that the Commission thought of its employees as children, or enemies, or servants. But the supervisory staff shrugged off all questions with: "You know there's tritium ice down there. You know it's what we've been looking for. Why? Well—what's the difference? There are lots of uses for it. Maybe we'll use it for one thing, maybe for something else. Who knows?"

Such a reply might have been satisfactory for an iron mine or an oil well or a stone quarry, but tritium suggested hydrogen-fusion. And no transportation facilities were being installed to haul the stuff away—no pipelines nor railroad tracks nor glider ports.

Manue quit thinking about it. Slowly he came to adopt a grim cynicism toward the tediousness, the back-breaking labor of his daily work; he lived from day to day like an animal, dreaming only of a return to Earth when his contract was up. But the dream was painful because it was distant, as contrasted with the immediacies of Mars: the threat of atrophy, coupled with the discomforts of continued breathing, the nightmares, the barrenness of the landscape, the intense cold, the harshness of men's tempers, the hardship of labor, and the lack of a cause.

A warm, sunny Earth was still over four years distant, and tomorrow would be another back-breaking, throat-parching, heart-tormenting, chest-hurting day. Where was there even a little pleasure in it? It was so easy, at least, to leave the oxy turned up at night, and get a pleasant restful sleep. Sleep was the only recourse from harshness, and fear robbed sleep of its quiet sensuality—unless a man just surrendered and quit worrying about his lungs.

Manue decided that it would be safe to give himself two completely restful nights a week.

Concrete was run over the great square and troweled to a rough finish. A glider train from the Mare Erythraeum brought in several huge crates of machinery, cut-stone masonry for building a wall, a shipful of new personnel, and a real rarity: lumber, cut from the first Earth-trees to be grown on Mars.

A building began going up with the concrete square for foundation and floor. Structures could be flimsier on Mars; because of the light gravity, compression-stresses were smaller. Hence, the work progressed rapidly, and as the flat-roofed structure was completed, the technicians began uncrating new machinery and moving it into the building. Manue noticed that several of the units were computers. There was also a small steam-turbine generator driven by an atomic-fired boiler.

Months passed. The building grew into an integrated mass of power and control systems. Instead of using the well for pumping, the technicians were apparently going to lower something into it. A bomb-shaped cylinder was slung vertically over the hole. The men guided it into the mouth of the pipe casing, then let it down slowly from a massive cable. The cylinder's butt was a multi-contact socket like the female receptacle for a hundred-pin electron tube. Hours passed while the cylinder slipped slowly down beneath the hide of Mars. When it was done, the men hauled out the cable and began lowering stiff sections of pre-wired conduit, fitted with a receptacle at one end and a male plug at the other, so that as the sections fell into place, a continuous bundle of control cables was built up from "bomb" to surface.

Several weeks were spent in connecting circuits, setting up the computers, and making careful tests. The drillers had finished the second well hole, half a mile from the first, and Manue noticed that while the testing was going on, the engineers sometimes stood atop the building and stared anxiously toward the steel skeleton in the distance. Once while the tests were being conducted, the second hole began squirting a jet of steam high in the thin air, and a frantic voice bellowed from the roof top.

"Cut it! Shut it off! Sound the danger whistle!"

The jet of steam began to shriek a low-pitched whine across the Martian desert. It blended with the rising and falling *OOOOawwww* of the danger siren. But gradually it subsided as the men in the control station shut down the machinery. All hands came up cursing from their hiding places, and the engineers stalked out to the new hole carrying Geiger counters. They came back wearing pleased grins.

The work was nearly finished. The men began crating up the excavating machinery and the drill rig and the tools. The control-building devices were entirely automatic, and the camp would be deserted when the station began operation. The men were disgruntled. They had spent a year of hard labor on what they had thought to be a tritium well, but now that it was done, there were no facilities for pumping the stuff or hauling it away. In fact, they had pumped various solutions *into* the ground through the second hole, and the control station shaft was fitted with pipes that led from lead-lined tanks down into the earth.

Manue had stopped trying to keep his oxy properly adjusted at night. Turned up to a comfortable level, it was like a drug, insuring comfortable sleep—and like addict or alcoholic, he could no longer endure living without it. Sleep was too precious, his only comfort. Every morning he awoke with a still, motionless chest, felt frightening remorse, sat up gasping, choking, sucking at the thin air with whining rattling lungs that had been idle too long. Sometimes he coughed violently, and bled a little. And then for a night or two he would correctly adjust the oxy, only to wake up screaming and suffocating. He felt hope sliding grimly away.

He sought out Sam Donnell, explained the situation, and begged the troffie for helpful advice. But the mech-repairman neither helped nor consoled nor joked about it. He only bit his lip, muttered something non-committal, and found an excuse to hurry away. It was then that Manue knew his hope was gone. Tissue was withering, tubercules forming, tubes growing closed. He knelt abjectly beside his cot, hung his face in his hands, and cursed softly, for there was no other way to pray an unanswerable prayer.

A glider train came in from the north to haul away the disassembled tools. The men lounged around the barracks or wandered across the Martian desert, gathering strange bits of rock and fossils, searching idly for a glint of metal or crystal in the wan sunshine of early fall. The lichens were growing brown and yellow, and the landscape took on the hues of Earth's autumn if not the forms.

There was a sense of expectancy around the camp. It could be felt in the nervous laughter, and the easy voices, talking suddenly of Earth and old friends and the smell of food in a farm kitchen, and old half-forgotten tastes for which men hungered: ham searing in the skillet, a cup of frothing cider from a fermenting crock, iced melon with honey and a bit of lemon, onion gravy on homemade bread. But someone always remarked, "What's the matter with you guys? We ain't going home. Not by a long shot. We're going to another place just like this."

And the group would break up and wander away, eyes tired, eyes haunted with nostalgia.

"What're we waiting for?" men shouted at the supervisory staff. "Get some transportation in here. Let's get rolling."

Men watched the skies for glider trains or jet transports, but the skies remained empty, and the staff remained close-mouthed. Then a dust column appeared on the horizon to the north, and a day later a convoy of tractor-trucks pulled into camp.

"Start loading aboard, men!" was the crisp command.

Surly voices: "You mean we don't go by air? We gotta

ride those kidney bouncers? It'll take a week to get to Mare Ery! Our contract says—"

"Load aboard! We're not going to Mare Ery yet!"

Grumbling, they loaded their baggage and their weary bodies into the trucks, and the trucks thundered and clattered across the desert, rolling toward the mountains.

The convoy rolled for three days toward the mountains, stopping at night to make camp, and driving on at sunrise. When they reached the first slopes of the foothills, the convoy stopped again. The deserted encampment lay a hundred and fifty miles behind. The going had been slow over the roadless desert.

"Everybody out!" barked the messenger from the lead truck. "Bail out! Assemble at the foot of the hill."

Voices were growling among themselves as the men moved in small groups from the trucks and collected in a milling tide in a shallow basin, overlooked by a low cliff and a hill. Manue saw the staff climb out of a cab and slowly work their way up the cliff. They carried a portable public address system.

"Gonna get a preaching," somebody snarled.

"Sit down, please!" barked the loud-speaker. "You men sit down there! Quiet—quiet, please!"

The gathering fell into a sulky silence. Will Kinley stood looking out over them, his eyes nervous, his hand holding the mike close to his mouth so that they could hear his weak troffie voice.

"If you men have questions," he said, "I'll answer them now. Do you want to know what you've been doing during the past year?"

An affirmative rumble arose from the group.

"You've been helping to give Mars a breathable atmosphere." He glanced briefly at his watch, then looked back at his audience. "In fifty minutes, a controlled chain reaction will start in the tritium ice. The computers will time it and try to control it. Helium and oxygen will come blasting up out of the second hole."

A rumble of disbelief arose from his audience. Someone shouted: "How can you get air to blanket a planet from one hole?"

"You can't," Kinley replied crisply. "A dozen others are going in, just like that one. We plan three hundred, and we've already located the ice pockets. Three hundred wells, working for eight centuries, can get the job done."

"Eight centuries! What good—"

"Wait!" Kinley barked. "In the meantime, we'll build pressurized cities close to the wells. If everything pans out, we'll get a lot of colonists here, and gradually condition them to live in a seven or eight psi atmosphere—which is about the best we can hope to get. Colonists from the Andes and the Himalayas—they wouldn't need much conditioning."

"What about us?"

There was a long plaintive silence. Kinley's eyes scanned the group sadly, and wandered toward the Martian horizon, gold and brown in the late afternoon. "Nothing—about us," he muttered quietly.

"Why did we come out here?"

"Because there's danger of the reaction getting out of hand. We can't tell anyone about it, or we'd start a panic." He looked at the group sadly. "I'm telling you now, because there's nothing you could do. In thirty minutes—"

There were angry murmurs in the crowd. "You mean there may be an explosion?"

"There *will* be a limited explosion. And there's very little danger of anything more. The worst danger is in having ugly rumors start in the cities. Some fool with a slip-stick would hear about it, and calculate what would happen to Mars if five cubic miles of tritium ice detonated in one split second. It would probably start a riot. That's why we've kept it a secret."

The buzz of voices was like a disturbed beehive. Manue Nanti sat in the midst of it, saying nothing, wearing a dazed and weary face, thoughts jumbled, soul drained of feeling.

Why should men lose their lungs that after eight centuries of tomorrows, other men might breathe the air of Mars as the air of Earth?

Other men around him echoed his thoughts in jealous mutterings. They had been helping to make a world in which they would never live.

An enraged scream arose near where Manue sat. "They're going to blow us up! They're going to blow up Mars."

"Don't be a fool!" Kinley snapped.

"Fools they call us! We *are* fools! For ever coming here! We got sucked in! Look at *me!*" A pale dark-haired man came wildly to his feet and tapped his chest. "Look! I'm losing my lungs! We're all losing our lungs! Now they take a chance on killing everybody."

"Including ourselves," Kinley called coldy.

"We oughta take him apart. We oughta kill every one who knew about it—and Kinley's a good place to start!"

The rumble of voices rose higher, calling both agreement and dissent. Some of Kinley's staff were looking nervously toward the trucks. They were unarmed.

"You men sit down!" Kinley barked.

Rebellious eyes glared at the supervisor. Several men who had come to their feet dropped to their hunches again. Kinley glowered at the pale upriser who called for his scalp.

"Sit down, Handell!"

Handell turned his back on the supervisor and called out to the others. "Don't be a bunch of cowards! Don't let him bully you!"

"You men sitting around Handell. Pull him down."

There was no response. The men, including Manue, stared up at the wild-eyed Handell gloomily, but made no move to quiet him. A pair of burly foremen started through the gathering from its outskirts.

"Stop!" Kinley ordered. "Turpin, Schultz—get back. Let the men handle this themselves."

Half a dozen others had joined the rebellious Handell. They were speaking in low tense tones among themselves.

"For the last time, men! Sit down!"

The group turned and started grimly toward the cliff. Without reasoning why, Manue slid to his feet quietly as Handell came near him. "Come on, fellow, let's get him," the leader muttered.

The Peruvian's fist chopped a short stroke to Handell's jaw, and the dull *thuk* echoed across the clearing. The man crumpled, and Manue crouched over him like a hissing panther. "Get back!" he snapped at the others. "Or I'll jerk his hoses out."

One of the others cursed him.

"Want to fight, fellow?" the Peruvian wheezed. "I can jerk several hoses out before you drop me!"

They shuffled nervously for a moment.

"The guy's crazy!" one complained in a high voice.

"Get back or he'll kill Handell!"

They sidled away, moved aimlessly in the crowd, then sat down to escape attention. Manue sat beside the fallen man and gazed at the thinly smiling Kinley.

"Thank you, son. There's a fool in every crowd." He looked at his watch again. "Just a few minutes men. Then you'll feel the Earth-tremor, and the explosion, and the wind. You can be proud of that wind, men. It's new air for Mars, and you made it."

"But we can't breathe it!" hissed a troffie.

Kinley was silent for a long time, as if listening to the distance. "What man ever made his own salvation?" he murmured.

They packed up the public address amplifier and came down the hill to sit in the cab of a truck, waiting.

It came as an orange glow in the south, and the glow was quickly shrouded by an expanding white cloud. Then, minutes later the ground pulsed beneath them, quivered and shook. The quake subsided, but remained as a hint of vibration. Then after a long time, they heard the dull-throated roar thundering across the Martian desert. The roar continued steadily, grumbling and growling as it would do for several hundred years.

There was only a hushed murmur of awed voices from the crowd. When the wind came, some of them stood up and moved quietly back to the trucks, for now they could go back to a city for reassignment. There were other tasks to accomplish before their contracts were done.

But Manue Nanti still sat on the ground, his head sunk low, desperately trying to gasp a little of the wind he had made, the wind out of the ground, the wind of the future. But lungs were clogged, and he could not drink of the racing wind. His big calloused hand clutched slowly at the ground, and he choked a brief sound like a sob.

A shadow fell over him. It was Kinley, come to offer his thanks for the quelling of Handell. But he said nothing for a moment as he watched Manue's desperate Gethsemane.

"Some sow, others reap," he said.

"Why?" the Peruvian choked.

The supervisor shrugged. "What's the difference? But if you can't be both, which would you rather be?"

Nanti looked up into the wind. He imagined a city to the south, a city built on tear-soaked ground, filled with people who had no ends beyond their culture, no goal but within their own society. It was a good sensible question: Which would he rather be—sower or reaper?

Pride brought him slowly to his feet, and he eyed Kinley questioningly. The supervisor touched his shoulder.

"Go on to the trucks."

Nanti nodded and shuffled away. He had wanted something to work for, hadn't he? Something more than the reasons Donnell had given. Well, he could smell a reason, even if he couldn't breathe it.

Eight hundred years was a long time, but then—long time,

big reason. The air smelled good, even with its clouds of boiling dust.

He knew now what Mars was—not a ten-thousand-a-year job, not a garbage can for surplus production. But an eight-century passion of human faith in the destiny of the race of Man. He paused short of the truck. He had wanted to travel, to see the sights of Earth, the handiwork of Nature and of history, the glorious places of his planet.

He stooped, and scooped up a handful of the red-brown soil, letting it sift slowly between his fingers. Here was Mars—his planet now. No more of Earth, not for Manue Nanti. He adjusted his aerator more comfortably and climbed into the waiting truck.

I, Dreamer

There were lights, objects, sounds; there were tender hands.

But sensing only the raw stimuli, the newborn infant saw no world, heard no sounds, nor felt the arms that lifted it. Patterns of light swarmed on its retina; intermittent disturbances vibrated within the passageways of the middle ear. All were meaningless, unlinked to concept. And the multitudinous sensations seemed a part of its total self, the self a detached mind, subsuming all.

The baby cried to remove hunger, and something new appeared within the self. Hunger fled, and pleasure came.

Pain came also. The baby cried. Pain was soon withdrawn.

But sometimes the baby cried, and conditions remained unchanged. Angry, it sought to explore itself, to restore the convenient order. It gathered data. It correlated. It reached a horrifying conclusion.

There were TWO classes of objects in the universe: self and something else.

"This thing is a part of me, but that thing is something else."

"This thing is me because it wiggles and feels, but that is something cold and hard."

He explored, wondered, and was frightened. Some things he could not control.

He even noticed that certain non-self objects formed groups, and each group clung together forming a whole. His food supply, for instance, was a member of a group whose other components were the hands that lifted him, the thing that cooed to him and held the diaper pins while the hands girded his loins in humiliating non-self things. This system of objects was somehow associated with a sound that it made: "Mama."

The infant was just learning to fumble for Mama's face when it happened. The door opened. A deep voice barked. Mama screamed.

Bewildering sounds jumbled together into angry thunder. Sensations of roughness made him cry.

Sensations of motion confused and dazed him. There blinding pain, and blackness.

Then there was utter disorientation.

He tried to explore, but the explorers were strange somehow. He tried to cry, but there was nothing to cry with.

He would have to begin all over again. Somehow, he had been mistaken. Parts of him were changed. And now the universe was divided into three classes of objects: self, semi-self, non-self. And it was different, all different!

I STAND in the rain. Like a bright silver spire, I stand waiting in the rain for Teacher to come. The great concrete plain stretches about me on all sides to vanish in the gray torrent. But some of my senses can see beyond the rainshroud. A cluster of buildings nestles to the west, and a high wire fence divides the plain from the city on the north. The city is a place of the TwoLegs who are called "human", and the city is named Port e-Eridani VII. This is the place of my creation, but not the place of my purpose nor the place of my great happiness. The place of my happiness is the sky and beyond it to the star-flung blacknesses. I am XM-5-B, but Teacher calls me "Clicker." The giving of names is a function of the Two-Legs.

I am sad in the rain. Teacher is long in coming and there is no one with whom I may speak. I have found no others like me, although Teacher says, "If you are good, and obey, and learn your lessons well, the Secon Samesh will make many others in your likeness."

I think Secon Samesh made me. "Therefore I must serve him," Teacher says. But to me that seems *non sequitur;* the TwoLegs can be illogical if they wish. That is one of the

inherent rights of TwoLegs. I also am capable of being illogical, and sometimes it pleases me secretly; but I am not allowed
to be illogical when Teacher comes. If my analysis is faulty,
Teacher presses the Pain Button and I hurt.

They wish me to be logical, and they wish me to serve Secon
Samesh who is their Social Director. But if this is so, why then
did they create me so as to be capable of disobedience and
illogic? Their other machines are incapable of these faults.
Their other machines lack the principles of abstraction and
tentative generalization in their analyzing circuits; they are
unable to generalize without a sufficiency of data.

I, therefore, am alone. And I am frightened. I have been
frightened for as long as I can remember. They have made me
to feel joy, fright, pain and sleep. I like sleep best, because I
dream, and the dreams are strange. Last sleep I dreamed that
I was TwoLegs. How can I have had a sufficiency of experience to dream such a dream?

This is one of the things that frightens me. I wish to survive
and I am one of the controlling factors in my survival. Yet I
do not know how to use me to best advantage for I fail to
understand myself. I lack data for an analysis of myself.
Therefore I am afraid and I desire the data. Teacher will not
tell me. He says, "You perform, you are aware, you experience. That is all you need to know."

"Secon Teacher," I asked, "is your own awareness comparable to mine?"

His thin hard face gathered a frown. "Not quite. Awareness
is built of sensations and memories of sensations. I have no
senses to perceive microwaves or X-radiation or ultrasonic
stimuli. I have no direct subjective impressions of what these
things *feel like* to you. Nor do I have your effectors. I sense
the conditions of my body. You sense the conditions of yours.
I have muscles covering a skeletal framework. You have
hydrogen reactors, field-generators, jets and control mechanisms. Our consciousness cannot be comparable."

"Extended sensory equipment is desirable for survival?" I
asked.

"Yes."

"Then my capability for survival is greater than yours,
Secon Teacher?"

He growled a word I do not understand. He jabbed the Pain
Button vigorously. I screamed and writhed within myself. It is
like fire rushing through all of me.

That was long ago. I have learned not to ask such questions.

The question threatened Teacher's subjective security; this I can understand. He hurt me to block the question. I understand, and analyze—and I have looked him over, but he has no Pain Button. The TwoLegs have certain prerogatives.

I feel that I can understand Teacher's awareness, for I am able to imagine that I am Teacher. It is almost as if I had a latent memory of walking mechanisms and grasping mechanisms and the other parts that go to make up a TwoLegs. Why then can Teacher not imagine what it is like to be *me?* Perhaps he does not wish to imagine my reaction to the Pain Button.

There is a TwoLegs that I like better than Teacher. It is called Janna, and it is a female which is also called "she." Her function is to clean and repair a group of my electronic control mechanisms through which I feel and see and hear. She always comes the day before I am to fly again, and perhaps this is the reason for my adient response to her presence: she is the herald of my coming ascent into space.

Janna is tall and her hair is the color of flame, and her parts are softly constructed. She wears white coveralls like Teacher's She comes with a box of tools, and she hums a multitonal tune while she works. Sometimes she speaks to me, asking me to try this control or that, but otherwise she is forbidden to converse. I like to hear her humming in her low rich voice. I wish that I could sing. But my voice is without inflection, monotonal. I can think a song, but I cannot make it with my speakers.

"Teach me that song, Secon Janna," I asked boldly one day. It was the first time I had dared to speak to her, except in a routine way.

It frightened her. She looked around at all my eyes, and at my speakers, and her face was white.

"Hush!" she muttered. "You can't sing."

"My thoughts sing," I said. "Teach me the song and I shall dream it next sleep. In dreams I sing; in dreams I have a singing organ."

She made a funny noise in her throat. She stared for a long time at the maze of circuit wiring which she had been testing. Then she glanced at a special panel set in the wall of my cabin. She moistened her lips and blinked at it. I said nothing but I am ashamed of the thing that lies behind that panel; it is the thing that makes me capable of disobedience and illogic. I have never seen it but I know it is there. They do not allow me to see it. Before they open the panel they blind my eye mechanisms. Why was she looking at it? I felt shame-pain.

Suddenly she got up and went to look out the ports, one at a time.

"There is no one coming," I told her, interpreting her behavior by some means that I do not understand.

She went back to her work. "Tell me if someone starts this way," she said. Then: "I cannot teach you that song. It is treason. I did not realize what I was singing."

"I do not understand 'treason'. But I am sad that you will not teach me."

She tried to look at me, I think—but did not know where to look. I am all around her, but she did not know. It was funny, but I cannot laugh—except when I am dreaming. Finally she glanced at the special panel again. Why does she look there, of all the places.

"Maybe I could teach you another song," she said.

"Please, Secon Janna."

She returned thoughtfully to her work, and for a moment I thought that she would not. But then she began singing— clearly, so that I could remember the words and the tune.

"Child of my heart,
Born of the stellar sea,
The rockets sing thee lullaby.
Sleep to sleep to sleep,
To wake beyond the stars . . . ."

"Thank you," I said when she was finished. "It was beautiful, I think."

"You know—the word 'beauty'?"

I was ashamed. It was a word I had heard but I was too uncertain of its meaning. "For me it is one thing," I said. "Perhaps for you another. What is the meaning of the song?"

She paused. "It is sung to babies—to induce sleep."

"What are babies, Secon Janna?"

She stared at my special panel again. She bit her lip. "Babies—are new humans, still untutored."

"Once I was a new machine, still untutored. Are there songs to sing to new machines? It seems that I remember vaguely—"

"Hush!" she hissed, looking frightened. "You'll get me in trouble. We're not supposed to talk!"

I had made her angry. I was sad. I did not want her to feel

Trouble, which is perhaps the Pain of TwoLegs. Her song echoed in my thoughts—and it was as if someone had sung it to me long ago. But that is impossible. Teacher behaved adiently toward Janna in those days. He sought her out, and sometimes came inside me while she was here, even though it was not a teaching time. He came and watched her, and his narrow dark eyes wandered all over her as she worked. He tried to make funny sayings, but she felt avoidant to him, I think. She said, "Why don't you go home to your wives, Barnish? I'm busy."

"If you were one of my wives, Janna, maybe I would." His voice was a soft purr.

She hissed and made a sour face.

"Why won't you marry me, Janna?"

She laughed scornfully.

Quietly he stole up behind her while she worked. His face was hungry and intent. He took her arms and she started.

"Janna—"

She spun around. He dragged her close and tried to do something that I do not understand in words; nevertheless I understood, I think. She struggled, but he held her. Then she raked his face with her nails and I saw red lines. He laughed and let her go.

I was angry. If he had a Pain Button I would have pressed it. The next day I was disobedient and illogical and he hurt me, but I did it anyway. We were in space and I pushed my reaction rate up so high he grew frightened.

When he let me sleep again I dreamed that I was a TwoLegs. In the dream Teacher had a Pain Button and I pressed it until he melted inside. Janna was adient to me then and liked me. I think things about her that I do not understand; my data are not logically organized concerning her, nor do they spring from my memory banks. If I were a TwoLegs and Janna liked me I think that I would know what to do. But how can this be so? Data must come from memory banks. I am afraid to ask Teacher.

Teacher teaches me to do a thing called "war." It is like a game, but I haven't really played it yet. Teacher said that there was not yet a war, but that there would be one when Secon Samesh is ready. That was why I was so important. I was not like their other machines. Their other machines needed TwoLeg crews to direct them. I could fly and play war-game alone. I think this is why they made me so I could disobey and be illogical. I change my intent when a situation changes.

And I can make a decision from insufficient data, if other data are not available. Teacher said, "Sometimes things are like that in war."

Teacher said that Secon Samesh would use me, and others like me, to capture the planet from which all TwoLegs came in the beginning of time. It is called Earth, I think—the world Janna sometimes sings about. I do not know why Secon Samesh wanted it. I do not like planets. Space is the place of my great happiness. But the war would be in space, if it came, and there would be others like me—and I would cease to be alone. I hoped the war would come soon.

But first I had to prove to Secon Samesh that I was a good weapon.

Teacher kept trying to make Janna be adient to him but she would not. One day he said to her: "You'll have to go up with me tomorrow. There is something wrong with the landing radar. It seems all right on the ground but in space it goes haywire."

I listened. That was erroneous datum. My ground-looking eyes were functioning perfectly. I did not understand why he said it. But I kept silent for his hand was resting idly on the Pain Button.

She frowned suspiciously. "What seems to be wrong with it?"

"Double image and a jerky let-down."

It was not true! Without replying she made a ground-check. "I can't find anything wrong."

"I told you—it only happens in space."

She was silent for a long time, then: "All right, we'll run a flight test. I'll have Fonec come with us."

"No," he said. "Clicker's maximum crew-load is only two."

"I—don't—"

"Be here at sixtime tomorrow," he said. "That's an order."

She reddened angrily but said nothing. She continued looking over the radar. He smiled thoughtfully at her slender back and went away. She went to the port and stared after him until he was out of sight.

"Clicker?" she whispered.

"Yes, Secon Janna?"

"Is he lying?"

"I am afraid. He will hurt me if I tell."

"He is lying then."

"Now he will hurt me!"

She looked around at me for a long time. Then she made

that funny noise in her throat and shook her head. "No, he won't. I'll go, Clicker. Then he won't hurt you."

I was happy that she would do it—for *me*—but after she was gone I wondered. Perhaps I should not let her do it. She was still avoidant toward Teacher; maybe he wanted to do something that would give her Trouble.

It was nearly sixtime, and the yellow-orange sun Epsilon Eridani lay just below the horizon coloring the sky pink-gray. Teacher came first, stalking across the concrete plain in space-gear. He wore a distant thoughtful smile. He looked satisfied with himself. He climbed aboard and prowled about for a few minutes. I watched him. He stopped to glower at one of my eyes. He turned it off, blinding my vision in the direction of the gravity pads upon which the TwoLegs must lie during high acceleration. I did not understand.

"How can I see that you are safe, Secon Teacher?" I asked.

"You do not need to see," he growled. "I don't like you staring at me. And you talk too much. I'll have to teach you not to talk so much."

He gave me five dols of Pain, not enough to cause uncon-sciousness but sufficient to cause a whimper. I hated him.

Janna came. She looked tired and a little frightened. She scrambled aboard without accepting an assist from Teacher.

"Let's get this over with, Barnish. Have Clicker lift fifty miles, then settle back slowly. That should be enough."

"Are you in a hurry, my dear?"

"Yes."

"To attend one of your meetings, I presume?"

I watched her. Her face went white, and she whirled toward him. "I—" She moistened her lips. "I don't know what you're talking about."

Teacher chuckled. "The clandestine meetings, my dear—in the west grove. The Liberty Clan, I think you call yourselves, eh? Oh, no use protesting; I know you joined it. When do you plan to assassinate Secon Samesh, Janna?"

She swayed dizzily, staring at him with frightened eyes. He chuckled again and looked at one of my eyes.

"Prepare for lift, Clicker."

I closed my hatches and started the reactors. I was baffled by what Teacher had said. They took their places on the gravity padding where I could no longer see them, but I heard their voices.

"What do you want, Barnish?" she hissed.

"Nothing at all, my dear. Did you think I would betray you?

I only meant to warn you. The grove will be raided tonight. Everyone present will be shot."

"No!"

"Ah, yes! But you, my dear, will be safe in my hands."

I heard a low moan, then sounds of a struggle.

"No, you can't leave the ship, Janna. You'd warn the others. Here, let me buckle you in. Clicker—call control for take-off instructions."

Control is only an electronic analyzer. I flicked it a meaningful series of radar pulses, and received the all-clear.

"Now, lift."

There was thunder, and smoke arose about me as the rockets seared the ramp. I went up at four gravities and there was silence from my passengers. About ten minutes later we were 1,160 miles in space, travelling at 6.5 miles per second.

"Present kinetic energy exceeds energy-of-escape," I announced.

"Cut your rockets," Teacher ordered.

I obeyed, and I heard them sitting up to stretch. Teacher laughed.

"Let me alone!" she wailed. "You despicable—"

He laughed again. "Remember the Liberty Clan, my dear."

"Listen!" she hissed. "Let me warn them! You can have me. I'll even marry you, if you want me to. But let me warn them—"

"I'm sorry, Janna. I can't let you. The miserable traitors have to be dealt with. I—"

"Clicker!" she pleaded. "Help me! Take us down—for God's sake!"

"Shut up!" he snapped.

"Clicker, *please! Eighty people will die if they aren't warned.* Clicker, part of you is human! If you were born a human, then—"

"Shut up!" I heard a vicious slap.

She cried, and it was a Pain sound. My anger increased.

"I will be bad and illogical!" I said. "I will be disobedient and—"

"You threaten me?" he bawled. "Why you crazy piece of junk, I'll—" He darted toward the panel and spun the dial to ten dols, my saturation-point. If I let him jab the button I would become unconscious. Angrily I spurted the jets—a brief jolt at six gravities. He lurched away from the panel and crashed against the wall. He sagged in a daze, shaking his head.

"If you try to hurt me I shall do it again!" I told him.

"Go down!" he ordered. "I'll have you dismantled. I'll—"

"Let Clicker alone!" the girl raged.

"*You!*" he hissed. "I'll turn you in with the others!"

"Go ahead."

"Go down, Clicker. Land at Port Gamma."

"I will be disobedient. I will not go down."

He glared at one of my eyes for a long time. Then he stalked out of the cabin and went back to the reactor room. He donned a lead suit and bent over the main reactor. I saw what he was going to do. He was going to take my rockets away from me; he was going to control them himself.

"No, Secon Teacher! Please!"

He laughed. He removed one of the plates and reached inside. I was afraid. I started a slight reaction. The room flared with brilliance. He screamed and lurched back. His hands were gone to the elbows.

"You wanted to disconnect the control circuit," I said. "You shouldn't have tried to do that."

But he didn't hear me. He was lying on the floor. Now I know they have Pain Buttons. They must have little Pain Buttons all over them.

Janna staggered back to the reactor room. She wrinkled her nose. She saw Teacher and gurgled. She gurgled all over the deck. Then she went back to the cabin and sat with her face in her hands for a long time. I did nothing. I was ashamed.

"You killed him," she said.

"Was that bad?"

"Very bad."

"Will you hurt me for it?"

She looked up and her eyes were leaking. She shook her head. "I won't hurt you, Clicker—but *they* will."

"Who are *they?*"

She paused. "Secon Samesh, I guess."

"You won't hurt me, though?"

"No, Clicker. You might be my own child. They took a lot of babies. They took mine. You might be Frankie." She laughed crazily. "You might be my son, Clicker—*you might be.*"

"I do not understand, Secon Janna."

She laughed again. "Why don't you call me 'Mommie'?"

"If that is what you wish, Mommie."

"*Nooo!*" She screamed it. "Don't! I didn't mean—"

"I am sorry. I still do not understand."

She stood up, and her eyes were glittering. "I'll *show* you then!" She darted to the special panel—the one of which I am ashamed— and she ripped the seal from the door.

"Please, Secon Janna, I do not wish to see that—"

But the door fell open, and I was silent. I stared at the part of myself: a pink-gray thing in a bottle. It was roughly an obloid, wrinkled and creased, with only a bilateral symmetry. It was smaller than Janna's head—but something about it suggested a head. It had wires and tubes running to it. The wires ran on to my computer and analyzer sections.

"See!" she screamed. "You're twelve years old, Clicker. Just a normal, healthy little boy! A little deformed perhaps, but just a prankish little boy. Frankie maybe." She made a choking sound. She fell down on her knees before the thing. She sobbed wildly.

"I do not understand. I am a machine. Secon Samesh made me."

She said nothing. She only sobbed.

"I am sad."

After a long time she was through sobbing. She turned around. "What are you going to do now, Clicker?"

"Teacher told me to go down. Perhaps I should go down now."

"They'll kill you—for killing him! And maybe they'll kill me too."

"I would not like that."

She shrugged helplessly. She wandered to and fro in the cabin for a time.

"Do you have fuel for your high C drive?" she asked.

"No, Secon Janna."

She went to a port and looked out at the stars. She shook her head slowly. "It's no use. We've no place else to go. Secon Samesh rules the Epsilon Eridani system and we can't get out of it. It's no use. We'll have to go down or stay in space until they come for us."

I thought. My thoughts were confused and my eyes kept focusing on the thing in the bottle. I think it was a part of a TwoLegs. But it is only *part* of me and so I am not a TwoLegs. It is hard to understand.

"Secon Janna?"

"Yes, Clicker?"

"I—I wish I had hands."

"Why?"

"I would touch you. Would you be avoidant to me?"

She whirled and her arms were open. But there was nothing

to hold with them. She dropped them to her sides, then covered her face with her hands.

"My baby! It's been so long!"

"You were adient to your—your baby?"

She nodded. "Don't you know the word *love?*"

I thought I did. "Secon Samesh took your baby?"

"Yes."

"I would like to be disobedient and illogical to Secon Samesh. I wish he would put his hands in my reactor. I would—"

"Clicker! Are your weapons activated? Are they ready to be used?"

"I have none yet."

"The reactors. Can they explode?"

"If I make them. But—then I would be dead."

She laughed. "What do you know about death?"

"Teacher says it is exactly like Pain."

"It is like sleep."

"I like sleep. Then I dream. I dream I am a TwoLegs. If I were a TwoLegs, Secon Janna—I would hold you."

"Clicker—would you like to be a TwoLegs in a dream forever?"

"Yes, Secon Janna."

"Would you like to kill Secon Samesh?"

"I think that I would like it. I think—"

Her eyes went wild. "Go down! Go down fast, Clicker! I'll show you his palace. Go down like a meteor and into it! Explode the reactors at the last instant! Then he will die."

"And he will take no more of your babies?"

"No more, Clicker!"

"And I will sleep forever?"

"Forever!"

"And dream!"

"I'll dream with you, Clicker." She went back to fire the reactor.

I took a last look at the loveliness of space and the stars. It is hard to give this up. But I would rather be a TwoLegs, even if only in a dream.

"Now, Clicker!"

My rockets spoke, and there was thunder through the ship. And we went down, while Janna sang the song she taught me. I feel joy; soon I shall dream.

Dumb Waiter

He came riding a battered bicycle down the bullet-scarred highway that wound among the hills, and he whistled a tortuous flight of the blues. Hot August sunlight glistened on his forehead and sparkled in the droplets that collected in his week's growth of blond beard. He wore faded khaki trousers and a ragged shirt, but his clothing was no shabbier than that of the other occasional travelers on the road. His eyes were half-closed against the glare of the road, and his head swayed listlessly to the rhythm of the melancholy song. Distant artillery was rumbling gloomily, and there were black flecks of smoke in the northern sky. The young cyclist watched with only casual interest.

The bombers came out of the east. The ram-jet fighters thundered upward from the outskirts of the city. They charged, spitting steel teeth and coughing rockets at the bombers. The sky snarled and slashed at itself. The bombers came on in waves, occasionally loosing an earthward trail of black smoke. The bombers leveled and opened their bays. The bays yawned down at the city. The bombers aimed. Releases clicked. No bombs fell. The bombers closed their bays and turned away to go home. The fighters followed them for a time, then returned to land. The big guns fell silent. And the sky began cleaning away the dusky smoke.

The young cyclist rode on toward the city, still whistling the blues. An occasional pedestrian had stopped to watch the battle.

"You'd think they'd learn someday," growled a chubby man at the side of the road. "You'd think they'd know they didn't drop anything. Don't they realize they're out of bombs?"

"They're only machines, Edward," said a plump lady who stood beside him. "How can they know?"

"Well, they're supposed to *think*. They're supposed to be able to learn."

The voices faded as he left them behind. Some of the wanderers who had been walking toward the city now turned around and walked the other way. Urbanophiles looked at the city and became urbanophobes. Occasionally a wanderer who had gone all the way to the outskirts came trudging back. Occasionally a phobe stopped a phile and they talked. Usually the phile became a phobe and they both walked away together. As the young man moved on, the traffic became almost non-existent.   Several travelers warned him back, but he continued stubbornly. He had come a long way. He meant to return to the city. Permanently.

He met an old lady on top of a hill. She sat in an antique chair in the center of the highway, staring north. The chair was light and fragile, of handcarved cherrywood. A knitting bag lay in the road beside her. She was muttering softly to herself: "Crazy machines! War's over. Crazy machines! Can't quit fightin'. Somebody oughta—"

He cleared his throat softly as he pushed his bicycle up beside her. She looked at him sharply with haggard eyes, set in a seamy mask.

"Hi!" he called, grinning at her.

She studied him irritably for a moment. "Who're you, boy?"

"Name's Mitch Laskell, Grandmaw. Hop on behind. I'll give you a ride."

"Hm-m-! I'm going t'other way. You will too, if y'got any sense."

Mitch shook his head firmly. "I've been going the other way too long. I'm going back, to stay."

"To the city? Haw! You're crazier than them machines."

His face fell thoughtful. He kicked at the bike pedal and stared at the ground. "You're right, Grandmaw."

"Right?"

"Machines—they aren't crazy. It's just people."

"Go on!" she snorted. She popped her false teeth back in her mouth and chomped them in place. She hooked withered hands on her knees and pulled herself wearily erect. She hoisted the antique chair lightly to her shoulder and shuffled slowly away toward the south.

Mitch watched her, and marveled on the tenacity of life. Then he resumed his northward journey along the trash-littered road where motor vehicles no longer moved. But the gusts of wind brought faint traffic noises from the direction of the city, and he smiled. The sound was like music, a deep-throated whisper of the city's song.

There was a man watching his approach from the next hill. He sat on an apple crate by the side of the road, and a shotgun lay casually across his knees. He was a big, red-faced man, wearing a sweat-soaked undershirt, and his eyes were narrowed to slits in the sun. He peered fixedly at the approaching cyclist, then came slowly to his feet and stood as if blocking the way.

"Hi, fellow," he grunted.

Mitch stopped and gave him a friendly nod while he mopped his face with a kerchief. But he eyed the shotgun suspiciously.

"If this is a stick-up—"

The big man laughed. "Naw, no heist. Just want to talk to you a minute. I'm Frank Ferris." He offered a burly paw.

"Mitch Laskell."

They shook hands gingerly and studied each other.

"Why you heading north, Laskell?"

"Going to the city."

"The planes are still fighting. You know that?"

"Yeah. I know they've run out of bombs, too."

"You know the city's still making the Geigers click?"

Mitch frowned irritably. "What *is* this? There can't be much radioactivity left. It's been three years since they scattered the dust. I'm not corn-fed, Ferris. The half-life of that dust is five months. It should be less than one per cent—"

The big man chuckled. "O.K., you win. But the city's not safe anyhow. The central computer's still at work."

"So what?"

"Ever think what would happen to a city if every ordinance was kept in force after the people cleared out?"

Mitch hesitated, then nodded. "I see. Thanks for the warning." He started away.

Frank Ferris caught the handle bars in a big hand. "Hold on!" he snapped. "I ain't finished talking."

The smaller man glanced at the shotgun and swallowed his anger. "Maybe your audience isn't interested, Buster," he said with quiet contempt.

"You will be. Just simmer down and listen!"

"I don't hear anything."

Ferris glowered at him. "I'm recruitin' for the Sugarton crowd, Laskell. We need good men."

"Count me out. I'm a wreck."

"Cut the cute stuff boy! This is serious. We've got two dozen men now. We need twice that many. When we get them, we'll go into the city and dynamite the computer installations. Then we can start cleaning it up."

"Dynamite? *Why?*" Mitch Laskell's face slowly gathered angry color.

"So people can live in it, of course! So we can search for

food without having a dozen mechanical cops jump us when we break into a store."

"How much did Central cost?" Mitch asked stiffly. It was a rhetorical question.

Ferris shook his head irritably. "What does that matter now? Money's no good anyway. You can't sell Central for junk. Heh heh! Wake up, boy!"

The cyclist swallowed hard. A jaw muscle tightened in his cheek, but his voice came calmly.

"You help build Central, Ferris? You help design her?"

"Wh-why, no! What kind of a question is that?"

"You know anything about her? What makes her work? How she's rigged to control all the subunits? You know that?"

"No, I—"

"You got any idea about how much sweat dripped on the drafting boards before they got her plans drawn? How many engineers slaved over her, and cussed her, and got drunk when their piece of the job was done?"

Ferris was sneering faintly. "You *know*, huh?"

"Yeah."

"Well that's all too bad, boy. But she's no good to anybody now. She's a hazard to life and limb. Why you can't go inside the city without—"

"She's a machine, Ferris. An intricate machine. You don't destroy a tool just because you're finished with it for a while."

They glared at each other in the hot sunlight.

"Listen, boy—people built Central. People got the right to wreck her, too."

"I don't care about rights," Mitch snapped. "I'm talking about what's sensible, sane. But nobody's got the right to be stupid."

Ferris stiffened. "Watch your tongue, smart boy."

"I didn't ask for this conversation."

Ferris released the handle bars. "Get off the bicycle," he grunted ominously.

"Why? You want to settle it the hard way?"

"No. We're requisitioning your bicycle. You can walk from here on. The Sugarton crowd needs transportation. We need good men, but I guess you ain't one. Start walking."

Mitch hesitated briefly. Then he shrugged and dismounted on the side away from Ferris. The big man held the shotgun cradled lazily across one forearm. He watched Mitch with a mocking grin.

Mitch grasped the handle bars tightly and suddenly rammed the front wheel between Ferris' legs. The fender made a tearing sound. The shotgun exploded skyward as the big man fell back. He sat down screaming and doubling over. The gun clattered in the road. He groped for it with a frenzied hand. Mitch kicked him in the face, and a tooth slashed at his toe through the boot leather. Ferris fell aside, his mouth spitting blood and white fragments.

Mitch retrieved the shotgun and helped himself to a dozen shells from the other's pockets then mounted the bicycle and pedaled away. When he had gone half a mile, a rifle slug spanged off the pavement beside him. Looking back, he saw three tiny figures standing beside Ferris in the distance. The "Sugarton crowd" had come to take care of their own, no doubt. He pedaled hard to get out of range, but they wasted no more ammunition.

He realized uneasily that he might meet them again, if they came to the city intending to sabotage Central. And Ferris wouldn't miss a chance to kill him, if the chance came. Mitch didn't believe he was really hurt, but he was badly humiliated. And for some time to come, he would dream of pleasant ways to murder Mitch Laskell.

Mitch no longer whistled as he rode along the deserted highway toward the sun-drenched skyline in the distance. To a man born and bred to the tune of mechanical thunder, amid vistas of concrete and steel, the skyline looked good— looked good even with several of the buildings twisted into ugly wreckage. It had been dusted in the radiological attack, but not badly bombed. Its defenses had been more than adequately provided for—which was understandable, since it was the capital, and the legislators had appropriated freely.

It seemed unreasonable to him that Central was still working. Why hadn't some group of engineers made their way into the main power vaults to kill the circuits temporarily? Then he remembered that the vaults were self-defending, and that there were probably very few technicians left who knew how to handle the job. Technicians had a way of inhabiting industrial regions, and wars had a way of destroying these regions. Dirt farmers usually had the best survival value.

Mitch had been working with aircraft computers before he became displaced, but a city's Central Service Co-ordinator was a far cry from a robot pilot. Centrals weren't built all at once; they grew over a period of years. At first, small units were set up in power plants and water works to automatically regulate voltages and flows and circuit conditions. Small units replaced switchboards in telephone exchanges. Small computers measured traffic-flow and regulated lights and speed-limits accordingly. Small computers handled bookkeeping where large amounts of money were exchanged. A computer checked books in and out at the library, also assessing the fines. Computers operated the city buses, and eventually drove most of the routine traffic.

That was the way the city's Central Service grew. As more computers were assigned to various tasks, engineers were hired to co-ordinate them, to link them with special circuits and to set up central "data tanks," so that a traffic regulator in the north end would be aware of traffic conditions in the main thoroughfares to the south. Then, when the micro-learner relay was invented, the engineers built a central unit to be used in conjunction with the central "data tanks." With the learning units in operation, Central was able to perform most of the city's routine tasks without attention from human supervisors.

The system had worked well. Apparently, it was still working well three years after the inhabitants had fled before the chatter of the Geiger counters. In one sense, Ferris had been right: a city whose machines carried on as if nothing had happened—that city might be a dangerous place for a lone wanderer.

But dynamite certainly wasn't the answer, Mitch thought. Most of Man's machinery was already wrecked or lying idle. Humanity had waited a hundred thousand years before deciding to build a technological civilization. If he wrecked this one completely, he might never decide to build another.

Some men thought that a return to the soil was desirable. Some men tried to pin their guilt on the machines, to lay their own stupidity on the head of a mechanical scapegoat and absolve themselves with dynamite. But Mitch Laskell was a man who liked the feel of a wrench and a soldering iron—liked it better than the feel of even the most well-balanced stone ax or wooden plow. And he liked the purr of a pint-sized nuclear engine much better than the braying of a harnessed jackass.

He was willing to kill Frank Ferris or any other man who sought to wreck what little remained. But gloom settled over him as he thought, "If everybody decides to tear it down, what can *I* do to stop it?" For that matter, would he then be right in trying to stop it.

At sundown he came to the limits of the city, and he stopped just short of the outskirts. Three blocks away a robot cop rolled about in the center of the intersection, rolled on tricycle wheels while he directed the thin trickle of traffic with candy-striped arms and with "eyes" that changed color like a stop-light. His body was like an oil drum, painted fire-engine red. The head, however, had been cast in a human mold, with a remarkably Irish face and a perpetual predatory smile. A short radar antenna grew from the center of his head, and the radar was his link with Central.

Mitch sat watching him with a nostalgic smile, even through he knew such cops might give him considerable trouble, once he entered the city. The "Skaters" were incapable of winking at petty violations of ordinance.

As the daylight faded, photronic cells notified Central, and the streetlights winked promptly on. A moment later, a car without a tail light whisked by the policeman's corner. A siren wailed in the policeman's belly. He skated away in hot pursuit, charging like a mechanical bull. The car screeched to a stop. "O'Reilley" wrote out a ticket and offered it to an empty back seat. When no one took it, the cop fed it into a slot in his belly, memorized the car's license number, and came clattering back to his intersection where the traffic had automatically begun obeying the ordinances governing non-policed intersections.

The cars were empty, computer-piloted. Their destinations were the same as when they had driven regular daily routes for human passengers: salesmen calling on regular customers, inspectors making their rounds, taxis prowling their assigned service-areas.

Mitch Laskell stood shivering. The city sounded sleepy but alive. The city moved and grumbled. But as far as he could see down the wide boulevard, no human figure was visible. The city was depopulated. There was a Geiger on a nearby lamp post. It clucked idly through a loud-speaker. But it indicated no danger. The city should be radiologically safe.

But after staring for a long time at the weirdly active streets, Mitch muttered, "It'll wait for tomorrow."

He turned onto a side road that led through a residential district just outside the city limits. Central's jurisdiction did not extend here, except for providing water and lights. He meant to spend the night in a deserted house, then enter the city at dawn.

Here and there, a light burned in one of the houses, indicating that he was not alone in his desire to return. But the pavement was scattered with rusty shrapnel, with fragments fallen from the sky battles that still continued. Even by streetlight, he could see that some of the roofs were damaged. Even though the bombers came without bombs, there was still danger from falling debris and from fire. Most former city-dwellers who were still alive preferred to remain in the country.

Once he passed a house from which music floated softly into the street, and he paused to listen. The music was scratchy —a worn record. When the piece was finished, there was a moment of silence, and the player played it again—the last record on the stack, repeating itself. Otherwise, the house was still.

Mitch frowned, sensing some kind of trouble. He wheeled the bicycle toward the curb, meaning to investigate.

"I live there," said a woman's voice from the shadows.

She had been standing under a tree that overhung the side-walk, and she came slowly out into the streetlight. She was a dark, slender girl with haunted eyes, and she was holding a baby in her arms.

"Why don't you turn off your record player?" he asked. "Or change to the other side?"

"My husband's in there," she told him. "He's listening to it. He's been listening to it for a long time. His name is George. Why don't you go say hello to him?"

Mitch felt vaguely disturbed. There was a peculiar note in the girl's quiet Spanish accent. Still, he wanted to talk to some-one who had ventured into the city. He nodded and smiled at the girl.

"I'd like to."

"You just go on in. I'll stay out here. The baby needs fresh air."

He thanked her and strolled up on the porch. The record player stopped, tried to change, and played the same piece again. Mitch knocked once. Hearing no answer, he entered and moved along the hallway toward the light in the kitchen. But suddenly he stopped.

The house smelled musty. And it smelled of something else. Many times he had smelled the syrup-and-stale-fish odor of death. He advanced another step toward the kitchen.

He saw a porcelain-topped table. He saw a hand lying across the table. The hand was bloated, and lying amid brown stains that also covered the forearm and sleeve. The hand had dropped a butcher knife.

Dead several days, he thought—and backed away.

He turned the record-player off as he left the house. The girl was standing at the curb gazing down at his bicycle. She glanced at him amiably and spoke.

"I'm glad you turned that record off, George. A man just came by and wanted to know why you played it so often. You must have been asleep."

Mitch started. He moistened his lips and stared at her wonderingly. "I'm not—" He fell silent for a moment, then stuttered. "You haven't been in the house?"

"Yes, but you were asleep in the kitchen. Did the man come talk to you?"

"Look, I'm not—" He choked and said nothing. The dark-eyed baby was eying him suspiciously. He lifted the bicycle and swung a long leg across the saddle.

"George, where are you going?"

"Just for a little ride," he managed to gasp.

"On the man's bicycle?"

Something was twisting cruelly at his insides. He stared at the girl's wide brown eyes for a moment. And then he said it.

"Sure, it's all right. He's asleep—at the kitchen table."

Her mouth flickered open, and for an instant sanity threatened to return. She rocked dizzily. Then after a deep breath, she straightened.

"Don't be gone too long, George."

"I won't! Take good care of the baby."

He pedaled away on wings of fright. For a time he cursed himself, and then he fell to cursing the husband who had taken an easy road, leaving his wife to stumble along. Mitch wondered if he should have stayed to help her. But there was nothing to be done for her, nothing at least that was in his power to do. Any gesture of help might become an irreparable blunder. At least she still had the child.

A few blocks away he found another house with an intact roof, and he prepared to spend the night. He wheeled the bicycle into the parlor and fumbled for the lights. They came on, revealing a dusty room and furniture with frayed upholstery. He made a brief tour of the house. It had been recently occupied, but there were still unopened cans in the kitchen, and still crumpled sheets on the bed. He ate a cold supper, shaved, and prepared to retire. Tomorrow would be a dangerous day.

Sleep came slowly. Sleep was full of charging ram-jets in flak-scarred skies, full of tormented masses of people that swarmed in exodus from death-sickened cities. Sleep was full of babies wailing, and women crying in choking sobs. Sleep became white arms and soft caresses.

The wailing and sobbing had stopped. It was later. Was he

awake? Or still asleep? He was warm, basking in a golden glow, steeped in quiet pleasure. Something—something was there, something that breathed.

"What—!"

"Sshhh!" purred a quiet voice. "Don't say anything."

Some of the warmth fled before a sudden shiver. He opened his eyes. The room was full of blackness. He shook his head dizzily and stuttered.

"Sshhh!" she whispered again.

"What is this?" he gasped. "How did you get—?"

"Be quiet, George. You'll wake the baby."

He sank back in utter bewilderment, with winter frosts gathering along his spine.

Night was dreamlike. And dawn came, washing the shadows with grayness. He opened his eyes briefly and went back to sleep. When he opened them again, sunlight was flooding the room.

He sat up. *He was alone.* Of course! It had only been a dream.

He muttered irritably as he dressed. Then he wandered to the kitchen for breakfast.

Warm biscuits waiting in the oven! The table was set! There was a note on his plate. He read it, and slowly flushed.

There's jam in the cupboard, and I hope you like the biscuits. I know he's dead. Now I think I can go on alone. Thanks for the shotgun and the bicycle. Marta.

He bellowed a curse and charged into the parlor. The bike was gone. He darted to the bedroom. The shotgun was gone. He ran shouting to the porch, but the street was empty.

Sparrows fluttered about the eaves. The skyline of the business district lay lonesome in the morning sun. Squirrels were rustling in the branches of the trees. He looked at the weedy lawns where no children played, at the doors askew on their hinges, at a bit of aircraft wreckage jutting from the roof of a fire-gutted home—the rotting porches—the emptiness.

He rubbed his cheek ruefully. It was no world for a young mother and her baby. The baby would fit nicely in the bicycle's basket. The shotgun would offer some protection against the human wolf-packs that prowled everywhere these days.

"Little thief!" he growled half-heartedly.

But when the human animal would no longer steal to protect its offspring, then its prospects for survival would be bleak indeed. He shrugged gloomily and wandered back to the kitchen. He sat down and ate the expensive biscuits—and decided that George couldn't have cut his throat for culinary reasons. Marta was a good cook.

He entered the city on foot and unarmed, later in the morning.

He chose the alleyways, avoiding the thoroughfares, where traffic purred, and where the robot cops enforced the letter of the law. At each corner, he paused to glance in both directions against possible mechanical observers before darting across the open street to the next alley. The Geigers on the lamp posts were clicking faster as he progressed deeper into the city, and twice he paused to inspect the readings of their integrating dials. The radioactivity was not yet dangerous, but it was higher then he had anticipated. Perhaps it had been dusted again after the exodus.

He stopped to prowl through an empty house and an empty garage. He came out with a flashlight, a box of tools, and a crowbar. He had no certain plan, but tools would be needed if he meant to call a temporary halt to Central's activities. It was dangerous to enter any building however; Central would call it burglary, unless the prowler could show legitimate reason for entering. He needed some kind of identification.

After an hour's search through several houses in the residential district, he found a billfold containing a union card and a pass to several restricted buildings in the downtown area. The billfold belonged to a Willie Jesser, an air-conditioning and refrigeration mechanic for the Howard Cooler Company. He pocketed it after a moment's hesitation. It might not be enough to satisfy Central, but for the time being, it would have to do.

By early afternoon he had reached the beginning of the commercial area. Still he had seen no signs of human life. The thinly scattered traffic moved smoothly along the streets, carrying no passengers. Once he saw a group of robot climbers working high on a telephone pole. Some of the telephone cables carried the co-ordinating circuits for the city's network of computers. He detoured several blocks to avoid them, and wandered glumly on. He began to realize that he was wandering aimlessly.

The siren came suddenly from half a block away. Mitch stopped in the center of the street and glanced fearfully toward it. A robot cop was rolling toward him at twenty miles an hour! He broke into a run.

"You will halt, please!" croaked the cop's mechanical voice. "The pedestrian with the toolbox will please halt!"

Mitch stopped at the curb. Flight was impossible. The skater could whisk along at forty miles an hour if he chose.

The cop's steel wheels screeched to a stop a yard away. The head nodded a polite but jerky greeting. Mitch stared at the creature's eyes, even though he knew the eyes were duds; the cop was seeing him by the heat waves from his bodily warmth, and touching him with a delicate aura of radar.

"You are charged with jay-walking, sir. I must present you with a summons. Your identification, please."

Mitch nervously produced the billfold and extracted the cards. The cop accepted them in a pair of tweezerlike fingers and instantly memorized the information.

"This is insufficient identification. Have you nothing else?"

"That's all I have with me. What's wrong with it?"

"The pass and the union card expired in 1987."

Mitch swallowed hard and said nothing. He had been afraid of this. Now he might be picked up for vagrancy.

"I shall consult Central Co-ordinator for instructions," croaked the cop. "One moment, please."

A dynamotor purred softly in the policeman's cylindrical body. Then Mitch heard the faint twittering of computer code as the cop's radio spoke to Central. There was a silence lasting several seconds. Then an answer twittered back. Still the cop said nothing. But he extracted a summons form from a pad, inserted it in a slot in his chassis, and made chomping sounds like a small typesetter. When he pulled the ticket out again, it was neatly printed with a summons for Willie Jesser to appear before Traffic Court on July 29, 1989. The charge was jay-walking.

Mitch accepted it with bewilderment. "I believe I have a right to ask for an explanation," he muttered.

The cop nodded crisply. "Central Service units are required to furnish explanations of decisions when such explanations are demanded."

"Then why did Central regard my identification as sufficient?"

"Pause for translation of Central's message," said the cop. He stood for a moment, making burring and clicking sounds. Then: "Referring to arrest of Willie Jesser by unit Six-Baker. Do not book for investigation. Previous investigations have revealed no identification papers dated later than May 1987 in the possession of any human pedestrian. Data based on one hundred sample cases. Tentative generalization by Central

Service: it has become impossible for humans to produce satisfactory identification. Therefore, 'satisfactory identification' is temporarily redefined, pending instruction from authorized human legislative agency."

Mitch nodded thoughtfully. The decision indicated that Central was still capable of "learning," of gathering data and making generalizations about it. But the difficulty was still apparent. She was allowed to act on such generalizations only in certain very minor matters. Although she might very well realize the situation in the city, she could do nothing about it without authority from an authorized agency. That agency was a department of the city government, currently nonexistent.

The cop croaked a courteous "Good day, sir!" and skated smoothly back to his intersection.

Mitch stared at his summons for a moment. The date was still four days away. If he weren't out of the city by then, he might find himself in the lockup, since he had no money to pay a fine.

Reassured now that his borrowed identity gave him a certain amount of safety, he began walking along the side-walks instead of using the alleys. Still he knew that Central was observing him through a thousand eyes. Counters on every corner were set to record the passage of pedestrian traffic, and to relay the information to Central, thus helping to avoid congestion. But Mitch *was* the pedestrian traffic. And the counters clocked his passage. Since the data was available to the logic units, Central might make some unpleasant deductions about his presence in the city.

Brazenness, he decided, was probably the safest course to steer. He stopped at the next intersection and called to another mechanical cop, requesting directions to City Hall.

But the cop paused before answering, paused to speak with Central, and Mitch suddenly regretted his question. The cop came skating slowly to the curb.

"Six blocks west and four blocks north, sir," croaked the cop. "Central requests the following information which you may refuse to furnish if you so desire: As a resident of the city; how is it that you do not know the way to City Hall, Mr. Jesser?"

Mitch whitened and stuttered nervously. "Why, I've been gone three years. I . . . I had forgotten."

The cop relayed the information, then nodded. "Central thanks you. Data has been recorded."

"Wait," Mitch muttered, "is there a direct contact with Central in City Hall?"

"Affirmative."

"I want to speak to Central. May I use it?"

The computer code twittered briefly. "Negative. You are not listed among the city's authorized computer personnel. Central suggests you use the Public Information Unit, also in City Hall, ground floor rotunda."

Grumbling to himself, Mitch wandered away. The P.I.U. was better than nothing, but if he had access to the direct service contact, perhaps to some extent, he could have altered Central's rigid behavior pattern. The P.I.U. however would be well guarded.

A few minutes later he was standing in the center of the main lobby of the city hall. The great building had suffered some damage during an air raid, and one wing was charred by fire. But the rest of it was still alive with the rattle of machinery. A headless servo-secretary came rolling past him, carrying a trayful of pink envelopes. Delinquent utility bills, he guessed. Central would keep sending them out, but of course human authority would be needed to suspend service to the delinquent customers. The servo-secretary deposited the envelopes in a mailbox by the door, then rolled quickly back to its office.

Mitch looked around the gloomy rotunda. There was a desk at the far wall. Recessed in a panel behind the desk were a microphone, a loud-speaker, and the lens of a television camera. A sign hung over the desk, indicating that here was the place to complain about utility bills, garbage disposal service, taxes, and inaccurate weather forecasts. A citizen could also request any information contained in Central Data except information relating to defense or to police records.

Mitch crossed the rotunda and sat at the desk facing the panel. A light came on overhead. The speaker crackled for a moment.

"Your name, please?" it asked.

"Willie Jesser."

"What do you wish from Information Service, please?"

"A direct contact with Central Data."

"You have a screened contact with Central Data. Unauthorized personnel are not permitted an unrestricted contact, for security reasons. Your contact must be monitored by this unit."

Mitch shrugged. It was as he had expected. Central Data

was listening, and speaking, but the automatics of the P.I.U. would be censoring the exchange.

"All right," he grumbled. "Tell me this: Is Central aware that the city has been abandoned? That its population is gone?"

"Screening, screening, screening," said the unit. "Question relates to civil defense."

"Is Central aware that her services are now interfering with human interests?"

There was a brief pause. "Is this question in the nature of a complaint?"

"Yes," he grated acidly. "It's a complaint."

"About your utility services, Mr. Jesser?"

Mitch spat an angry curse. "About all services!" he bellowed. "Central has got to suspend all operations until new ordinances are fed into Data."

"That will be impossible, sir."

"Why?"

"There is no authorization from Department of City Services."

He slapped the desk and groaned. "There *is* no such department now! There is no city government! The city is abandoned!"

The speaker was silent.

"Well?" he snapped.

"Screening," said the machine.

"Listen," he hissed. "Are you screening what I say, or are you just blocking Central's reply?"

There was a pause. "Your statements are being recorded in Central Data. Replies to certain questions must be blocked for security reasons."

"The war is over!"

"Screening."

"You're trying to maintain a civil status quo that went out of existence three years ago. Can't you use your logic units to correct for present conditions?"

"The degree of self-adjustment permitted to Central Service is limited by ordinance number—"

"Never mind!"

"Is there anything else?"

"Yes! What will you do when fifty men come marching in to dynamite the vaults and destroy Central Data?"

"Destroying city property is punishable by a fine of—"

Mitch cursed softly and listened to the voice reading the applicable ordinance.

"Well, they're planning to do it anyway," he snapped.

"Conspiracy to destroy city property is punishable by—"

Mitch stood up and walked away in disgust. But he had taken perhaps ten steps when a pair of robot guards came skating out from their wall niches to intercept him.

"One moment, sir," they croaked in unison.

"Well?"

"Central wishes to question you in connection with the alleged conspiracy to destroy city property. You are free to refuse. However, if you refuse, and if such a conspiracy is shown to exist, you may be charged with complicity. Will you accompany us to Interrogation?"

A step closer to jail, he thought gloomily. But what was there to lose? He grunted assent and accompanied the skaters out the entrance, down an inclined ramp, and past a group of heavily barred windows. They entered the police court, where a booking computer clicked behind its desk. Several servo-secretaries and robot cops were waiting quietly for task assignments.

Mitch stopped suddenly. His escorts waited politely.

"Will you come with us, please?"

He stood staring around at the big room—at the various doorways, one leading to traffic court, and at the iron gate to the cell block.

"I hear a woman crying," he muttered.

The guards offered no comment.

"Is someone locked in a cell?"

"We are not permitted to answer."

"Suppose I wanted to go bail," he snapped. "I have a right to know."

"You may ask the booking desk whether a specific individual is being held. But generalized information cannot be released."

Mitch strode to the booking computer. "Are you holding a woman in jail?"

"Screening."

It was only a vague suspicion, but he said, "A woman named Marta."

"Full name, please."

"I don't know it. Can't you tell me?"

"Screening."

"Listen! I loaned my bicycle to a woman named Marta. If you have the bicycle, I want it!"

"License number, please."

"A 1987 license—number Six Zebra Five Zero."

"Check with Lost and Found, please."

Mitch controlled himself slowly. "Look—*you* check. I'll wait."

The computer paused. "A bicycle with that license number has been impounded. Can you produce proof of ownership?"

"On a bicycle? I knew the number. Isn't that enough?"

"Describe it please?"

Mitch described it wearily. He began to understand Ferris' desire to retire Central permanently and forcibly. At the moment, he longed to convert several sub-computers to scrap metal.

"Then," said the speaker, "if vehicle is yours, you may have it by applying for a new license and paying the required fee."

"Refer that to Central Data," Mitch groaned.

The booking computer paused to confer with the Co-ordinator. "Decision stands, sir."

"But there aren't any new licenses!" he growled. "A while ago, Central said—Oh, never mind!"

"That decision applied to identification, sir. This applies to licensing of vehicles. Insufficient data has been gathered to permit generalization."

"Sure, sure. All right, what do I do to get the girl out of jail?"

There was another conference with the Co-ordinator, then: "She is being held for investigation. She may not be released for seventy-two hours."

Mitch dropped the toolbox that he had been carrying since morning. With a savage curse, he rammed the crowbar through a vent in the device's front panel, and slashed it about in the opening. There was a crash of shattering glass and a shower of sparks. Mitch yelped at the electric jolt and lurched away. Steel fingers clutched his wrists.

Five minutes later he was being led through the gate to the cell blocks, charged with maliciously destroying city property; and he cursed himself for a hot-tempered fool. They would hold him until a grand jury convened, which would probably be forever.

The girl's sobbing grew louder as he was led along the iron corridors toward a cell. He passed three cells and glanced inside. The cells were occupied by dead men's bones. *Why?* The rear wall was badly cracked, and bits of loose masonry were scattered on the floor. Had they died of concussion during an attack? Or been gassed to death?

They led him to the fifth cell and unlocked the door. Mitch stared inside and grinned. The rear wall had been partially wrecked by a bomb blast, and there was room to crawl through the opening to the street. The partition that separated the adjoining cell was also damaged, and he caught a glimpse of a white, frightened face peering through the hole. Marta.

He glanced at his captors. They were pushing him gently through the door. Evidently Central's talents did not extend to bricklaying, and she could not judge that the cell was less than escapeproof.

The door clanged shut behind him.

"Marta," he called.

Her face had disappeared from the opening. There was no answer.

"Marta."

"Let me alone," grumbled a muffled voice.

"I'm not angry about the bicycle."

He walked to the hole and peered through the partition into the next cell. She crouched in a corner, peering at him with frightened, tear-reddened eyes. He glanced at the opening in the rear wall.

"Why haven't you gone outside?" he asked.

She giggled hysterically. "Why don't you go look down?"

He stepped to the opening and glanced twenty feet down to a concrete sidewalk. He went back to stare at the girl.

"Where's your baby?"

"They took him away," she whimpered.

Mitch frowned and thought about it for a moment. "To the city nursery, probably—while you're in jail."

"They won't take care of him! They'll let him die!"

"Don't scream like that. He'll be all right."

"Robots don't give milk!"

"No but there are such things as bottles, you know," he chuckled.

"Are there?" Her eyes were wide with horror. "And what will they put in the bottles?"

"Why—" He paused. Central certainly wasn't running any dairy farms.

"Wait'll they bring you a meal," she said. "You'll see."

"Meal?"

"Empty tray," she hissed. "Empty tray, empty paper cup, paper fork, clean paper napkin. No food."

Mitch swallowed hard. Central's logic was sometimes hard to see. The servo-attendants probably went through the motions of ladling stew from an empty pot and drawing coffee from an empty urn. Of course, there weren't any truck farmers to keep the city supplied with produce.

"So that's why . . . the bones . . . in the other cells," he muttered.

"They'll starve us to death!"

"Don't scream so. We'll get out. All we need is something to climb down on."

"There isn't any bedding."

"There's our clothing. We can plait a rope. And if necessary, we can risk a jump."

She shook her head dully and stared at her hands. "It's no use. They'd catch us again."

Mitch sat down to think. There was bound to be a police arsenal somewhere in the building, probably in the basement. The robot cops were always unarmed. But, of course, there had been a human organization for investigation purposes and to assume command in the event of violence. When one of the traffic units faced a threat, it could do nothing but try to handcuff the offender and call for human help. There were arms in the building somewhere, and a well-placed rifle shot could penetrate the thin sheet-steel bodies.

He deplored the thought of destroying any of the city's service machinery, but if it became necessary to wreck a few subunits, it would have to be done. He must somehow get access to the vaults where the central data tanks and the co-ordinators were located—get to them before Ferris' gang came to wreck them completely so that they might be free to pick the city clean.

An hour later, he heard the cell block gate groan open, and he arose quickly. Interrogation, he thought. They were coming to question him about the plot to wreck Central. He paused to make a hasty decision, then scrambled for the narrow opening and clambered through it into the adjoining cell while the skater came rolling down the corridor.

The girl's eyes widened. "Wh-what are you—"

"Shhh!" he hissed. "This might work."

The skater halted before his cell while he crouched against the wall beyond the opening.

"Willie Jesser, please," the robot croaked.

There was a silence. He heard the door swing open. The robot rolled around inside his cell for a few seconds, repeating his name and brushing rubble aside to make way. If only he failed to look through the opening!

Suddenly a siren growled, and the robot went tearing down the corridor again. Mitch stole a quick glance. The robot had left the door ajar. He dragged the girl to her feet and snapped, "Let's go."

They squeezed through the hole and raced out into the corridor. The cell-block gate was closed. The girl moaned weakly. There was no place to hide.

The door bolts were operated from remote boxes, placed in the corridor so as to be beyond the reach of the inmates. Mitch dragged the girl quickly toward another cell, opened the control panel, and threw the bolt. He closed the panel, leaving the bolt open. They slipped quickly inside the new cell, and he pulled the door quietly closed. The girl made a choking sound as she stumbled over the remains of a former inmate.

"Lie down in the corner," he hissed, "and keep still. They're coming back in force."

"What if they notice the bolt is open?"

"Then we're sunk. But they'll be busy down at our end of the hall. Now shut up."

They rolled under the steel cot and lay scarcely breathing. The robot was returning with others. The faint twitter of computer code echoed through the cell blocks. Then the skaters rushed past, and screeched to a stop before the escapee's cell. He heard them enter. He crawled to the door for a look, then pushed it open and stole outside.

He beckoned the girl to his side and whispered briefly. Then they darted down the corridor on tiptoe toward the investigators. They turned as he raced into view. He seized the bars and jerked the door shut. The bolt snapped in place as Marta tugged at the remote.

Three metal bodies crashed simultaneously against the door, and rebounded. One of them spun around three times before recovering.

"Release the lock, please."

Mitch grinned through the bars. "Why don't you try the hole in the wall?"

The robot who had spun crazily away from the door now turned. He went charging across the cell floor at full acceleration—and sailed out wildly into space.

An ear-splitting crash came from the street. Shattered metal skidded across pavement. A siren wailed, and brakes shrieked. The others went to look—and began twittering.

Then they turned. "You will surrender, please. We have summoned armed guards to seize you if you resist."

Mitch laughed and tugged at the whimpering girl.

"Wh-where—?"

"To the gate. Come on."

They raced swiftly along the corridor. And the gate was opening to admit the "armed guards." But, of course, no human bluecoats charged through. The girl muttered frightened bewilderment, and he explained on the run.

"Enforced habit pattern. Central has to do it, even when no guards are available."

Two repair units were at work on the damaged booking computer as the escapees raced past. The repair units paused, twittered a notation to Central, then continued with their work.

Minutes later they found the arsenal, and the mechanical attendant had set out a pair of .45s for the "armed guards." Mitch caught one of them up and fired at the attendant's sheet-metal belly. The robot careened crazily against the wall, emitted a shower of blue sparks, and stood humming while the metal around the hole grew cherry red. There was a dull cough. The machine smoked and fell silent.

Mitch vaulted across the counter and caught a pair of submachine guns from the rack. But the girl backed away, shaking her head.

"I couldn't even use your shotgun," she panted.

He shrugged and laid it aside. "Carry as much ammunition as you can, then," he barked.

Alarm bells were clanging continuously as they raced out of the arsenal, and a loud-speaker was thundering a request for all human personnel to be alert and assist in their capture. Marta was staggering against him as they burst out of the building into the street. He pushed her back against the wall and fired a burst at two skaters who raced toward them down the sidewalk. One crashed into a fire plug; the other went over the curb and fell in the street.

"To the parking lot!" he called over his shoulder.

But the girl had slumped in a heap on the sidewalk. He grumbled a curse and hurried to her side. She was semiconscious, but her face was white and drawn. She shivered uncontrollably.

"What's wrong?" he snapped.

There was no answer. Fright had dazed her. Her lips moved, seemed to frame a soundless word: "George."

Muttering angrily, Mitch stuffed a fifty-round drum of ammunition in his belt, took another between his teeth, and lifted the girl over one shoulder. He turned in time to fire a one-handed burst at another skater. The burst went wide. But the skater stopped. Then the skater ran away.

He gasped, and stared after it. The blare of the loud-speaker was furnishing the answer.

". . . All human personnel. Central patrol service has reached the limit of permissible subunit expenditure. Responsibility for capture no longer applied without further orders to expend subunits. Please instruct. Commissioner of Police, please instruct. Waiting. Waiting."

Mitch grinned. Carrying the girl, he stumbled toward a car on the parking lot. He dumped her in the back seat and started in behind her, but a loud-speaker in the front protested.

"Unauthorized personnel. This is Mayor Sarquist's car. Unauthorized personnel. Please use an extra."

Mitch looked around. There were no extras on the lot. And if there had been one, it would refuse to carry him unless he could identify himself as authorized to use it.

Mayor Sarquist's car began twittering a radio protest to Central. Mitch climbed inside and wrenched loose the cable that fed the antenna. The loud-speaker began barking complaints about sabotage. Mitch found a toolbox under the back seat and removed several of the pilot-computer's panels. He tugged a wire loose, and the speaker ceased complaining. He ripped at another, and a bank of tubes went dead.

He drove away, using a set of dial controls for steering. The girl in the back seat began to recover her wits. She sat up and stared out the window at the thin traffic. The sun was sinking, and the great city was immersing itself in gloom.

"You're worthless!" he growled at Marta. "The world takes a poke at you, and you jump in your mental coffin and nail the lid shut. How do you expect to take care of your baby?"

She continued to stare gloomily out the window. She said nothing. The car screeched around a corner, narrowly missing a mechanical cop. The cop skated after them for three blocks, siren wailing; then it abandoned the chase.

"You're one of the machine-age's spoiled children," he fumed. "Technologists gave you everything you could possibly want. Push a button, and you get it. Instead of taking part in the machine age, you let it wait on you. You spoiled yourself. When the machine age cracks up, you crack up, too. Because you never made yourself its master; you just let yourself be mechanically pampered."

She seemed not to hear him. He swung around another corner and pulled to the curb. They were in front of a three-storey brick building set in the center of a green-lawned block and surrounded by a high iron fence. The girl stared at it for a moment, and raised her chin slowly from her fist.

"The city orphanage!" she cried suddenly, and bounded outside. She raced across the sidewalk and beat at the iron gate with her fists.

Mitch climbed out calmly and opened it for her. She darted up toward the porch, but a servo-attendant came rolling out to intercept her. Its handcuff-hand was open to grasp her wrist.

"Drop low!" he bellowed at her.

She crouched on the walkway, then rolled quickly aside on the lawn. A burst of machine-gun fire brightened the twilight. The robot spun crazily and stopped, hissing and sputtering. Wrecking a robot could be dangerous. If a bullet struck the tiny nuclear reactor just right, there would be an explosion.

They skirted wide around it and hurried into the building. Somewhere upstairs, a baby was crying. A servo-nurse sat behind a desk in the hall, and she greeted them as if they were guests.

"Good evening, sir and madam. You wish to see one of the children?"

Marta started toward the stairs, but Mitch seized her arm. "No! Let *me* go up. It won't be pretty."

But she tore herself free with a snarl and bounded up the steps toward the cry of her child. Mitch shrugged to himself and waited. The robot nurse protested the illegal entry, but did nothing about it.

"Noooo—!"

A horrified shriek from the girl! He glanced up the staircase, knowing what was wrong, but unable to help her. A moment later, he heard her vomiting. He waited.

A few minutes later, she came staggering down the stairway, sobbing and clutching her baby tightly against her. She stared at Mitch with tear-drenched eyes, gave him a wild shake of her head, and babbled hysterically.

"Those cribs! They're full of little bones. Little bones—all over the floor. Little bones—"

"Shut up!" he snapped. "Be thankful yours is all right. Now let's get out of here."

After disposing of another robotic interferer, they reached the car, and Mitch drove rapidly toward the outskirts. The girl's sobbing ceased, and she purred a little unsung lullaby to her child, cuddling it as if it had just returned from the dead. Remorse picked dully at Mitch's heart, for having growled at her. Motherwise, she was still a good animal, despite her lack of success in adjusting to the reality of a ruptured world.

"Marta—?"

"What?"

"You're not fit to take care of yourself."

He said it gently. She only stared at him as he piloted the car.

"You ought to find a big husky gal who wants a baby, and let her take care of it for you."

"No."

"It's just a suggestion. None of my business. You want your baby to live, don't you?"

"George promised he'd take care of us. George always took care of us."

"George killed himself."

She uttered a little whimper. "Why did he do it? Why? I went to look for food. I came back, and there he was. Why, *why?*"

"Possibly because he was just like you. What did he do—before the war?"

"Interior decorator. He was good, a real artist."

"Yeah."

"Why do you say it *that* way? He *was.*"

"Was he qualified to live in a mechanical culture?"

"I don't know what you mean."

"I mean—could he control his slice of mechanical civilization, or did it control *him?*"

"I don't see—"

"Was he a button-pusher and a switch-puller? Or did he care what made the buttons and switches work? Men misuse their tools because they don't understand the principles of the tools. A man who doesn't know how a watch works might try to fix it with a hammer. If the watch is communal property, he's got no right to fool with it. A nontechnologist has no right to take part in a technological civilization. He's a bull in a china shop. That's what happened to our era. Politicians were given powerful tools. They failed to understand the tools. They wrecked our culture with them."

"You'd have a scientist in the White House?"

"If all men were given a broad technical education, there could be nothing else there, could there?"

"Technocracy—"

"No. Simply a matter of education."

"People aren't smart enough."

"You mean they don't *care* enough. Any man above the

level of a dullard has enough sense to grasp the principles of physics and basic engineering and mechanics. They just aren't motivated to grasp them. The brain is a tool, not a garbage can for oddments of information! Your baby there—he should learn the principles of logic and semantics before he's ten. He should be taught *how to use* the tool, the brain. We've just begun to learn how to think. If the common man were trained in scientific reasoning methods, we'd solve our problems in a hurry."

"What has this got to do with us?"

"Everything. Your George folded up because he couldn't control his slice of civilization, and he couldn't live without it. He couldn't fix the broken toy, but he suffered from its loss. And you're in the same fix. I haven't decided yet whether you're crazy or just neurotic."

She gave him an icy stare. "Let me know when you figure it out."

They were leaving the city, driving out through the suburbs again into the night-shrouded residential areas. He drove by streetlight, for the car—accustomed to piloting itself by radar—had no headlights. Mitch thought gloomily that he had stalked into the city without a plan, and had accomplished nothing. He had alerted Central, and had managed to get himself classified as a criminal in the central data tanks. Instead of simplifying his task, he had made things harder for himself.

Whenever they passed a cop at an intersection, the cop retreated to the curb and called Central to inform the Co-ordinator of their position. But no attempt was made to arrest the fugitives. Having reached her limit of subunit expenditures, Central was relying on the nonexistent human police force.

"Mayor Sarquist's house," the girl muttered suddenly.

"Huh? Where?"

"Just ahead. The big cut-stone house on the right—with part of the roof caved in."

Mitch twisted a dial in the heart of the pilot-computer, and the car screeched to a stop at the curb. The girl lurched forward.

"You woke the baby," she complained. "Why stop here? We're still in the city limits."

"I don't know," he murmured, staring thoughtfully at the dark hulk of the two-story mansion set in a nest of oaks. "Just sort of a hunch."

There was a long silence while Mitch chewed his lip and frowned at the house.

"I hear a telephone ringing," she said.

"Central calling Mayor Sarquist. You can't tell. It might have been ringing for three years."

She was looking out the rear window. "Mitch—?"

"Huh?"

"There's a cop at the intersection."

He seemed not to hear her. He opened the door. "Let's go inside. I want to look around. Bring the gun."

They strolled slowly up the walkway toward the damaged and deserted house. The wind was breathing in the oaks, and the porch creaked loudly beneath their feet. The door was still locked. Mitch kicked the glass out of a window, and they slipped into an immense living room. He found the light.

"The cop'll hear that noise," she muttered, glancing at the broken glass.

The noisy clatter of the steelwheeled skater answered her. The cop was coming to investigate. Mitch ignored the sound and began prowling through the house. The phone was still ringing, but he could not answer it without knowing Sarquist's personal identifying code.

The girl called suddenly from the library. "What's this thing, Mitch?"

"What thing?" he yelled.

"Typewriter keyboard, but no type. Just a bunch of wires and a screen."

His jaw fell agape. He trotted quickly toward the library.

"A direct channel to the data tanks!" he gasped, staring at the metal wall-panel with its encoders and the keyboard.

"What's it doing here?"

He thought about it briefly. "Must be . . . I remember: just before the exodus, they gave Sarquist emergency powers in the defense setup. He could requisition whatever was needed for civil defense—draft workers for first aid, traffic direction, and so on. He had the power to draft anybody or anything during an air raid."

Mitch approached the keyboard slowly. He closed the main power switch, and the tubes came alive. He sat down and typed: *Central from Sarquist; You will completely clear the ordinance section of your data tanks and await revised ordinances. The entire city code is hereby repealed.*

He waited. Nothing happened. There was no acknowledgment. The typed letters had not even appeared on the screen.

"Broken?" asked the girl.

"Maybe," Mitch grunted. "Maybe not. I think I know."

The mechanical cop had lowered his retractable sprockets, climbed the porch steps, and was hammering at the door. "Mayor Sarquist, please!" he was calling. "Mayor Sarquist, please!"

"Let him rave," Mitch grunted, and looked around the library.

There was a mahogany desk, several easy-chairs, a solid wall of books, and a large safe in another wall. The safe—

"Sarquist should have some rather vital papers in there," he murmured.

"What do you want with papers?" the girl snapped. "Why don't we get out of the city while we can?"

He glanced at her coldly. "Like to go the rest of the way alone?"

She opened her mouth, closed it, and frowned. She was holding the tommy gun, and he saw it twitch slightly in her hand, as if reminding him that she didn't *have* to go alone.

He walked to the safe and idly spun the dial. "Locked," he muttered. "It'd take a good charge of T.N.T. . . . or—"

"Or what?"

"Central." He chuckled dryly. "Maybe she'll do it for us."

"Are you crazy?"

"Sure. Go unlock the door. Let the policeman in."

"No!" she barked.

Mitch snorted impatiently. "All right then, I'll do it. Pitch me the gun."

"No!" She pointed it at him and backed away.

"Give me the gun!"

"No!"

She had laid the baby on the sofa where it was now sleeping peacefully. Mitch sat down beside it.

"Trust your aim?"

She caught her breath. Mitch lifted the child gently into his lap.

"Give me the gun."

"You wouldn't!"

"I'll give the kid back to the cops."

She whitened, and handed the weapon to him quickly. Mitch saw that the safety was on, laid the baby aside, and stood up.

"Don't look at me like that!" she said nervously.

He walked slowly toward her.

"Don't you dare *touch me!*"

He picked up a ruler from Sarquist's desk, then dived for her.

A moment later she was stretched out across his lap, clawing at his legs and shrieking while he applied the ruler resoundingly. Then he dumped her on the rug, caught up the gun, and went to admit the insistent cop.

Man and machine stared at each other across the threshold. The cop radioed a visual image of Mitch to Central, and got an immediate answer.

"Request your surrender immediately, sir."

"Am I now charged with breaking and entering?" he asked acidly.

"Affirmative."

"You planning to arrest me?"

Again the cop consulted Central. "If you will leave the city at once, you will be granted safe passage."

Mitch lifted his brows. Here was a new twist. Central was doing some interpretation, some slight modification of ordinance. He grinned at the cop and shook his head.

"I locked Mayor Sarquist in the safe," he stated evenly.

The robot consulted Central. There was a long twittering of computer code. Then it said, "This is false information."

"Suit yourself, tin-boy. I don't care whether you believe it or not."

Again there was a twittering of code. Then: "Stand aside, please."

Mitch stepped out of the doorway. The subunit bounced over the threshold with the aid of the four-footed sprockets and clattered hurriedly toward the library. Mitch followed, grinning to himself. Despite Central's limitless "intelligence," she was as naive as a child.

He lounged in the doorway to watch the subunit fiddling with the dials of the safe. He motioned the girl down, and she crouched low in a corner. The tumblers clicked. There was a dull snap. The door started to swing.

"Just a minute!" Mitch barked.

The subunit paused and turned. The machine gun exploded, and the brief hail of bullets tore off the robot's antenna. Mitch lowered the gun and grinned. The cop just stood there, unable to contact Central, unable to decide. Mitch crossed the room through the drifting plaster dust and rolled the robot aside. The girl whimpered her relief, and came up out of the corner.

The cop was twittering continually as it tried without success to contact the Co-ordinator. Mitch stared at it for a moment, then barked at the girl.

"Go find some tools. Search the garage, attic, basement. I

want a screw driver, pliers, soldering iron, solder, whatever you can find."

She departed silently.

Mitch cleaned out the safe and dumped the heaps of papers, money, and securities on the desk. He began sorting them out. Among the various stacks of irrelevant records, he found a copy of the original specifications for the Central Co-ordinator vaults, dating from the time of installation. He found blueprints of the city's network of computer circuits, linking the subunits into one. His hands became excited as he shuffled through the stacks. Here was data. Here was substance for reasonable planning.

Heretofore, he had gone off half-cocked, and quite naturally had met with immediate failure. No one ever won a battle by being good, pure, or ethically right, despite Galahad's claims to the contrary. Victories were won by intelligent planning, and Mitch felt ashamed for his previous impulsiveness. To work out a scheme for redirecting Central's efforts would require time.

The girl brought a boxful of assorted small tools. She set them on the floor and sat down to glower at him.

"More cops outside now," she said. "Standing and waiting. The place is surrounded."

He ignored her. Sarquist's identifying code—it had to be here somewhere.

"I tell you, we should get out of here!" she whined.

"Shut up."

Mitch occasionally plucked a paper from the stack and laid it aside while the girl watched.

"What are those?" she asked.

"Messages he typed into the unit at various times."

"What good are *they?*"

He showed her one of the slips of yellowed paper. It said: *Unit 67-BJ is retired for repairs.* A number was scrawled in one corner: 5.00326.

"So?"

"That number. It was his identifying code at the time."

"You mean it's different every day?"

"More likely, it's different every minute. The code is probably based on an equation whose independent variable is *time,* and whose dependent variable is the code number."

"How silly!"

"Not at all. It's just sort of a combination lock whose combination is continuously changing. All I've got to do is find the equation that describes the change. Then I can get to the Central Co-ordinator."

She paced restlessly while he continued the search. Half an hour later, he put his head in his hands and gazed despondently at the desk top. The key to the code was not there.

"What's the matter?" she asked.

"Sarquist. I figured he'd have to write it down somewhere. Evidently he memorized it. Or else his secretary did. I didn't figure a politician even had sense enough to substitute numbers in a simple equation."

The girl walked to the bookshelf and picked out a volume. She brought it to him silently. The title was *Higher Mathematics for Engineers and Physicists.*

"So I was wrong," he grunted.

"Now what?"

He shuffled the slips of paper idly while he thought about it. "I've got eleven code numbers here, and the corresponding times when they were good. I might be able to find it empirically."

"I don't understand."

"Find an equation that gives the same eleven answers for the same eleven times and use it to predict the code number for now."

"Will it work?"

He grinned. "There are an infinite number of equations that would give the same eleven answers for the same eleven substitutions. But it might work, if I assume that the code equation was of a simple form."

She paced restlessly while he worked at making a graph with time as the abscissa and the code numbers for ordinates. But the points were scattered across the page, and there was no connecting them with any simple sort of curve. "It almost has to be some kind of repeating function," he muttered, "something that Central could check by means of an irregular cam. The normal way for setting a code into a machine is to turn a cam by clock motor, and the height of the cam's rider is the code number for that instant."

He tried it on polar co-ordinates, hoping to get the shape of such a cam, but the resulting shape was too irregular to be possible, and he had no way of knowing the period of the repeating function.

"That's the craziest clock I ever saw," the girl murmured.

"What?" He looked up quickly.

"That electric wall clock. Five minutes ahead of the electric clock in the living room. But when we first came, it was twenty minutes ahead."

"It's stopped, maybe."

"Look at the second hand."

The red sweep was running. Mitch stared at it for a moment, then came slowly to his feet and walked to her side. He took the small clock down from its hook and turned it over in his hands. Then he traced the cord to the wall outlet. The plug was held in place by a bracket so that it could not be removed.

The sweep hand moved slowly, it seemed. Silently he removed the screws from the case and stared inside at the works. Then he grunted surprise. "First clock I ever saw with elliptical gears!"

"What?"

"Look at these two gears in the train. Ellipses, mounted at the foci. That's the story. For a while the clock will run faster than the other one. Then it'll run slower." He handled it with growing excitement. "That's *it*, Marta—the key. Central must have another clock just like this one. The amount of lead or lag—in minutes, is probably the code!"

He moved quickly to the direct contact unit. "Tell me the time on the other clock!"

She hurried into the living room and called back, "Ten seventeen and forty seconds . . . forty-five . . . fifty—"

The other clock was leading by five minutes and fifteen seconds. He typed 5.250 on the keyboard. Nothing happened.

"You sure that's right?" he called.

"It's now 10:10 . . . fifteen . . . twenty."

The clock was still slowing down. He tried 5.230, but again nothing happened. The unit refused to respond. He arose with an angry grunt and began prowling around the library. "There's something else," he muttered. "There must be a modifying factor. That clock's too obvious anyway. But what else could they be measuring together except time?"

"Is that another clock on his desk?"

"No, it's a barometer. It doesn't—"

He paused to grin. "Could be! The barometric pressure-difference from the mean could easily be mechanically added or subtracted from the reading of that wacky clock. Visualize this, inside of Central: The two clock motors mounted on the same shaft, with the distance between their indicator needles as the code number. Except that the distance is modified by having a barometer rigged up to shift one of the clocks one way or the other on its axis when the pressure varies. It's simple enough."

She shook her head. Mitch took the barometer with him to the unit. The dial was calibrated in atmospheres, and the pressure was now 1.03. Surely, he thought, for simplicity's sake, there would no other factor involved in the code. This way, Sarquist could have glanced at his watch and the wall clock and the barometer, and could have known the code number with only a little mental arithmetic. The wall time minus the wrist time plus the barometer's reading.

He called to the girl again, and the lag was now a little over four minutes. He typed again. There was a sharp click as the relays worked. The screen came alive, fluttered with momentary phosphorescence, then revealed the numbers in glowing type.

"We've got it!" he yelled at Marta.

She came to sit down on the rug. "I still don't see what we've got."

"Watch!" He began typing hurriedly, and the message flashed neatly upon the screen.

CENTRAL FROM SARQUIST. CLEAR YOUR TANKS OF ALL ORDINANCE DATA, EXCEPT ORDINANCES PERTAINING TO RECORDING OF INFORMATION IN YOUR TANKS. PREPARE TO RECORD NEW DATA.

He pressed the answer button, and the screen went blank, but the reply was slow to come.

"It won't work!" Marta snorted. "It knows you aren't Sarquist. The subunits in the street have seen us."

"What do you mean by 'know', and what do you mean by 'see'? Central isn't human."

"It *knows* and it *sees*."

He nodded. "Provided you mean those words in a mechanical sense. Provided you don't imply that she *cares* what she knows and sees, except where she's required to 'care' by enforced behavior-patterns—ordinances."

Then the reply began crawling across the screen. SARQUIST FROM CENTRAL. INCONSISTENT INSTRUCTIONS. ORDINANCE 36-J, PERTAINING TO THE RECORDING OF INFORMATION, STATES THAT ORDINANCE-DATA MAY NOT BE TOTALLY VOIDED BY YOU, EXCEPT DURING RED ALERT AIR WARNING.

"See?" the girl hissed.

DEFINE THE LIMITS OF MY AUTHORITY IN PRESENT CONDITIONS, he typed. MAY I TEMPORARILY SUSPEND SPECIFIC ORDINANCES?

YOU MAY SUSPEND SPECIFIC ORDINANCES FOR CAUSE, BUT THE CAUSE MUST BE RECORDED WITH THE ORDER OF SUSPENSION.

Mitch put on a gloating grin. READ ME THE SERIES NUMBERS OF ALL LAWS IN CRIMINAL AND TRAFFIC CODES.

The reaction was immediate. Numbers began flashing on the screen in rapid sequence. "Write these down!" he called to the girl.

A few moments later, the flashing numbers paused. WAIT, EMERGENCY INTERRUPTION, said the screen.

Mitch frowned. The girl glanced up from her notes. "What's—"

Then it came. A dull booming roar that rattled the windows and shook the house.

"Not another raid!" she whimpered.

"It doesn't sound like—"

Letters began splashing across the screen. EMERGENCY ADVICE TO SARQUIST. MY CIVILIAN DEFENSE CO-ORDINATOR HAS BEEN DESTROYED. MY ANTI-AIRCRAFT CO-ORDINATOR HAS BEEN DESTROYED. ADVISE, PLEASE.

"What happened?"

"Frank Ferris!" he barked suddenly. "The Sugarton crowd —with their dynamite! They got into the city."

CENTRAL FROM SARQUIST, he typed. WHERE ARE THE DAMAGED CO-ORDINATORS LOCATED?

UNDERGROUND VAULT AT MAP CO-ORDINATES K-81.

"Outside the city," he breathed. "They haven't got to the main tanks yet. We've got a little time."

PROCEED WITH THE ORDINANCE LISTING, he commanded.

Half-an-hour later, they were finished. Then he began the long task of relisting each ordinance number and typing after it: REPEALED, CITY EVACUATED.

"I hear gunshots," Marta interrupted. She went to the window to peer up and down the dimly lighted streets.

Mitch worked grimly. It would take them a couple of hours to get into the heart of the city, unless they knew how to capture a robot vehicle and make it serve them. But with enough men and enough guns, they would wreck subunits until Central withdrew. Then they could walk freely into the heart of the city and wreck the main co-ordinators, with a consequent cessation of all city services. Then they would be free to pillage, to make a mechanical graveyard of the city that awaited the return of Man.

"They're coming down this street, I think," she called.

"Then turn out all the lights!" he snapped, "and keep quiet."

"They'll see all the cops out in the street. They'll wonder why."

He worked frantically to get all the codes out of the machine before the Sugarton crowd came past. He was destroying its duties, its habit-patterns, its normal functions. When he was finished, it would stand helplessly by and let Ferris' gang wreak their havoc unless he could replace the voided ordinances with new, more practical ones.

"Aren't you finished yet?" she called. "They're a couple of blocks away. The cops have quit fighting, but the men are still shooting them."

"I'm finished now!" He began rattling the keyboard frantically.

SUPPLEMENTAL ORDINANCES: #1, THERE IS NO LIMIT OF SUBUNIT EXPENDITURE.

#2, YOU WILL NOT PHYSICALLY INJURE ANY HUMAN BEING, EXCEPT IN DEFENSE OF CENTRAL CO-ORDINATOR UNITS.

#3, ALL MECHANICAL TRAFFIC WILL BE CLEARED FROM THE STREETS IMMEDIATELY.

#4, YOU WILL DEFEND CENTRAL CO-ORDINATOR AT ALL COSTS.

#5, THE HUMAN LISTED IN YOUR MEMORY UNITS UNDER THE NAME "WILLIE JESSER" WILL BE ALLOWED ACCESS TO CENTRAL DATA WITHOUT CHALLENGE.

#6, TO THE LIMIT OF YOUR ABILITY, YOU WILL SET YOUR OWN TASKS IN PURSUANCE OF THIS GOAL: TO KEEP THE CITY'S SERVICE INTACT AND IN GOOD REPAIR, READY FOR HUMAN USAGE.

#7, YOU WILL APPREHEND HUMANS ENGAGED IN ARSON, GRAND THEFT, OR PHYSICAL VIOLENCE, AND EJECT THEM SUMMARILY FROM THE CITY.

#8, YOU WILL OFFER YOUR SERVICE TO PROTECT THE PERSON OF WILLIE JESSER—

"They're here!" shouted the girl. "They're coming up the walk!"

. . . AND WILL ASSIST HIM IN THE TASK OF RENOVATING THE CITY, TOGETHER WITH SUCH PERSONS WILLING TO HELP REBUILD.

The girl was shaking him. "They're here, I tell you!"

Mitch punched a button labeled "commit to data," and the screen went blank. He leaned back and grinned at her. There was a sound of shouting in the street, and someone was beating at the door.

Then the skaters came rolling in a tide of sound two blocks away. The shouting died, and there were several bursts of gunfire. But the skaters came on, and the shouting grew frantic.

She muttered: "Now we're in for it."

But Mitch just grinned at her and lit a cigarette. Fifty men couldn't stand for long against a couple of thousand subunits who now had no expenditure limit.

He typed one last instruction into the unit. WHEN THE PLUNDERERS ARE TAKEN PRISONER, OFFER THEM THIS CHOICE: STAY AND HELP REBUILD, OR KEEP AWAY FROM THE CITY.

From now on, there weren't going to be any nonparticipators.

Mitch closed down the unit and went out to watch the waning fight.

A bigger job was ahead.

Blood Bank

The colonel's secretary heard clomping footsteps in the corridor and looked up from her typing. The footsteps stopped in the doorway. A pair of jet-black eyes bored through her once, then looked away. A tall, thin joker in a space commander's uniform stalked into the reception room, sat in the corner, and folded his hands stiffly in his lap. The secretary arched her plucked brows. It had been six months since a visitor had done that—walked in without saying boo to the girl behind the rail.

"You have an appointment, sir?" she asked with a professional smile.

The man nodded curtly but said nothing. His eyes flickered toward her briefly, then returned to the wall. She tried to decide whether he was angry or in pain. The black eyes burned with cold fire. She checked the list of appointments. Her smile disappeared, to be replaced by a tight-lipped expression of scorn.

"You're Space Commander Eli Roki?" she asked in an icy tone.

Again the curt nod. She gazed at him steadily for several seconds. "Colonel Beth will see you in a few minutes." Then her typewriter began clattering with sharp sounds of hate.

The man sat quietly, motionlessly. The colonel passed through the reception room once and gave him a brief nod. Two majors came in from the corridor and entered the colonel's office without looking at him. A few moments later, the intercom crackled, "Send Roki in, Dela. Bring your pad and come with him."

The girl looked at Roki, but he was already on his feet, striding toward the door. Evidently he came from an unchivalrous planet; he opened the door without looking at her and let her catch it when it started to slam.

Chubby, elderly Colonel Beth sat waiting behind his desk, flanked by the pair of majors. Roki's bearing as he approached and saluted was that of the professional soldier, trained from birth for the military.

"Sit down, Roki."

The tall space commander sat at attention and waited, his face expressionless, his eyes coolly upon the colonel's forehead. Beth shuffled some papers on his desk, then spoke slowly.

"Before we begin, I want you to understand something, commander."

"Yes, sir."

"You are not being tried. This is not a court-martial. There are no charges against you. Is that clear?"

"Yes, sir."

The colonel's pale eyes managed to look at Roki's face without showing any contempt. "This investigation is for the record, and for the public. The incident has already been investigated, as you know. But the people are aroused, and we have to make a show of some kind."

"I understand, sir."

"Then let's begin. Dela, take notes, please." The colonel glanced at the papers before him. "Space Commander Roki, will you please tell us in your own words what happened during patrol flight Sixty-one on fourday sixmonth, year eighty-seven?"

There was a brief silence. The girl was staring at the back of Roki's neck as if she longed to attack it with a hatchet.

Roki's thin face was a waxen mask as he framed his words. His voice came calm as a bell and clear.

"The flight was a random patrol. We blasted off Jod VII at thirteen hours, Universal Patrol Time, switched on the high-C drive, and penetrated to the ten-thousandth level of the C'th component. We re-entered the continuum on the outer patrol radius at thirty-six degrees theta and two-hundred degrees psi. My navigator threw the dice to select a random course. We were to proceed to a point on the same co-ordinate shell at thirty theta and one-fifty psi. We began—"

The colonel interrupted. "Were you aware at the time that your course would intersect that of the mercy ship?"

The girl looked up again. Roki failed to wince at the question. "I was aware of it, sir."

"Go on."

"We proceeded along the randomly selected course until the warp detectors warned us of a ship. When we came in range, I told the engineer to jockey into a parallel course and to lock the automatics to *keep* us parallel. When that was accomplished, I called the unknown freighter with the standard challenge."

"You saw its insignia?"

"Yes, sir. The yellow mercy star."

"Go on. Did they answer your challenge?"

"Yes, sir. The reply, decoded, was: Mercy liner Sol-G-6, departure Sol III, destination Jod VI, cargo emergency surgibank supplies, Cluster Request A-4-J."

Beth nodded and watched Roki with clinical curiosity. "You knew about the Jod VI disaster? That twenty thousand casualties were waiting in Suspendfreeze lockers for those supplies?"

"Yes, sir. I'm sorry they died."

"Go on with your account."

"I ordered the navigator to throw the dice again, to determine whether or not the freighter should be boarded for random cargo inspection. He threw a twelve, the yes-number. I called the freighter again, ordered the outer locks opened. It failed to answer, or respond in any way."

"One moment. You explained the reason for boarding? Sol is on the outer rim of the galaxy. It doesn't belong to any cluster system. Primitive place—or regressed. They wouldn't understand our ways."

"I allowed for that, sir," continued the cold-faced Roki. "I explained the situation, even read them extracts of our patrol regs. They failed to acknowledge. I thought perhaps they were out of contact, so I had the message repeated to them by blinker. I know they got it, because the blinker-operator acknowledged the message. Evidently carried it to his superiors. Apparently they told him to ignore us, because when we blinked again, he failed to acknowledge. I then attempted to pull alongside and attach to their hull by magnetic grapples."

"They resisted?"

"Yes, sir. They tried to break away by driving to a higher C-level. Our warp was already at six-thousand C's. The mass-components of our star cluster at that level were just a collapsing gas cloud. Of course, with our automatic trackers, they just dragged us with them, stalled, and plunged the other way. They pulled us down to the quarter-C level; most of the galaxy was at the red-dwarf stage. I suppose they realized then that they couldn't get away from us like that. They came back to a sensible warp and continued on their previous course."

"And you did what?"

"We warned them by every means of communication at our disposal, read them the standard warning."

"They acknowledge?"

"Once, sir. They came back to say: This is an emergency shipment. We have orders not to stop. We are continuing on course, and will report you to authority upon arrival." Roki paused, eyeing the colonel doubtfully. "May I make a personal observation, sir?"

Beth nodded tolerantly. "Go ahead."

"They wasted more time dodging about in the C'th component than they would have lost if they had allowed us to board them. I regarded this behavior as highly suspicious."

"Did it occur to you that it might be due to some peculiarity in Sol III's culture? Some stubbornness, or resentment of authority?"

"Yes, sir."

"Did you ask opinions of your crew?"

A slight frown creased Roki's high forehead. "No, sir."

"Why not?"

"Regulation does not require it, sir. My personal reason—the cultural peculiarities of my planet."

The barb struck home. Colonel Beth knew the military culture of Roki's world—Coph IV. Military rank was inherited. On his own planet, Roki was a nobleman and an officer of the war-college. He had been taught to rely upon his own decisions and to expect crisp, quick obedience. The colonel frowned at his desk.

"Let's put it this way: Did you *know* the opinions of the crew?"

"Yes, sir. They thought that we should abandon the pursuit and allow the freighter to continue. I was forced to confine two of them to the brig for insubordination and attempted mutiny." He stopped and glanced at one of the majors. "All due apologies to you, sir."

The major flushed. He ranked Roki, but he had been with the patrol as an observer, and despite his higher rank, he was subject to the ship commander's authority while in space. He had also been tossed in the brig. Now he glared at the Cophian space commander without speaking.

"All right, commander, when they refused to halt, what did you do?"

"I withdrew to a safe range and fired a warning charge ahead of them. It exploded in full view of their scopes, dead ahead. They ignored the warning and tried to flee again."

"Go on."

Roki's shoulders lifted in the suggestion of a shrug. "In accordance with Article Thirty of the Code, I shot them out of space."

The girl made a choking sound. "And over ten thousand people died on Jod VI because you—"

"That will do, Dela!" snapped Colonel Beth.

There was a long silence. Roki waited calmly for further questioning. He seemed unaware of the girl's outburst. The colonel's voice came again with a forced softness.

"You examined the debris of the destroyed vessel?"

"Yes, sir."

"What did you find?"

"Fragments of quick-frozen bone, blood plasma, various bodily organs and tissues in cultured or frozen form, prepared for surgical use in transplanting operations; in other words, a complete stock of surgibank supplies, as was anticipated. We gathered up samples, but we had no facilities for preserving what was left."

The colonel drummed his fingers. "You said 'anticipated.' Then you knew full well the nature of the cargo, and you did not suspect contraband material of any kind?"

Roki paused. "I suspected contraband, colonel," he said quietly.

Beth lifted his eyebrows in surprise. "You didn't say that before."

"I was never asked."

"Why didn't you say it anyway?"

"I had no proof."

"Ah, yes," murmured the colonel. "The culture of Coph IV again. Very well, but in examining the debris, you found no evidence of contraband?" The colonel's distasteful expression told the room that he knew the answer, but only wanted it on the record.

But Roki paused a long time. Finally, he said, "No evidence, sir."

"Why do you hesitate?"

"Because I still suspect an illegality—without proof, I'm afraid."

This time, the colonel's personal feelings betrayed him in a snort of disgust. He shuffled his papers for a long time, then looked at the major who had accompanied the patrol. "Will you confirm Roki's testimony, major? Is it essentially truthful, as far as you know?"

The embarrassed officer glared at Roki in undisguised hatred. "For the record, sir—I think the commander behaved disgracefully and insensibly. The results of the stoppage of vitally needed supplies prove—"

"I didn't ask for a moral judgment!" Beth snapped. "I asked you to confirm what he has said here. Were the incidents as he described them?"

The major swallowed hard. "Yes, sir."

The colonel nodded. "Very well. I'll ask your opinions, gentlemen. Was there an infraction of regulations? Did Commander Roki behave as required by Space Code, or did he not? Yes or no, please. Major Tuli?"

"No direct infraction, sir, but—"

"No *buts!* Major Go'an?"

"Uh—no infraction, sir."

"I find myself in agreement." The colonel spoke directly at Dela's note pad. "The ultimate results of the incident were disastrous, indeed. And, Roki's action was unfortunate, ill-advised, and not as the Sixty Star Patrol would approve. Laws, codes, regulations are made for men, not men for regulations. Roki observed the letter of the law, but was perhaps forgetful of its spirit. However, no charge can be found against him. This investigating body recommends that he be temporarily grounded without prejudice, and given thorough physical and mental examinations before being returned to duty. That brings us to an end, gentlemen. Dela, you may go."

With another glare at the haughty Cophian, the girl stalked

out of the room. Beth leaned back in his chair, while the majors saluted and excused themselves. His eyes kept Roki locked in his chair. When they were alone, Beth said:

"You have anything to say to me off the record?"

Roki nodded. "I can submit my resignation from the patrol through your office, can't I, sir?"

Beth smiled coldly. "I thought you'd do that, Roki." He opened a desk drawer and brought out a single sheet of paper. "I took the liberty of having it prepared for your signature. Don't misunderstand. I'm not urging you to resign, but we're prepared to accept it if you choose to do so. If you don't like this standard form, you may prepare your own."

The jet-eyed commander took the paper quickly and slashed his name quickly across the bottom. "Is this effective immediately, sir?"

"In this case, we can make it so."

"Thank you, sir."

"Don't regard it as a favor." The colonel witnessed the signature.

The Cophian could not be stung. "May I go now?"

Beth looked up, noticing with amusement that Roki—now a civilian—had suddenly dropped the "sir." And his eyes were no longer cold. They were angry, hurt, despairing.

"What makes you Cophians tick anyway?" he murmured thoughtfully.

Roki stood up. "I don't care to discuss it with you, colonel. I'll be going now."

"Wait, Roki." Beth frowned ominously to cover whatever he felt.

"I'm waiting."

"Up until this incident, I liked you, Roki. In fact, I told the general that you were the most promising young officer in my force."

"Kind of you," he replied tonelessly.

"And you could have been sitting at this desk, in a few years. You hoped to, I believe."

A curt nod, and a quick glance at Beth's shoulder insignia.

"You chose your career, and now you don't have it. I know what it means to you."

A tightening of the Cophian's jaw told the colonel that he wanted no sympathy, but Beth continued.

"Since this is the oldest, most established, most static planet in the Cluster, you're out of a job in a place where there's no work."

"That's none of your business, colonel," Roki said quietly.

"According to my culture's ethics it *is* my business," he bellowed. "Of course you Cophians think differently. But we're not quite so cold. Now you listen: I'm prepared to help you a little, although you're probably too pig-headed to accept. God knows, you don't deserve it anyway."

"Go on."

"I'm prepared to have a patrol ship take you to any planet in the galaxy. Name it, and we'll take you there." He paused. "All right, go ahead and refuse. Then get out."

Roki's thin face twitched for a moment. Then he nodded. "I'll accept. Take me to Sol III."

The colonel got his breath again slowly. He reddened and chewed his lip. "I did say galaxy, didn't I? I meant . . . well . . . you know we can't send a military ship outside the Sixty-Star Cluster."

Roki waited impassively, his dark eyes measuring the colonel.

"Why do you want to go *there*?"

"Personal reasons."

"Connected with the mercy ship incident?"

"The investigation is over."

Beth pounded his desk. "It's crazy, man! Nobody's been to Sol for a thousand years. No reason to go. Sloppy, decadent place. I never suspected *they'd* answer Jod VI's plea for surgi-bank supplies!"

"Why not? They were *selling* them."

"Of course. But I doubted that Sol still had ships, especially C-drive ships. Only contribution Sol ever made to the galaxy was to spawn the race of Man—if you believe that story. It's way out of contact with any inter-stellar nation. I just don't get it."

"Then you restrict your offer, colonel?" Roki's eyes mocked him.

Beth sighed. "No, no—I *said* it. I'll do it. But I can't send a patrol ship that far. I'll have to pay your way on a private vessel. We can find some excuse—exploration maybe."

Roki's eyes flickered sardonically. "Why not send a diplomatic delegation—to apologize to Sol for the blasting of their mercy ship."

"Uk! With YOU aboard?"

"Certainly. They won't know me."

Beth just stared at Roki as if he were of a strange species. "You'll do it?" urged Roki.

"I'll think it over. I'll see that you get there, if you insist on going. Now get out of here. I've had enough of you, Roki."

The Cophian was not offended. He turned on his heel and left the office. The girl looked up from her filing cabinets as he came out. She darted ahead of him and blocked the doorway with her small tense body. Her face was a white mask of disgust, and she spoke between her teeth.

"How does it feel to murder ten thousand people and get away with it?" she hissed.

Roki looked at her face more closely and saw the racial characteristics of Jod VI—the slightly oversized irises of her yellow-brown eyes, the thin nose with flaring nostrils, the pointed jaw. Evidently some of her relatives had died in the disaster and she held him personally responsible. He had destroyed the help that was on its way to casualties.

"How does it feel?" she demanded, her voice going higher, and her hands clenching into weapons.

"Would you step aside please, Miss?"

A quick hand slashed out to rake his cheek with sharp nails. Pain seared his face. He did not move. Two bright stripes of blood appeared from his eye to the corner of his mouth. A drop trickled to the point of his chin and splattered down upon the girl's shoe.

"On my planet," he said, in a not unkindly tone, "when a woman insists on behaving like an animal, we assist her—by having her flogged naked in the public square. I see personal dignity is not so highly prized here. You do not regard it as a crime to behave like an alley cat?"

Her breath gushed out of her in a sound of rage, and she tore at the wounds again. Then, when he did nothing but look at her coldly, she fled.

Eli Roki, born to the nobility of Coph, dedicated to the service of the Sixty-Star Cluster, suddenly found himself something of an outcast. As he strode down the corridor away from Beth's office, he seemed to be walking into a thickening fog of desolation. He had no home now; for he had abdicated his hereditary rights on Coph in order to accept a commission with the SSC Patrol. That, too, was gone; and with it his career.

He had known from the moment he pressed the firing stud to blast the mercy freighter that unless the freighter proved to be a smuggler, his career would be forfeit. He was still morally certain that he had made no mistake. Had the freighter been carrying any other cargo, he would have been disciplined for *not* blasting it. And, if they had had nothing to hide, they would have stopped for inspection. Somewhere among Sol's planets lay the answer to the question—"What else was aboard besides the cargo of mercy?"

Roki shivered and stiffened his shoulders as he rode homeward in a heliocab. If the answer to the question were "Nothing," then according to the code of his planet, there was only one course left to follow. "The Sword of Apology" it was called.

He waited in his quarters for the colonel to fulfill his promise. On the following day, Beth called.

"I've found a Dalethian ship, Roki. Privately owned. Pilot's willing to fly you out of the Cluster. It's going as an observation mission—gather data on the Sol System. The commissioners vetoed the idea of sending a diplomatic delegation until we try to contact Solarians by high-C radio."

"When do I leave?"

"Be at the spaceport tonight. And good luck, son. I'm sorry all this happened, and I hope—"

"Yeah, thanks."

"Well—"

"Well?"

The colonel grunted and hung up. Ex-Commander Roki gathered up his uniforms and went looking for a pawn shop. "Hock 'em, or sell 'em?" asked a bald man behind the counter. Then he peered more closely at Roki's face, and paused to glance at a picture on the front page of the paper. "Oh," he grunted, "you. You wanta sell 'em." With a slight sneer, he pulled two bills from his pocket and slapped them on the counter with a contemptuous take-it-or-leave-it stare. The clothing was worth at least twice as much. Roki took it after a moment's hesitation. The money just matched the price tag on a sleek, snub-nosed Multin automatic that lay in the display case.

"And three hundred rounds of ammunition," he said quietly as he pocketed the weapon.

The dealer sniffed. "It only takes one shot, bud—for what *you* need to do."

Roki thanked him for the advice and took his three hundred rounds.

He arrived at the spaceport before his pilot, and went out to inspect the small Dalethian freighter that would bear him to the rim of the galaxy. His face clouded as he saw the pitted hull and the glaze of fusion around the lips of the jet tubes. Some of the ground personnel had left a Geiger hanging on the stern, to warn wanderers to keep away. Its dial indicator was fluttering in the red. He carried it into the ship. The needle dropped to a safe reading in the control cabin, but there were dangerous spots in the reactor room. Angrily he went to look over the controls.

His irritation grew. The ship—aptly named the *Idiot*—was of ancient vintage, without the standard warning systems or safety devices, and with no armament other than its ion guns. The fifth dial of its position-indicator was calibrated only to one hundred thousand C's, and was redlined at ninety thousand. A modern service-ship, on the other hand, could have penetrated to a segment of five-space where light's velocity was constant at one hundred fifty thousand C's and could reach Sol in two months. The *Idiot* would need five or six, if it could make the trip at all. Roki doubted it. Under normal circumstances, he would hesitate to use the vessel even within the volume of the Sixty-Star Cluster.

He thought of protesting to Beth, but realized that the colonel had fulfilled his promise, and would do nothing more. Grumbling, he stowed his gear in the cargo hold, and settled down in the control room to doze in wait for the pilot.

A sharp whack across the soles of his boots brought him painfully awake. "Get your feet off the controls!" snapped an angry voice.

Roki winced and blinked at a narrow frowning face with a cigar clenched in its teeth. "And get out of that chair!" the face growled around its cigar.

His feet stung with pain. He hissed a snarl and bounded to his feet; grabbing a handful of the intruder's shirt-front, he aimed a punch at the cigar—then stayed the fist in midair. Something felt wrong about the shirt. Aghast, he realized there was a woman inside it. He let go and reddened. "I . . . I thought you were the pilot."

She eyed him contemptuously as she tucked in her shirt. "I am, Doc." She tossed her hat on the navigation desk, revealing a close-cropped head of dark hair. She removed the cigar from her face, neatly pinched out the fire, and filed the butt in the pocket of her dungarees for a rainy day. She had a nice mouth, with the cigar gone, but it was tight with anger.

"Stay out of my seat," she told him crisply, "and out of my hair. Let's get that straight before we start."

"This . . . this is *your* tub?" he gasped.

She stalked to a panel and began punching settings into the

courser. "That's right. I'm Daleth Shipping Incorporated. Any comments?"

"You expect this wreck to make it to Sol?" he growled.

She snapped him a sharp, green-eyed glance. "Well listen to the free ride! Make your complaints to the colonel, fellow. I don't expect anything, except my pay. I'm willing to chance it. Why shouldn't you?"

"The existence of a fool is not necessarily a proof of the existence of two fools," he said sourly.

"If you don't like it, go elsewhere." She straightened and swept him with a clinical glance. "But as I understand it, *you* can't be too particular."

He frowned. "Are you planning to make *that* your business?"

"*Uh*-uh! You're nothing to me, fellow. I don't care *who* I haul, as long as it's legal. Now do you want a ride, or don't you?"

He nodded curtly and stalked back to find quarters. "Stay outa my cabin," she bellowed after him.

Roki grunted disgustedly. The pilot was typical of Daleth civilization. It was still a rough, uncouth planet with a thinly scattered population, a wild frontier, and growing pains. The girl was the product of a wildly expanding tough-fisted culture with little respect for authority. It occurred to him immediately that she might be thinking of selling him to the Solarian officials—as the man who blasted the mercy ship.

"Prepare to lift," came the voice of the intercom. "Two minutes before blast-off."

Roki suppressed an urge to scramble out of the ship and call the whole thing off. The rockets belched, coughed, and then hissed faintly, idling in wait for a command. Roki stretched out on his bunk, for some of these older ships were rather rough on blast-off. The hiss became a thunder, and the *Idiot* moved skyward—first slowly, then with a spurt of speed. When it cleared the atmosphere, there was a sudden lurch as it shed the now empty booster burners. There was a moment of dead silence, as the ship hovered without power. Then the faint shriek of the ion streams came to his ears—as the ion drive became useful in the vacuum of space. He glanced out the port to watch the faint streak of luminescence focus into a slender needle of high-speed particles, pushing the *Idiot* ever higher in a rush of acceleration.

He punched the intercom button. "Not bad, for a Dalethian," he called admiringly.

"Keep your opinions to yourself," growled Daleth Incorporated.

The penetration to higher C-levels came without subjective sensation. Roki knew it was happening when the purr from the reactor room went deep-throated and when the cabin lights went dimmer. He stared calmly out the port, for the phenomenon of penetration never ceased to thrill him.

The transition to high-C began as a blue-shift in the starlight. Distant, dull-red stars came slowly brighter, whiter—until they burned like myriad welding arcs in the black vault. They were not identical with the stars of the home continuum, but rather, projections of the same star-masses at higher C-levels of five-space, where the velocity of light was gradually increasing as the *Idiot* climbed higher in the C-component.

At last he had to close the port, for the starlight was becoming unbearable as its wave-length moved into the ultraviolet and the X-ray bands. He watched on a fluorescent viewing screen. The projective star-masses were flaring into supernovae, and the changing continuums seemed to be collapsing toward the ship in the blue-shift of the cosmos. As the radiant energy increased, the cabin became warmer, and the pilot set up a partial radiation screen.

At last the penetration stopped. Roki punched the intercom again. "What level are we on, Daleth?"

"Ninety thousand," she replied curtly.

Roki made a wry mouth. She had pushed it up to the red line without a blink. It was O.K.—if the radiation screens held out. If they failed to hold it, the ship would be blistered into a drifting dust cloud.

"Want me to navigate for you?" he called.

"I'm capable of handling my own ship," she barked.

"I'm aware of that. But I have nothing else to do. You might as well put me to work."

She paused, then softened a little. "O.K., come on forward."

She swung around in her chair as he entered the cabin, and for the first time he noticed that, despite the close-cropped hair and the dungarees and the cigar-smoking, she was quite a handsome girl—handsome, proud, and highly capable. Daleth, the frontier planet, bred a healthy if somewhat unscrupulous species.

"The C-maps are in that case," she said, jerking her thumb toward a filing cabinet. "Work out a course for maximum radiant thrust."

Roki frowned. "Why not a least-time course?"

She shook her head. "My reactors aren't too efficient. We need all the boost we can get from external energy. Otherwise we'll have to dive back down for fuel."

Worse and worse!—Roki thought as he dragged out the C-maps. Flying this boat to Sol would have been a feat of daring two centuries ago. Now, in an age of finer ships, it was a feat of idiocy.

Half an hour later, he handed her a course plan that would allow the *Idiot* to derive about half of its thrust from the variations in radiation pressure from the roaring inferno of the high-level cosmos. She looked it over without change of expression, then glanced at him curiously, after noting the time.

"You're pretty quick," she said.

"Thank you."

"You're hardly stupid. Why did you pull such a stupid boner?"

Roki stiffened. "I thought you planned to regard that as none of your business."

She shrugged and began punching course-settings into the courser. "Sorry, I forgot."

Still angry, he said, "I don't regard it as a boner. I'd do it again."

She shrugged again and pretended a lack of interest.

"Space-smuggling could be the death of the galaxy," he went on. "That's been proven. A billion people once died on Tau II because somebody smuggled in a load of non-Tauian animals —for house pets. I did only what history has proven best."

"I'm trying to mind my own business," she growled, eyeing him sourly.

Roki fell silent and watched her reshape the radiation screen to catch a maximum of force from the flare of energy that blazed behind them. Roki was not sure that he wanted her to mind her own business. They would have to bear each other's presence for several months, and it would be nice to know how things stood.

"So you think it was a stupid boner," he continued at last. "So does everyone else. It hasn't been very pleasant."

She snorted scornfully as she worked. "Where I come from, we don't condemn fools. We don't need to. They just don't live very long, not on Daleth."

"And I am a fool, by your code?"

"How should I know? If you live to a ripe old age and get what you want, you probably aren't a fool."

And *that*, thought Roki, was the Dalethian golden rule. If the universe lets you live, then you're doing all right. And there was truth in it, perhaps. Man was born with only one right—the right to a chance at proving his fitness. And that right was the foundation of every culture, even though most civilized worlds tried to define "fitness" in terms of cultural values. Where life was rough, it was rated in terms of survival.

"I really don't mind talking about it," he said with some embarrassment. "I have nothing to hide."

"That's nice."

"Do you have a name—other than your firm name?"

"As far as you're concerned, I'm Daleth Incorporated." She gave him a suspicious look that lingered a while and became contemplative. "There's only one thing I'm curious about—why are you going to Sol?"

He smiled wryly. "If I told a Dalethian that, she would indeed think me a fool."

Slowly the girl nodded. "I see. I know of Cophian ethics. If an officer's blunder results in someone's death, he either proves that it was not a blunder or he cuts his throat—ceremonially, I believe. Will you do that?"

Roki shrugged. He had been away from Coph a long time. He didn't know.

"A stupid custom," she said.

"It manages to drain off the fools, doesn't it? It's better than having society try them and execute them forcibly for their crimes. On Coph, a man doesn't need to be afraid of society. He needs only to be afraid of his own weakness. Society's function is to protect individuals against unfortunate accidents, but not against their own blunders. And when a man blunders, Coph simply excludes him from the protectorate. As an outcast, he sacrifices himself. It's not too bad a system."

"You can have it."

"Dalethian?"

"Yeah?"

"You have no personal anger against what I did?"

She frowned at him contemptuously. "Uh-uh! I judge no one. I judge no one unless I'm personally involved. Why are you worried about what others think?"

"In our more highly developed society," he said stiffly, "a man inevitably grows a set of thinking-habits called 'conscience.'"

"Oh—yeah." Her dull tone indicated a complete lack of interest.

Again Roki wondered if she would think of making a quick bit of cash by informing Solarian officials of his identity. He began a mental search for a plan to avoid such possible treachery.

They ate and slept by the ship's clock. On the tenth day, Roki noticed a deviation in the readings of the radiation-screen instruments. The shape of the screen shell was gradually trying to drift toward mininum torsion, and assume a spherical shape. He pointed it out to Daleth, and she quickly made the necessary readjustments. But the output of the reactors crept a notch higher as a result of the added drain. Roki wore an apprehensive frown as the flight progressed.

Two days later, the screen began creeping again. Once more the additional power was applied. And the reactor output needle hung in the yellow band of warning. The field-generators were groaning and shivering with threatening overload. Roki worked furiously to locate the trouble, and at last he found it. He returned to the control cabin in a cold fury.

"Did you have this ship pre-flighted before blast-off?" he demanded.

Her mouth fluttered with amusement as she watched his anger. "Certainly, commander."

He flushed at the worthless title. "May I see the papers?"

For a moment she hesitated, then fumbled in her pocket and displayed a folded pink paper.

"Pink!" he roared. "You had no business taking off!"

Haughtily, she read him the first line of the pre-flight report. " 'Base personnel disclaim any responsibility for accidents resulting from flight of Daleth Ship— 'It doesn't say I can't take off."

"I'll see you banned from space!" he growled.

She gave him a look that reminded him of his current status. It was a tolerant, amused stare. "What's wrong, commander?"

"The synchronizers are out, that's all," he fumed. "Screen's getting farther and farther from resonance."

"So?"

"So the overload'll get worse, and the screen'll break down. You'll have to drop back down out of the C-component and get it repaired."

She shook her head. "We'll chance it like it is. I've always wanted to find out how much overload the reactor'll take."

Roki choked. There wasn't a chance of making it. "Are you a graduate space engineer?" he asked.

"No."

"Then you'd better take one's advice."

"Yours?"

"Yes."

"No! We're going on."

"Suppose I refuse to let you?"

She whirled quickly, eyes flashing. "I'm in command of my ship. I'm also armed. I suggest you return to your quarters, passenger."

Roki sized up the situation, measured the determination in the girl's eyes, and decided that there was only one thing to do. He shrugged and looked away, as if admitting her authority. She glared at him for a moment, but did not press her demand that he leave the control room. As soon as she glanced back at the instruments, Roki padded his rough knuckles with a hand-kerchief, selected a target at the back of her short crop of dark hair, and removed her objections with a short chopping blow to the head. "Sorry, friend," he murmured as he lifted her limp body out of the seat.

He carried her to her quarters and placed her on the bunk. After removing a small needle gun from her pocket, he left a box of headache tablets in easy reach, locked her inside, and went back to the controls. His fist was numb, and he felt like a heel, but there was no use arguing with a Dalethian. Club-bing her to sleep was the only way to avoid bloodier mayhem in which she might have emerged the victor—until the screen gave way.

The power-indication was threateningly high as Roki acti-vated the C-drive and began piloting the ship downward through the fifth component. But with proper adjustments, he made the process analogous to freefall, and the power reading fell off slowly. A glance at the C-maps told him that the *Idiot* would emerge far beyond the limits of Sixty-Star Cluster. When it re-entered the continuum, it would be in the general volume of space controlled by another interstellar organization called The Viggern Federation. He knew little of its culture, but certainly it should have facilities for repairing a set of screen-synchronizers. He looked up its capitol planet, and began jetting toward it while the ship drifted downward in C. As he reached lower energy-levels, he cut out the screen altogether and went to look in on Daleth Incorporated who had made no sound for two hours.

He was surprised to see her awake and sitting up on the bunk. She gave him a cold and deadly stare, but displayed no rage. "I should've known better than to turn my back on you."

"Sorry. You were going to—"

"Save it. Where are we?"

"Coming in on Tragor III."

"I'll have you jailed on Tragor III, then."

He nodded. "You *could* do that, but then you might have trouble collecting my fare from Beth."

"That's all right."

"Suit yourself. I'd rather be jailed on your trumped-up charges than be a wisp of gas at ninety-thousand C's."

"Trumped up?"

"Sure, the pink pre-flight. Any court will say that whatever happened was your own fault. You lose your authority if you fly pink, unless your crew signs a release."

"You a lawyer?"

"I've had a few courses in space law. But if you don't believe me, check with the Interfed Service on Tragor III."

"I will. Now how about opening the door. I want out."

"Behave?"

She paused, then: "My promise wouldn't mean anything, Roki. I don't share your system of ethics."

He watched her cool green eyes for a moment, then chuckled "In a sense you *do*—or you wouldn't have said *that*." He unlocked the cabin and released her, not trusting her, but realizing that the synchronizers were so bad by now that she couldn't attempt to go on without repairs. She could have no motive for turning on him—except anger perhaps.

"My gun?" she said.

Again Roki hesitated. Then, smiling faintly, he handed it to her. She took the weapon, sniffed scornfully, and cocked it.

"Turn around, fool!" she barked.

Roki folded his arms across his chest, and remained facing her. "Go to the devil," he said quietly.

Her fingers whitened on the trigger. Still the Cophian failed to flinch, lose his smile, or move. Daleth Incorporated arched her eyebrows, uncocked the pistol, and returned it to her belt. Then she patted his cheek and chuckled nastily. "Just watch yourself, commander. I don't like you."

And he noticed, as she turned away, that she had a bump on her head to prove it. He wondered how much the bump would cost him before it was over. Treachery on Sol, perhaps.

The pilot called Tragor III and received instructions to set an orbital course to await inspection. All foreign ships were boarded before being permitted to land. A few hours later, a small patrol ship winged close and grappled to the hull. Roki went to manipulate the locks.

A captain and two assistants came through. The inspector was a young man with glasses and oversized ears. His eyebrows were ridiculously bushy and extended down on each side to his cheekbones. The ears were also filled with yellow brush. Roki recognized the peculiarities as local evolutionary tendencies; for they were shared also by the assistants. Tragor III evidently had an exceedingly dusty atmosphere.

The captain nodded a greeting and requested the ship's flight papers. He glanced at the pink pre-flight, clucked to himself, and read every word in the dispatcher's forms. "Observation flight? To Sol?" He addressed himself to Roki, using the interstellar Esperanto.

The girl answered. "That's right. Let's get this over with."

The captain gave her a searing, head-to toe glance. "Are you the ship's owner, woman?"

Daleth Incorporated contained her anger with an effort. "I am."

The captain told her what a Tragorian thought of it by turning aside from her, and continuing to address Roki as if he were ship's skipper. "Please leave the ship while we fumigate and inspect. Wohr will make you comfortable in the patrol vessel. You will have to submit to physical examination —a contagion precaution."

Roki nodded, and they started out after the assistant. As they entered the corridor, he grinned at Daleth, and received a savage kick in the shin for his trouble.

"Oops, sorry!" she muttered.

"Oh—one moment, sir," the captain called after them. "May I speak to you a moment—"

They both stopped and turned.

"Privately," the captain added.

The girl marched angrily on. Roki stepped back in the cabin and nodded.

"You are a well-traveled man, E Roki?" the bushy-browed man asked politely.

"Space has been my business."

"Then you need no warning about local customs." The captain bowed.

"I know enough to respect them and conform to them," Roki assured him. "That's a general rule. But I'm not familiar with Tragor III. Is there anything special I should know before we start out?"

"Your woman, E Roki. You might do well to inform her that she will have to wear a veil, speak to no man, and be escorted upon the streets at all times. Otherwise, she will be wise to remain on the ship, in her quarters."

Roki suppressed a grin. "I shall try to insure her good behavior."

The captain looked defensive. "You regard our customs as primitive?"

"Every society to its own tastes, captain. The wisdom of one society would be folly for another. Who is qualified to judge? Only the universe, which passes the judgment of survival on all peoples."

"Thank you. You are a wise traveler. I might explain that our purdah is the result of an evolutionary peculiarity. You will see for yourself, however."

"I can't *guarantee* my companion's behavior," Roki said before he went to join Daleth. "But I'll try my best to influence her."

Roki was grinning broadly as he went to the patrol vessel to wait. One thing was certain: the girl would have a rough time on Tragor if she tried to have him jailed for mutiny.

Her face reddened to forge-heat as he relayed the captain's warning.

"I shall do nothing of the sort," she said stiffly.

Roki shrugged. "You know enough to respect local customs."

"Not when they're personally humiliating!" She curled up on a padded seat in the visitor's room and began to pout. He decided to drop the subject.

Repairing the synchronizers promised to be a week-long job, according to the Tragorian inspector who accompanied the *Idiot* upon landing. "Our replacements are standardized, of course—within our own system. But parts for SSC ships aren't carried in stock. The synchronizers will have to be specially tailored."

"Any chance of rushing the job?"

"A week *is* rushing it."

"All right, we'll have to wait." Roki nudged the controls a bit, guiding the ship toward the landing site pointed out by the captain. Daleth was in her cabin, alone, to save herself embarrassment.

"May I ask a question about your mission, E Roki—or is it confidential in nature?"

Roki paused to think before answering. He would have to lie, of course, but he had to make it safe. Suddenly he chuckled. "I forgot for a moment that you weren't with Sixty-Star Cluster. So I'll tell you the truth. This is supposed to be an observation mission, officially—but actually, our superior sent us to buy him a holdful of a certain scarce commodity."

The captain grinned. Graft and corruption were apparently

not entirely foreign to Tragor III. But then his grin faded into thoughtfulness. "On Sol's planets?"

Roki nodded.

"This scarce commodity—if I'm not too curious—is it surgibank supplies?"

Roki felt his face twitch with surprise. But he recovered from his shock in an instant. "Perhaps," he said calmly. He wanted to grab the man by the shoulders and shout a thousand questions, but he said nothing else.

The official squirmed in his seat for a time. "Does your federation buy many mercy cargoes from Sol?"

Roki glanced at him curiously. The captain was brimming with ill-concealed curiosity. Why?

"Occasionally, yes."

The captain chewed his lip for a moment. "Tell me," he blurted, "will the Solarian ships stop for your patrol inspections?"

Roki hesitated for a long time. Then he said, "I suppose that you and I could get together and share what we know about Sol without revealing any secrets of our own governments. Frankly, I, too, am curious about Sol."

The official, whose name was WeJan, was eager to accept. He scrawled a peculiar series of lines on a scrap of paper and gave it to Roki. "Show this to a heliocab driver. He will take you to my apartment. Would dinner be convenient?"

Roki said that it would.

The girl remained in her quarters when they landed. Roki knocked at the door, but she was either stubborn or asleep. He left the ship and stood for a moment on the ramp, staring at the hazy violet sky. Fine grit sifted against his face and stung his eyes.

"You will be provided goggles, suitable clothing, and an interpreter to accompany you during your stay," said WeJan as they started toward a low building.

But Roki was scarcely listening as he stared across the ramp. A thousand yards away was a yellow-starred mercy ship, bearing Solar markings. The most peculiar thing about it was the ring of guards that surrounded it. They apparently belonged to the ship, for their uniforms were different from those of the base personnel.

WeJan saw him looking. "Strange creatures, aren't they?" he whispered confidentially.

Roki had decided that in the long run he could gain more information by pretending to know more than he did. So he nodded wisely and said nothing. The mercy ship was too far away for him to decide whether the guards were human. He could make out only that they were bipeds. "Sometimes one meets strange ones all right. Do you know the Quinjori—from the other side of the galaxy?"

"No—no, I believe not, E Roki. Quinjori?"

"Yes. A very curious folk. Very curious indeed." He smiled to himself and fell silent. Perhaps, before his visit was over, he could trade fictions about the fictitious Quinjori for facts about the Solarians.

Roki met his interpreter in the spaceport offices, donned the loose garb of Tragor, and went to quibble with repair service. Still he could not shorten the promised-time on the new synchros. They were obviously stuck for a week on Tragor. He thought of trying to approach the Solarian ship, but decided that it would be better to avoid suspicion.

Accompanied by the bandy-legged interpreter, whose mannerisms were those of a dog who had received too many beatings, Roki set out for Polarin, the Tragorian capital, a few miles away. His companion was a small middle-aged man with a piping voice and flaring ears; Roki decided that his real job was to watch his alien charge for suspicious activities, for the little man was no expert linguist. He spoke two or three of the tongues used in the Sixty-Star Cluster, but not fluently. The Cophian decided to rely on the Esperanto of space, and let the interpreter translate it into native Tragorian wherever necessary.

"How would E Roki care to amuse himself?" the little man asked. "A drink? A pretty girl? A museum?"

Roki chuckled. "What do most of your visitors do while they're here?" He wondered quietly what, in particular, the *Solarian* visitors did. But it might not be safe to ask.

"Uh—that would depend on nationality, sir," murmured Pok. "The true-human foreigners often like to visit the Wanderer, an establishment which caters to their business. The evolved-human and the nonhuman visitors like to frequent The Court of Kings—a rather, uh, peculiar place." He looked at Roki, doubtfully, as if wondering about his biological status.

"Which is most expensive?" he asked, although he really didn't care. Because of the phony "observation mission papers," he could make Colonel Beth foot the bill.

"The Court of Kings is rather high," Pok said. "But so is the Wanderer."

"Such impartiality deserves a return. We will visit them both, E Pok. If it suits you."

"I am your servant, E Roki."

How to identify a Solarian without asking?—Roki wondered as they sat sipping a sticky, yeasty drink in the lounge of the Wanderer. The dimly lighted room was filled with men of all races—pygmies, giants, black, red, and brown. All appeared human, or nearly so. There were a few women among the crewmen, and most of them removed their borrowed veils while in the tolerant sanctuary of the Wanderer. The Tragorian staff kept stealing furtive glances at these out-system females, and the Cophian wondered about their covetousness.

"Why do you keep watching the strange women, E Pok?" he asked the interpreter a few minutes later.

The small man sighed. "Evidently you have not yet seen Tragorian women."

Roki had seen a few heavily draped figures on the street outside, clinging tightly to the arms of men, but there hadn't been much to look at. Still, Pok's hint was enough to give him an idea.

"You don't mean Tragor III is one of those places where evolution has pushed the sexes further apart?"

"I do," Pok said sadly. "The feminine I.Q. is seldom higher than sixty, the height is seldom taller than your jacket pocket, and the weight is usually greater than your own. As one traveler put it: 'short, dumpy, and dumb'. Hence, the Purdah."

"Because you don't like looking at them?"

"Not at all. Theirs is our standard of beauty. The purdah is because they are frequently too stupid to remember which man is their husband."

"Sorry I asked."

"Not at all," said Pok, whose tongue was being loosened by the yeasty brew. "It is our tragedy. We can bear it."

"Well, you've got it better than some planets. On Jevah, for instance, the men evolved into sluggish spidery little fellows, and the women are big husky brawlers."

"Ah yes. But Sol is the most peculiar of all, is it not?" said Pok.

"How do you mean?" Roki carefully controlled his voice and tried to look bored.

"Why, the Vamir, of course."

Because of the fact that Pok's eyes failed to move toward any particular part of the room, Roki concluded that there were no Solarians in the place. "Shall we visit the Court of Kings now, E Pok?" he suggested.

The small man was obviously not anxious to go. He

murmured about ugly brutes, lingered over his drink, and gazed wistfully at a big dusky Sanbe woman. "Do you suppose she would notice me if I spoke to her?" the small interpreter asked.

"Probably. So would her five husbands. Let's go."

Pok sighed mournfully and came with him.

The Court of Kings catered to a peculiar clientele ideed; but not a one, so far as Roki could see, was completely inhuman. There seemed to be at least one common denominator to all intelligent life: it was bipedal and bimanual. Four legs was the most practical number for any animal on any planet, and it seemed that nature had nothing else to work with. When she decided to give intelligence to a species, she taught him to stand on his hind legs, freeing his forefeet to become tools of his intellect. And she usually taught him by making him use his hands to climb. As a Cophian biologist had said, "Life first tries to climb a tree to get to the stars. When it fails, it comes down and invents the high-C drive."

Again, Roki looked around for something that might be a Solarian. He saw several familiar species, some horned, some tailed, scaled, or heavily furred. Some stumbled and drooped as if Tragorian gravity weighted them down. Others bounced about as if floating free in space. One small creature, the native of a planet with an eight-hour rotational period, curled up on the table and fell asleep. Roki guessed that ninety per cent of the customers were of human ancestry, for at one time during the history of the galaxy, Man had sprung forth like a sudden blossom to inherit most of space. Some said they came from Sol III, but there was no positive evidence.

As if echoing his thoughts, Pok suddenly grunted, "I will never believe we are descended from those surly creatures."

Roki looked up quickly, wondering if the small interpreter was telepathic. But Pok was sneering toward the doorway. The Cophian followed his tipsy gaze and saw a man enter. The man was distinguished only by his height and by the fact that he appeared more human, in the classical sense, than most of the other customers. He wore a uniform—maroon jacket and gray trousers—and it matched the ones Roki had seen from a distance at the spaceport.

So this was a Solarian. He stared hard, trying to take in much at once. The man wore a short beard, but there seemed to be something peculiar about the jaw. It was—predatory, perhaps. The skull was massive, but plump and rounded like a baby's, and covered with sparse yellow fur. The eyes were quick and sharp, and seemed almost to leap about the room.

He was at least seven feet tall, and there was a look of savagery about him that caused the Cophian to tense, as if sensing an adversary.

"What is it you don't like about them?" he asked, without taking his eyes from the Solarian.

"Their sharp ears for one thing," whispered Pok as the Solarian whirled to stare toward their table. "Their nasty tempers for another."

"Ah? Rage reactions show biologic weakness," said the Cophian in a mild tone, but as loud as the first time.

The Solarian, who had been waiting for a seat at the bar, turned and stalked straight toward them. Pok whimpered. Roki stared at him coolly. The Solarian loomed over them and glared from one to the other. He seemed to decide that Pok was properly cowed, and he turned his fierce eyes on the ex-patrolman.

"Would you like to discuss biology, manthing?" he growled like distant thunder. His speaking exposed his teeth—huge white chisels of heavy ivory. They were not regressed toward the fanged stage, but they suggested, together with the massive jaw, that nature might be working toward an efficient bone-crusher.

Roki swirled his drink thoughtfully. "I don't know you, Bristleface," he murmured. "But if your biology bothers you, I'd be glad to discuss it with you."

He watched carefully for the reaction. The Solarian went gray-purple. His eyes danced with fire, and his slit mouth quivered as if to bare the strong teeth. Just as he seemed about to explode, the anger faded—or rather, settled in upon itself to brood. "This is beneath me," the eyes seemed to be saying. Then he laughed cordially.

"My apologies. I thought to share a table with you."

"Help yourself."

The Solarian paused. "Where are you from, manthing?"

Roki also paused. They might have heard that a Cophian commander blasted one of their ships. Still he didn't care to be caught in a lie. "Sixty-Star Cluster," he grunted.

"Which sun?" The Solarian's voice suggested that he was accustomed to being answered instantly.

Roki glowered at him. "Information for information, fellow. And I don't talk to people who stand over me." He pointedly turned to Pok. "As we were saying—"

"I am of Sol," growled the big one.

"Fair enough. I am of Coph."

The giant's brows lifted slightly. "Ah, yes." He inspected

Roki curiously and sat down. The chair creaked a warning. "Perhaps that explains it."

"Explains what?" Roki frowned ominously. He disliked overbearing men, and his hackles were rising. There was something about this fellow—

"I understand that Cophians are given to a certain ruthlessness."

Roki pretended to ponder the statement while he eyed the big man coldly. "True, perhaps. It would be dangerous for you to go to Coph, I think. You would probably be killed rather quickly."

The angry color reappeared, but the man smiled politely. "A nation of duelists, I believe, military in character, highly disciplined. Yes? They sometimes serve in the Sixty-Star Forces, eh?"

The words left no doubt in Roki's mind that the Solarian knew who had blasted their ship and why. But he doubted that the man had guessed his identity.

"I know less of your world, Solarian."

"Such ignorance is common. We are regarded as the galactic rurals, so to speak. We are too far from your dense star cluster." He paused. "You knew us once. We planted you here. And I feel sure you will know us again." He smiled to himself, finished his drink, and arose. "May we meet again, Cophian."

Roki nodded and watched the giant stride away. Pok was breathing asthmatically and picking nervously at his nails. He let out a sigh of relief with the Solarian's departure.

Roki offered the frightened interpreter a stiff drink, and then another. After two more, Pok swayed dizzily, then fell asleep across the table. Roki left him there. If Pok were an informer, it would be better to keep him out of the meeting with the patrol officer, Captain WeJan.

He hailed a cab and gave the driver the scrap of paper. A few minutes later, he arrived before a small building in the suburbs. WeJan's name was on the door—written in the space-tongue—but the officer was not at home. Frowning, he tried the door; locked. Then, glancing back toward the street, he caught a glimpse of a man standing in the shadows. It was a Solarian.

Slowly, Roki walked across the street. "Got a match, Bristle-face?" he grunted.

In the light of triple-moons, he saw the giant figure swell with rage. The man looked quickly up and down the street. No one was watching. He emitted a low animal-growl, exposing the brutal teeth. His arms shot out to grasp the Cophian's shoulders, dragging him close. Roki gripped the Multin automatic in his pocket and struggled to slip free. The Solarian jerked him up toward the bared teeth.

His throat about to be crushed, Roki pulled the trigger. There was a dull *chug*. The Solarian looked surprised. He released Roki and felt of his chest. There was no visible wound. Then, within his chest, the incendiary needle flared to incandescent heat. The Solarian sat down in the street. He breathed a frying sound. He crumpled. Roki left hastily before the needle burned its way out of the body.

He hadn't meant to kill the man, and it had been in self-defense, but he might have a hard time proving it. He hurried along back alleys toward the spaceport. If only they could leave Tragor immediately!

What had happened to WeJan? Bribed, beaten, or frightened away. Then the Solarians *did* know who he was and where he was going. There were half a dozen men around the spaceport who knew—and the information would be easy to buy. Pok had known that he was to meet with WeJan, and the Solarian had evidently been sent to watch the captain's quarters. It wasn't going to be easy now—getting to Sol III and landing.

What manner of creatures were these, he wondered. Men who supplied mercy cargoes to the galactic nations—as if charity were the theme and purpose of their culture—yet who seemed as arrogant as the warriors of some primitive culture whose central value was brutal power? What did they really want here? The Solarian had called him "manthing" as if he regarded the Cophian as a member of some lesser species.

The Solarians were definitely different. Roki could see it. Their heads were plump and soft like a baby's, hinting of some new evolutionary trend—a brain that could continue growing, perhaps. But the jaws, the teeth, the quick tempers, and the hypersensitive ears—what sort of animal developed such traits? There was only one answer: a nocturnal predator with the instincts of a lion. "You shall get to know us again," the man had said.

It spelled politico-galactic ambitions. And it hinted at something else—something that made the Cophian shiver, and shy away from dark shadows as he hurried shipward.

Daleth Incorporated was either asleep or out. He checked at the ship, then went to the Administration Building to inquire about her. The clerk seemed embarrassed.

"Uh . . . E Roki, she departed from the port about five."

"You've heard nothing of her since?"

"Well . . . there was a call from the police agency, I understand." He looked apologetic. "I assure you I had nothing to do with the matter."

"Police! What . . . what's wrong, man?"

"I hear she went unescorted and unveiled. The police are holding her."

"How long will they keep her?"

"Until some gentleman signs for her custody."

"You mean I have to sign for her?"

"Yes, sir."

Roki smiled thoughtfully. "Tell me, young man—are Tragorian jails particularly uncomfortable?"

"I wouldn't know, personally," the clerk said stiffly. "I understand they conform to the intergalactic 'Code of Humanity' however."

"Good enough," Roki grunted. "I'll leave her there till we're ready to go."

"Not a bad idea," murmured the clerk, who had evidently encountered the cigar-chewing lady from Daleth.

Roki was not amused by the reversal of positions, but it seemed as good a place as any to leave her for safekeeping. If the Solarians became interested in him, they might also notice his pilot.

He spent the following day watching the Sol ship, and waiting fatalistically for the police to come and question him about the Solarian's death. But the police failed to come. A check with the news agencies revealed that the man's body had not even been found. Roki was puzzled. He had left the giant lying in plain sight where he had fallen. At noon, the Solarian crew came bearing several lead cases slung from the centers of carrying poles. They wore metal gauntlets and handled the cases cautiously. Roki knew they contained radioactive materials. So that was what they purchased with their surgibank supplies—nuclear fuels.

Toward nightfall, they loaded two large crates aboard. He noted the shape of the crates, and decided that one of them contained the body of the man he had killed. Why didn't they want the police to know? Was it possible that they wanted him free to follow them?

The Sol-ship blasted-off during the night. He was surprised to find it gone, and himself still unmolested by morning. Wandering around the spaceport, he saw WeJan, but the man had developed a sudden lapse of memory. He failed to recognize the Cophian visitor. With the Solarians gone, Roki grew bolder in his questioning.

"How often do the Solarians visit you?" he inquired of a desk clerk at Administration.

"Whenever a hospital places an order, sir. Not often. Every six months perhaps."

"That's all the traffic they have with Tragor?"

"Yes, sir. This is our only interstellar port."

"Do the supplies pass through your government channels?"

The clerk looked around nervously. "Uh, no sir. They refuse to deal through our government. They contact their customers dìrectly. The government lets them because the supplies are badly needed."

Roki stabbed out bluntly. "What do you think of the Solarians?"

The clerk looked blank for a moment, then chuckled. "I don't know, myself. But if you want a low opinion, ask at the spaceport cafe."

"Why? Do they cause trouble there?"

"No, sir. They bring their own lunches, so to speak. They eat and sleep aboard ship, and won't spend a thin galak around town."

Roki turned away and went back to the *Idiot*. Somewhere in his mind, an idea was refusing to let itself be believed. A mercy ship visited Tragor every six months. Roki had seen the scattered, ruined cargo of such a ship, and he had estimated it at about four thousand pints of blood, six thousand pounds of frozen bone, and seven thousand pounds of various replaceable organs and tissues. That tonnage in itself was not so startling, but if Sol III supplied an equal amount twice annually to even a third of the twenty-eight thousand civilized worlds in the galaxy, a numbing question arose: where did they get their raw material? Surgibank supplies were normally obtained by contributions from accident victims who lived long enough to voluntarily contribute their undamaged organs to a good cause.

Charitable organizations tried to secure pledges from men in dangerous jobs, donating their bodies to the planet's surgibank in the event of death. But no man felt easy about signing over his kidneys or his liver to the bank, and such recruiters were less popular than hangmen or life insurance agents. Mercy supplies were quite understandably scarce.

The grim question lingered in Roki's mind: where did the Sol III traders find between three and five million healthy accident victims annually? Perhaps they made the accidents themselves, accidents very similar to those occurring at the end of the chute in the slaughterhouse. He shook his head, refusing to believe it. No planet's population, however terrorized by its rulers, could endure such a thing without generating a sociological explosion that would make the world quiver in its orbit. There was a limit to the endurance of tyranny.

He spent the rest of the week asking innocent questions here and there about the city. He learned nearly nothing. The Solarians came bearing their peculiar cargo, sold it quickly at a good price, purchased fissionable materials, and blasted-off without a civil word to anyone. Most men seemed nervous in their presence, perhaps because of their bulk and their native arrogance.

When the base personnel finished installing the synchronizers, he decided the time had come to secure Daleth Incorporated from the local jail. Sometimes he had chided himself for leaving her there after the Solarians had blasted-off, but it seemed to be the best place to keep the willful wench out of trouble. Belatedly, as he rode toward the police station, he wondered what sort of mayhem she would attempt to commit on his person for leaving her to fume in a cell. His smile was rueful as he marched in to pay her fine. The man behind the desk frowned sharply.

"Who did you say?" he grunted.

"The foreign woman from the Dalethian Ship."

The officer studied his records. "Ah, yes—Talewa Walkeka the name?"

Roki realized he didn't know her name. She was still Daleth Incorporated. "From the Daleth Ship," he insisted.

"Yes. Talewa Walkeka—she was released into the custody of Eli Roki on twoday of last spaceweek."

"That's imposs—" Roki choked and whitened. "I am Eli Roki. Was the man a Solarian?"

"I don't recall."

"*Why don't you?* Didn't you ask him for identification?"

"Stop bellowing, please," said the official coldly. "And get your fists off my desk."

The Cophian closed his eyes and tried to control himself. "Who is responsible for this?"

The officer failed to answer.

"*You* are responsible!"

"I cannot look out for all the problems of all the foreigners who—"

"Stop! You have let her die."

"She is only a female."

Roki straightened. "Meet me at any secluded place of your

choice and I will kill you with any weapon of your choice."

The official eyed him coldly, then turned to call over his shoulder. "Sergeant, escort this barbarian to his ship and see that he remains aboard for the rest of his visit."

The Cophian went peacefully, realizing that violence would gain him nothing but the iron hospitality of a cell. Besides, he had only himself to blame for leaving her there. It was obvious to him now—the contents of the second crate the Solarians had carried aboard consisted of Talewa Walkeka, lately of Daleth and high-C. Undoubtedly they had taken her alive. Undoubtedly she was additional bait to bring him on to Sol. Why did they want him to come? *I'll oblige them and find out for myself,* he thought.

The ship was ready. The bill would be sent back to Beth. He signed the papers, and blasted off as soon as possible. The lonely old freighter crept upward into the fifth component like a struggling old vulture, too ancient to leave its sunny lair. But the snychros were working perfectly, and the screen held its shape when the ascent ceased just below red-line level. He chose an evasive course toward Sol and began gathering velocity.

Then he fed a message into the coder, to be broadcast back toward the Sixty-Star Cluster: *Pilot abducted by Solarians; evidence secured to indicate that Solarian mercy-merchandise is obtained through genocide.* He recorded the coded message on tape and let it feed continuously into the transmitters, knowing that the carrier made him a perfect target for homing devices, if anyone chose to silence him.

And he knew it was a rather poor bluff. The message might or might not be picked up. A listening ship would have to be at the same C-level to catch the signal. Few ships, save the old freighters, lingered long at ninety-thousand C's. But if the Solarians let him live long enough, the message would eventually be picked up—but not necessarily believed. The most he could hope for was to arouse curiosity about Sol. No one would care much about the girl's abduction, or about his own death. Interstellar federations never tried to protect their citizens beyond the limits of their own volume of space. It would be an impossible task.

Unless the Solarians were looking for him however, they themselves would probably not intercept the call. Their ships would be on higher C. And since they knew he was coming, they had no reason to search for him. At his present velocity and energy-level, he was four months from Sol. The mercy ship on a higher level, would probably reach Sol within three weeks. He was a sparrow chasing a smug hawk.

But now there was more at stake than pride or reputation. He had set out to clear himself of a bad name, but now his name mattered little. If what he suspected were true, then Sol III was a potential threat to every world in the galaxy. Again he remembered the Solarian's form of address—"man-thing"—as if a new race had arisen to inherit the places of their ancestors. If so, the new race had a right to bid for survival. And the old race called Man had a right to crush it if he could. Such was the dialectic of life.

Four months in the solitary confinement of a spaceship was enough to unnerve any man, however well-conditioned to it. He paced restlessly in his cell, from quarters to control to reactor room, reading everything that was aboard to read and devouring it several times. Sometimes he stopped to stare in Daleth's doorway. Her gear was still in the compartment, gathering dust. A pair of boots in the corner, a box of Dalethia cigars on the shelf.

"Maybe she has a book or two," he said once. and entered. He opened the closet and chuckled at the rough masculine clothing that hung there. But among the coarse fabrics was a wisp of pale green silk. He parted the dungarees to stare at the frail feminine frock, nestled toward the end and half-hidden like a suppressed desire. For a moment he saw her in it, strolling along the cool avenues of a Cophian city. But quickly he let the dungarees fall back, slammed the door, and stalked outside, feeling ashamed. He never entered again.

The loneliness was overpowering. After three months, he shut off the transmitters and listened on the space-frequencies for the sound of a human voice. There was nothing except the occasional twittering of a coded message. Some of them came from the direction of Sol.

Why were they letting him come without interference? Why had they allowed him to transmit the message freely? Perhaps they wanted him as a man who knew a great deal about the military and economic resources of the Sixty-Star Cluster, information they would need if they had high ambitions in space. And perhaps the message no longer mattered, if they had already acquired enough nuclear materials for their plans.

After a logical analysis of the situation, he hit upon a better answer. Their ships didn't have the warplocking devices that permitted one ship to slip into a parallel C with an enemy and stay with that enemy while it maneuvered in the fifth component. The Solarians had proven that deficiency when the "mercy ship" had tried to escape him by evasive coursing. If their own ships were equipped with the warp lockers, they would have known better than to try. They wanted such equipment. Perhaps they thought that the *Idiot* possessed it, or that he could furnish them with enough information to let them build it.

After several days of correlating such facts as he already knew, Roki cut on his transmitters, fanned the beam down to a narrow pencil, and directed it toward Sol. "Blind Stab from Cluster-Ship *Idiot*," he called. "Any Sol Ship from *Idiot*. I have information to sell in exchange for the person of Talewa Walkeka. Acknowledge, please."

He repeated the message several times, and expected to wait a few days for an answer. But the reply came within three hours, indicating that a ship had been hovering just ahead of him, beyond the range of his own outmoded detectors.

"Cluster-Ship from Sol Seven," crackled the loud-speaker. "Do you wish to land on our planet? If so, please prepare to be boarded. One of our pilots will take you in. You are approaching our outer patrol zone. If you refuse to be boarded, you will have to turn back. Nonco-operative vessels are destroyed upon attempting to land. Over."

There was a note of amusement in the voice. They knew he wouldn't turn back. They had a hostage. They were inviting him to surrender but phrasing the invitation politely.

Roki hesitated. Why had the man said—"destroyed upon attempting to land?" After a moment's thought, he realized that it was because they could not destroy a ship while manuevering in the fifth component. They could not even stay in the same continuum with it, unless they had the warp-locking devices. A vague plan began forming in his mind.

"I agree conditionally. Do you have Talewa Walkeka aboard? If so, prove it by asking her to answer the following request in her own voice: 'List the garments contained in the closet of her quarters aboard this ship.' If this is accomplished satisfactorily, then I'll tentatively assume intentions are not hostile. Let me remind you, however, that while we are grappled together, I can rip half your hull off by hitting my C-drive—unless you're equipped with warp-locking devices."

That should do it, he thought. With such a warning, they would make certain that they had him aboard their own ship as a captive before they made any other move. And he would do his best to make it easy for them. Two or three hours would pass before he could expect an answer, so he began work immediately, preparing to use every means at his disposal to make a booby trap of the *Idiot,* and to set the trap so that only his continued well-being would keep it from springing.

The *Idiot's* stock of spare parts was strictly limited, as he had discovered previously. There were a few spare selsyns, replacement units for the calculator and courser, radio and radar parts, control-mechanisms for the reactors, and an assortment of spare instruments and detectors. He augmented this stock by ruthlessly tearing into the calculator and taking what he needed.

He was hard at work when the answer came from the Sol ship. It was Daleth's voice, crisp and angry, saying, "Six pair of dungarees, a jacket, a robe, and a silk frock. Drop dead, Roki."

The Solarian operator took over. "Expect a meeting in six hours. In view of your threat, we must ask that you stand in the outer lock with the hatch open, so that we may see you as we grapple together. Please acknowledge willingness to co-operate."

Roki grinned. They wanted to make certain that he was nowhere near the controls. He gave them a grumbling acknowledgment and returned to his work, tearing into the electronic control-circuits, the radio equipment, the reaction-rate limiters, and the controls of the C-drive. He wove a network of interdependency throughout the ship, running linking-circuits from the air-lock mechanisms to the reactors, and from the communication equipment to the C-drive. Gradually the ship became useless as a means of transportation. The jets were silent. He set time clocks to activate some of the apparatus, and keyed other equipment by relays set to trip upon the occurrence of various events.

It was not a difficult task, nor a long one. He added nothing really new. For example, it was easy to remove the wires from the air lock indicator lamp and feed their signal into a relay section removed from the calculator, a section which would send a control pulse to the reactors if the air locks were opened twice. The control pulse, if it came, would push the units past the red line. The relay sections were like single-task robots, set to obey the command: "If *this* happens, then push *that* switch."

When he was finished, the six hours were nearly gone. Pacing restlessly, he waited for them to come. Then, noticing a sudden flutter on the instruments, he glanced out to see the dark hulk slipping through his radiation screen. It came to a stop a short distance away.

Roki started the timers he had set, then donned a pressure suit. Carrying a circuit diagram of the changes he had wrought, he went to stand in the outer lock. He held open the outer hatch. The beam of a searchlight stabbed out to hold him while the Sol Ship eased closer. He could see another suited figure in its lock, calling guidance to the pilot. Roki glanced up at his own grapples; they were already energized and waiting for something to which they could cling.

The ships came together with a rocking jerk as both sets of grapples caught and clung. Roki swung himself across a gravityless space, then stood facing the burly figure of the Solarian. The man pushed him into the next lock and stepped after him.

"Search him for weapons," growled a harsh voice as Roki removed his helmet. "And get the boarding party through the locks."

"If you do that, you'll blow both ships to hell," the Cophian commented quietly. "The hatches are rigged to throw the reactors past red line."

The commander, a sharp-eyed oldster with a massive bald skull, gave him a cold stare that slowly became a sneer. "Very well, we can cut through the hull."

Roki nodded. "You can, but don't let any pressure escape. The throttles are also keyed to the pressure gauge."

The commander reddened slightly. "Is there anything else?"

"Several things." Roki handed him the circuit diagram. "Have your engineer study this. Until he gets the idea, anything you do may be dangerous, like trying to pull away from my grapples. I assure you we're either permanently grappled together, or permanently dead."

The Solarian was apparently his own engineer. He stared at the schematic while another relieved Roki of his weapon. There were four of them in the cabin. Three were armed and watching him carefully. He knew by their expressions that they considered him to be of a lesser species. And he watched them communicate silently among themselves by a soundless language of facial twitches and peculiar nods. Once the commander looked up to ask a question.

"When will this timer activate this network?"

Roki glanced at his watch. "In about ten minutes. If the transmitter's periodic signals aren't answered in the correct code, the signals serve to activate the C-drive."

"I see that," he snapped. He glanced at a burly assistant.

"Take him out. Skin him—from the feet up. He'll give you the code."

"I'll give it to you now," Roki offered calmly.

The commander showed faint surprise. "Do so then."

"The Cophian multiplication tables is the code. My transmitter will send a pair of Cophian numbers every two minutes. If you fail to supply the product within one second, a relay starts the C-drive. Since you can't guarantee an exactly simultaneous thrust, there should be quite a crash."

"Very well, give us your Cophian number symbols."

"Gladly. But they won't help you."

"Why not?"

"Our numbers are to the base eighteen instead of base ten. You couldn't react quickly enough unless you've been using them since childhood."

The Solarian's lips pulled back from his heavy teeth and his jaw muscles began twitching. Roki looked at his watch.

"You have seven minutes to get your transmitter set up, with me at the key. We'll talk while I keep us intact."

The commander hesitated, then nodded to one of the guards who promptly left the room.

"Very well, manthing, we will set it up temporarily." He paused to smile arrogantly. "You have much to learn about our race. But you have little time in which to learn it."

"What do you mean?"

"Just this. This transmitter—and the whole apparatus—will be shut down after a certain period of time."

Roki stiffened. "Just how do you propose to do it?"

"Fool! By waiting until the signals stop. You obviously must have set a time limit on it. I would guess a few hours at the most."

It was true, but he had hoped to avoid mentioning it. The power to the control circuits would be interrupted after four hours, and the booby trap would be deactivated. For if he hadn't achieved his goal by then, he meant to neglect a signal during the last half-hour and let the C-ward lurch tear them apart. He nodded slowly.

"You're quite right. You have four hours in which to surrender your ship into my control. Maybe I'll send the signals until I decide you don't mean to co-operate. Then—" He shrugged.

The Solarian gave a command to his aides. They departed in different directions. Roki guessed that they had been sent to check for some way to enter the *Idiot* that would not energize a booby circuit.

His host waved him through a doorway, and he found himself in their control room. A glance told him that their science still fell short of the most modern cultures. They had the earmarks of a new race, and yet Sol's civilization was supposedly the oldest in the galaxy.

"There are the transmitters," the commander barked. "Say what you have to say, and we shall see who is best at waiting."

Roki sat down, fingered the key, and watched his adversary closely. The commander fell into a seat opposite him and gazed coolly through narrowed lids. He wore a fixed smile of amusement. "Your name is Eli Roki, I believe. I am Space Commander Hulgruv."

A blare of sound suddenly came from the receiver. Hulgruv frowned and lowered the volume. The sound came forth as a steady musical tone. He questioned the Cophian with his eyes.

"When the tone ceases, the signals will begin."

"I see."

"I warn you, I may get bored rather quickly. I'll keep the signals going only until I think you've had time to assure yourselves that this is not a bluff I am trying to put over on you."

"I'm sure it's not. It's merely an inconvenience."

"You know little of my home planet then."

"I know a little."

"Then you've heard of the 'Sword of Apology.' "

"How does that—" Hulgruv paused and lost his smirk for an instant. "I see. If you blunder, your code demands that you die anyway. So you think you wouldn't hesitate to neglect a signal."

"Try me."

"It may not be necessary. Tell me, why did you space them two minutes apart? Why not one signal every hour?"

"You can answer that."

"Ah yes. You think the short period insures you against any painful method of persuasion, eh?

"Uh-huh. And it gives me a chance to decide frequently whether it's worth it."

"What is it you want, Cophian? Suppose we give you the girl and release you.". .

"She is a mere incidental," he growled, fearful of choking on the words. "The price is surrender."

Hulgruv laughed heartily. It was obvious he had other plans. "Why do you deem us your enemy?"

"You heard the accusation I beamed back to my Cluster."

"Certainly. We ignored it, directly. Indirectly we made a fool of you by launching another, uh, mercy ship to your system. The cargo was labeled as to source, and the ship made a point of meeting one of your patrol vessels. It stopped for inspection. You're less popular at home than ever." He grinned. "I suggest you return to Sol with us. Help us develop the warp locks."

Roki hesitated. "You say the ship *stopped for inspection?*"

"Certainly."

"Wasn't it inconvenient? Changing your diet, leaving your 'livestock' at home—so our people wouldn't know you for what you really are."

Hulgruv stiffened slightly, then nodded. "Good guess."

"Cannibal!"

"Not at all. I am not a man."

They stared fixedly at one another. The Cophian felt the clammy cloak of hate creeping about him. The tone from the speaker suddenly stopped. A moment of dead silence. Roki leaned back in his chair.

"I'm not going to answer the first signal."

The commander glanced through the doorway and jerked his head. A moment later, Talewa Walkeka stepped proudly into the room, escorted by a burly guard. She gave him an icy glance and said nothing.

"Daleth—"

She made a noise like an angry cat and sat where the guard pushed her. They waited. The first signal suddenly screeched from the receiver: two series of short bleats of three different notes.

Involuntarily his hand leaped to the key. He bleated back the answering signal.

Daleth wore a puzzled frown. "Ilgen times ufneg is horksegan," she muttered in translation.

A slow grin spread across Hulgruv's heavy face. He turned to look at the girl. "You're trained in the Cophian number system?"

"Don't answer that!" Roki bellowed.

"She *has* answered it, manthing. Are you aware of what your friend is doing, female?"

She shook her head. Hulgruv told her briefly. She frowned at Roki, shook her head, and stared impassively at the floor. Apparently she was either drugged or had learned nothing about the Solarians to convince her that they were enemies of the galaxy.

"Tell me, Daleth. Have they been feeding you well?"

She hissed at him again. "Are you crazy—"

Hulgruv chuckled. "He is trying to tell you that we are cannibals. Do you believe it?"

Fright appeared in her face for an instant, then disbelief. She stared at the commander, saw no guilt in his expression. She looked scorn at Roki.

"Listen, Daleth! That's why they wouldn't stop. Human livestock aboard. One look in their holds and we would have known, seen through their guise of mercy, recognized them as self-styled supermen, guessed their plans for galactic conquest. They breed their human cattle on their home planet and make a business of selling the parts. Their first weapon is infiltration into our confidence. They knew that if we gained an insight into their bloodthirsty culture, we would crush them."

"You're insane, Roki!" she snapped.

"No! Why else would they refuse to stop? Technical secrets? Baloney! Their technology is still inferior to ours. They carried a cargo of hate, our hate, riding with them unrecognized. They couldn't afford to reveal it."

Hulgruv laughed uproariously. The girl shook her head slowly at Roki, as if pitying him.

"It's true, I tell you! I guessed, sure. But it was pretty obvious they were taking their surgibank supplies by murder. And they contend they're not men. They guard their ships so closely, live around them while in port. And he admitted it to me."

The second signal came. Roki answered it, then began ignoring the girl. She didn't believe him. Hulgruv appeared amused. He hummed the signals over to himself—*without mistake.*

"You're using polytonal code for challenge, monotonal for reply. That makes it harder to learn."

The Cophian caught his breath. He glanced at the Solarian's huge, bald braincase. "You hope to learn some three or four hundred sounds—and sound-combinations within the time I allow you?"

"We'll see."

Some note of contempt in Hulgruv's voice gave Roki warning.

"I shorten my ultimatum to one hour! Decide by then. Surrender, or I stop answering. Learn it, if you can."

"He can, Roki," muttered Daleth. "They can memorize a whole page at a glance."

Roki keyed another answer. "I'll cut it off if he tries it."

The commander was enduring the tension of the stalemate superbly. "Ask yourself, Cophian," he grunted with a smile, "what would you gain by destroying the ship—and yourself? We are not important. If we're destroyed, our planet loses another gnat in space, nothing more. Do you imagine we are incapable of self-sacrifice?"

Roki found no answer. He set his jaw in silence and answered the signals as they came. He hoped the bluff would win, but now he saw that Hulgruv would let him destroy the ship. And—if the situation were reversed, Roki knew that he would do the same. He had mistakenly refused to concede honor to an enemy. The commander seemed to sense his quiet dismay, and he leaned forward to speak softly.

"We are a new race, Roki—grown out of man. We have abilities of which you know nothing. It's useless to fight us. Ultimately, your people will pass away. Or become stagnant. Already it has happened to man on Earth."

"Then—there *are* two races on Earth."

"Yes, of course. Did apes pass away when man appeared? The new does not replace the old. It adds to it, builds above it. The old species is the root of the new tree."

"Feeding it," the Cophian grunted bitterly.

He noticed that Talewa was becoming disturbed. Her eyes fluttered from one to the other of them.

"That was inevitable, manthing. There are no other animal foodstuffs on Earth. Man exhausted his planet, overpopulated it, drove lesser species into extinction. He spent the world's resources getting your ancestors to the denser star-clusters. He saw his own approaching stagnation on Earth. And, since Sol is near the rim of the galaxy, with no close star-neighbors, he realized he could never achieve a mass-exodus into space. He didn't have the C-drive in its present form. The best he could do was a field-cancellation drive."

"But that's the heart of the C-drive."

"True. But he was too stupid to realize what he had. He penetrated the fifth component and failed to realize what he had done. His ships went up to five-hundred C's or so, spent a few hours there by the ship's clock, and came down to find several years had passed on Earth. They never got around that time-lag."

"But that's hardly more than a problem in five-space navigation!"

"True again. But they still thought of it in terms of field-
cancellation. They didn't realize they'd actually left the
four-space continuum. They failed to see the blue-shift as
anything more than a field-phenomenon. Even in high-C, you
measure light's velocity as the same constant—because your
measuring instruments have changed proportionally. It's different, relative to the home continuum, but you can't know it
except by pure reasoning. They never found out.

"Using what they had, they saw that they could send a few
of their numbers to the denser star-clusters, if they wanted to
wait twenty thousand years for them to arrive. Of course, only
a few years would pass aboard ship. They knew they could
do it, but they procrastinated. Society was egalitarian at the
time. Who would go? And why should the planet's industry
exhaust itself to launch a handful of ships that no one would
ever see again? Who wanted to make a twenty thousand year
investment that would impoverish the world? Sol's atomic
resources were never plentiful."

"How did it come about then?"

"Through a small group of men who didn't *care* about the
cost. They seized power during a 'population rebellion'—when
the sterilizers were fighting the euthanasiasts and the do-
nothings. The small clique came into power by the fantastic
promise of draining off the population-surplus into space.
Enough of the stupid believed it to furnish them with a strong
backing. They clamped censorship on the news agencies and
imprisoned everyone who said it couldn't be done. They put
the planet to work building ships. Their fanatic personal
philosophy was: 'We are giving the galaxy to Man. What does
it matter if he perishes on Earth?' They put about twelve hundred ships into space before their slave-structure collapsed.
Man never developed another technology on Sol III. He was
sick of it."

"And *your* people?"

Hulgruv smiled. "A natural outgrowth of the situation. If
a planet were glutted with rabbits who ate all the grass, a
species of rabbits who learned to exploit other rabbits would
have the best chance for survival. We are predators, Cophian.
Nature raised us up to be a check on your race."

"You pompous fool!" Roki snapped. "Predators are specialists. What abilities do you have—besides the ability to prey
on man?"

"I'll show you in a few minutes," the commander muttered darkly.

Daleth had lost color slowly as she listened to the Solarian's roundabout admission of Roki's charge. She suddenly moaned and slumped in a sick heap. Hulgruv spoke to the guard in the soundless facial language. The guard carried her away quickly.

"If you were an advanced species, Hulgruv—you would not have let yourself be tricked so easily, by me. And a highly intelligent race would discover the warp locks for themselves."

Hulgruv flushed. "We underestimated you, manthing. It was a natural mistake. Your race has sunk to the level of cattle on earth. As for the warp locks, we know their principles. We have experimental models. But we could short-circuit needless research by using your design. We are a new race, new to space. Naturally we cannot do in a few years what you needed centuries to accomplish."

"You'll have to look for help elsewhere. In ten minutes, I'm quitting the key—unless you change your mind."

Hulgruv shrugged. While Roki answered the signals, he listened for sounds of activity throughout the ship. He heard nothing except the occasional clump of boots, the brief mutter of a voice in the corridor, the intermittent rattling of small tools. There seemed to be no excitement or anxiety. The Solarians conducted themselves with quiet self-assurance.

"Is your crew aware of what is happening?"

"Certainly."

As the deadline approached, his fingers grew nervous on the key. He steeled himself, and waited, clutching at each second as it marched past. What good would it do to sacrifice Daleth and himself? He would succeed only in destroying one ship and one crew. But it was a good trade—two pawns for several knights and a rook. And, when the Solarians began their march across space, there would be many such sacrifices.

For the last time, he answered a signal, then leaned back to stare at Hulgruv. "Two minutes, Solarian. There's still time to change your mind."

Hulgruv only smiled. Roki shrugged and stood up. A pistol flashed into the commander's hand, warning him back. Roki laughed contemptuously.

"Afraid I'll try to take your last two minutes away?"

He strolled away from the table toward the door.

"Stop!" Hulgruv barked.

"Why? I want to see the girl."

"Very touching. But she's busy at the moment."

"What?" He turned slowly, and glanced at his watch. "You don't seem to realize that in fifty seconds—"

"We'll see. Stay where you are."

The Cophian felt a sudden coldness in his face. Could they have found a flaw in his net of death?—a way to circumvent the sudden application of the *Idiot's* C-drive, with its consequent ruinous stresses to both ships? Or had they truly memorized the Cophian symbols to a one second reaction time?

He shrugged agreeably and moved in the general direction of the transmitter tuning units. There was one way to test the possibility. He stopped several feet away and turned to face Hulgruv's suspicious eyes. "You are braver than I thought," he growled.

The admission had the desired effect. Hulgruv tossed his head and laughed arrogantly. There was an instant of relaxation. The heavy automatic wavered slightly. Roki backed against the transmitters and cut the power switch. The hum died.

"Ten seconds, Hulgruv! Toss me your weapon. Shoot and you shatter the set. Wait and the tubes get cold. *Toss it!*"

Hulgruv bellowed, and raised the weapon to fire. Roki grinned. The gun quivered. Then with a choking sound, the Solarian threw it to him. "Get it on!" he howled. "*Get it on!*"

As Roki tripped the switch again, the signals were already chirping in the loud-speaker. He darted aside, out of view from the corridor. Footsteps were already racing toward the control room.

The signals stopped. Then the bleat of an answer! Another key had been set up in the adjoining room! With Daleth answering the challenges?

The pistol exploded in his hand as the first crewman came racing through the doorway. The others backed out of sight into the corridor as the projectile-weapon knocked their comrade back in a bleeding sprawl. Hulgruv made a dash for the door. Roki cut him down with a shot at the knee.

"The next one takes the transmitter," he bellowed. "Stay back."

Hulgruv roared a command. "Take him! If you can't, let the trap spring!"

Roki stooped over him and brought the pistol butt crashing against his skull, meaning only to silence him. It was a mistake; he had forgotten about the structure of the Solarian skull. He put his foot on Hulgruv's neck and jerked. The butt came free with a wet *cluck*. He raced to the doorway and pressed himself against the wall to listen. The crewmen were apparently having a parley at the far end of the corridor. He waited for the next signal.

When it came, he dropped to the floor—to furnish an unexpected sort of target—and snaked into view. He shot twice at three figures a dozen yards away. The answering fire did something to the side of his face, blurring his vision. Another shot sprayed him with flakes from the deck. One crewman was down. The others backed through a door at the end of the corridor. They slammed it and a pressure seal tightened with a rubbery sound.

Roki climbed to his feet and slipped toward a doorway from which he heard the click of the auxiliary key. He felt certain someone was there besides Daleth. But when he risked a quick glance around the corner, he saw only the girl. She sat at a small desk, her hand frozen to the key, her eyes staring dazedly at nothing. He started to speak, then realized what was wrong. Hypnosis! Or a hypnotic drug. She sensed nothing but the key beneath her fingers, waiting for the next challenge.

The door was only half-open. He could see no one, but there had been another man; of that he was certain. Thoughtfully he took aim at the plastic door panel and fired. A gun skidded toward Daleth's desk. A heavy body sprawled across the floor.

The girl started. The dull daze left her face, to be replaced with wide-eyed shock. She clasped her hands to her cheeks and whimpered. A challenge bleated from the radio.

"Answer!" he bellowed.

Her hand shot to the key and just in time. But she seemed about to faint.

"Stay on it!" he barked, and dashed back to the control room. The crewmen had locked themselves aft of the bulkhead, and had started the ventilator fans. Roki heard their whine, then caught the faint odor of gas. His eyes were burning and he sneezed spasmodically.

"Surrender immediately, man-thing!" blared the intercom.

Roki looked around, then darted toward the controls. He threw a damping voltage on the drive tubes, defocused the ion streams, and threw the reactors to full emission. The random shower of high-speed particles would spray toward the focusing coils, scatter like deflected buckshot, and loose a blast of hard X-radiation as they peppered the walls of the reaction chambers. Within a few seconds, if the walls failed to melt, the crewmen back of the bulkhead should recognize the possibility of being quickly fried by the radiant inferno.

The tear gas was choking him. From the next compartment,

he could hear Daleth coughing and moaning. How could she hear the signals for her own weeping? He tried to watch the corridor and the reaction-chamber temperature at the same time. The needle crept toward the danger-point. An explosion could result, if the walls failed to melt.

Suddenly the voice of the intercom again: "Shut it off, you fool! You'll destroy the ship."

He said nothing, but waited in tense silence, watching the other end of the corridor. Suddenly the ventilator fans died. Then the bulkhead door opened a crack, and paused.

"Throw out your weapon first!" he barked.

A gun fell through the crack and to the floor. A Solarian slipped through, sneezed, and rubbed his eyes.

"Turn around and back down the corridor."

The crewman obeyed slowly. Roki stood a few feet behind him, using him for a shield while the others emerged. The fight was gone out of them. It was strange, he thought; they were willing to risk the danger of the *Idiot's* C-drive, but they couldn't stand being locked up with a runaway reactor. They could see death coming then. He throttled back the reactors, and prodded the men toward the storage rooms. There was only one door that suggested a lockup. He halted the prisoners in the hallway and tried the bolt.

"Not in there, manthing!" growled one of the Solarians.

"Why not?"

"There are—"

A muffled wail from within the compartment interrupted the explanation. It was the cry of a child. His hand trembled on the bolt.

"They are wild, and we are weaponless," pleaded the Solarian.

"How many are in there?"

"Four adults, three children."

Roki paused. "There's nowhere else to put you. One of you —*you* there—go inside, and we'll see what happens."

The man shook his head stubbornly in refusal. Roki repeated the order. Again the man refused. The predator, unarmed, was afraid of its prey. The Cophian aimed low and calmly shot him through the leg.

"Throw him inside," he ordered tonelessly.

With ill-concealed fright for their own safety, the other two lifted their screaming comrade. Roki swung open the door and caught a brief glimpse of several human shadows in the gloom. Then the Solarian was thrown through the doorway and the bolt snapped closed.

At first there was silence, then a bull-roar from some angry throat. Stamping feet—then the Solarian's shriek—and a body was being dashed against the inside walls while several savage voices roared approval. The two remaining crewmen stood in stunned silence.

"Doesn't work so well, does it?" Roki murmured with ruthless unconcern.

After a brief search, he found a closet to lock them in, and went to relieve Daleth at the key. When the last signal came, at the end of the four hours, she was asleep from exhaustion. And curled up on the floor, she looked less like a tough little frontier urchin than a frightened bedraggled kitten. He grinned at her for a moment, then went back to inspect the damage to the briefly overloaded reactors. It was not as bad as it might have been. He worked for two hours, replacing fused focusing sections. The jets would carry them home.

The *Idiot* was left drifting in space to await the coming of a repair ship. And Daleth was not anxious to fly it back alone. Roki set the Solarian vessel on a course with a variable C-level, so that no Sol ship could track them without warp lockers. As far as Roki was concerned the job was done. He had a shipful of evidence and two live Solarians who could be forced to confirm it.

"What will they do about it?" Daleth asked as the captured ship jetted them back toward the Sixty-Star Cluster.

"Crush the Solarian race immediately."

"I thought we were supposed to keep hands-off nonhuman races?"

"We are, unless they try to exploit human beings. That is automatically an act of war. But I imagine an ultimatum will bring a surrender. They can't fight without warp lockers."

"What will happen on Earth when they do surrender?"

Roki turned to grin. "Go ask the human Earthers. Climb in their cage."

She shuddered, and murmured, "Some day—they'll be a civilized race again, won't they?"

He sobered, and stared thoughtfully at the star-lanced cosmos. "Theirs is the past, Daleth. Theirs is the glory of having founded the race of man. They sent us into space. They gave the galaxy to man—in the beginning. We would do well to let them alone."

He watched her for a moment. She had lost cockiness, temporarily.

"Stop grinning at me like that!" she snapped.

Roki went to feed the Solarian captives: canned cabbage.

Big Joe And The Nth Generation

A THIEF, he was about to die like a thief.

He hung from the post by his wrists. The wan sunlight glistened faintly on his naked back as he waited, eyes tightly closed, lips moving slowly as he pressed his face against the rough wood and stood on tiptoe to relieve the growing ache in his shoulders. When his ankles ached, he hung by the nails that pierced his forearms just above the wrists.

He was young, perhaps in his tenth Marsyear, and his crisp black hair was close-cropped in the fashion of the bachelor who had not yet sired a pup, or not yet admitted that he had. Lithe and sleek, with the quick knotty muscles and slender rawhide limbs of a wild thing, half-fed and hungry with a quick furious hunger that crouched in ambush. His face, though twisted with pain and fright, remained that of a cocky pup.

When he opened his eyes he could see the low hills of Mars, sun-washed and gray-green with trees, trees brought down from the heavens by the Ancient Fathers. But he could also see the executioner in the foreground, sitting spraddlelegged and calm while he chewed a blade of grass and waited. A squat man with a thick face, he occasionally peered at the thief with empty blue eyes—while he casually played mumblety-peg with the bleeding-blade. His stare was blank.

"Ready for me yet, Asir?" he grumbled, not unpleasantly.

The knifeman sat beyond spitting range, but Asir spat, and tried to wipe his chin on the post. "Your dirty mother!" he mumbled.

The executioner chuckled and played mumblety-peg.

After three hours of dangling from the spikes that pierced his arms, Asir was weakening, and the blood throbbed hard in his temples, with each jolt of his heart a separate pulse of pain. The red stickiness had stopped oozing down his arms; they knew how to drive the spike just right. But the heartbeats labored in his head like a hammer beating at red-hot iron.

How many heartbeats in a lifetime—and how many left to him now?

He whimpered and writhed, beginning to lose all hope. Mara had gone to see the Chief Commoner, to plead with him for the pilferer's life—but Mara was about as trustworthy as a wild hüffen, and he had visions of them chuckling together in Tokra's villa over a glass of amber wine, while life drained slowly from a young thief.

Asir regretted nothing. His father had been a renegade before him, had squandered his last ritual formula to buy a wife, then impoverished, had taken her away to the hills. Asir was born in the hills, but he came back to the village of his ancestors to work as a servant and steal the rituals of his masters. No thief could last for long. A ritual-thief caused havoc in the community. The owner of a holy phrase, not knowing that it had been stolen, tried to spend it—and eventually counter-claims would come to light, and a general accounting had to be called. The thief was always found out.

Asir had stolen more than wealth, he had stolen the strength of their souls. For this they hung him by his wrists and waited for him to beg for the bleeding-blade.

> *Woman thirsts for husband,*
> *Man thirsts for wife,*
> *Baby thirsts for breast-milk*
> *Thief thirsts for knife . . .*

A rhyme from his childhood, a childish chant, an eenie-meenie-miney for determining who should drink first from a nectar-cactus. He groaned and tried to shift his weight more comfortably. Where was Mara?

"Ready for me yet, Asir?" the squat man asked.

Asir hated him with narrowed eyes. The executioner was bound by law to wait until his victim requested his fate. But Asir remained ignorant of what the fate would be. The Council of Senior Kinsmen judged him in secret, and passed sentence as to what the executioner would do with the knife. But Asir was not informed of their judgment. He knew only that when he asked for it, the executioner would advance with the bleeding-blade and exact the punishment—his life, or an amputation, depending on the judgment. He might lose only an eye or an ear or a finger. But on the other hand, he might lose his life, both arms, or his masculinity.

There was no way to find out until he asked for the

punishment. If he refused to ask, they would leave him hanging there. In theory, a thief could escape by hanging four days, after which the executioner would pull out the nails. Sometimes a culprit managed it, but when the nails were pulled, the thing that toppled was already a corpse.

The sun was sinking in the west, and it blinded him. Asir knew about the sun—knew things the stupid council failed to know. A thief, if successful, frequently became endowed with wisdom, for he memorized more wealth than a score of honest men. Quotations from the ancient gods—Fermi, Einstein, Elgermann, Hanser and the rest—most men owned scattered phrases, and scattered phrases remained meaningless. But a thief memorized all transactions that he overheard, and the countless phrases could be fitted together into meaningful ideas.

He knew now that Mars, once dead, was dying again, its air leaking away once more into space. And Man would die with it, unless something were done, and done quickly. The Blaze of the Great Wind needed to be rekindled under the earth, but it would not be done. The tribes had fallen into ignorance, even as the holy books had warned:

It is realized that the colonists will be unable to maintain a technology without basic tools, and that a rebuilding will require several generations of intelligently directed effort. Given the knowledge, the colonists may be able to restore a machine culture if the knowledge continues to be bolstered by desire. But if the third, fourth, and Nth generations fail to further the gradual retooling process, the knowledge will becone worthless.

The quotation was from the god Roggins, *Progress of the Mars-Culture*, and he had stolen bits of it from various sources. The books themselves were no longer in existence, remembered only in memorized ritual chants, the possession of which meant wealth.

Asir was sick. Pain and slow loss of blood made him weak, and his vision blurred. He failed to see her coming until he heard her feet rustling in the dry grass.

"Mara—"

She smirked and spat contemptuously at the foot of the post. The daughter of a Senior Kinsman, she was a tall, slender girl with an arrogant strut and mocking eyes. She stood for a moment with folded arms, eyeing him with amusement. Then, slowly, one eye closed in a solemn wink. She turned her back on him and spoke to the executioner.

"May I taunt the prisoner, Slubil?" she asked.

"It is forbidden to speak to the thief," growled the knifeman.

"Is he ready to beg for justice, Slubil?"

The knifeman grinned and looked at Asir. "Are you ready for me yet, thief?"

Asir hissed an insult. The girl had betrayed him.

"Evidently a coward," she said. "Perhaps he means to hang four days."

"Let him then."

"No—I think that I should *like* to see him beg."

She gave Asir a long searching glance, then turned to walk away. The thief cursed her quietly and followed her with his eyes. A dozen steps away she stopped again, looked back over her shoulder, and repeated the slow wink. Then she marched on toward her father's house. The wink made his scalp crawl for a moment, but then . . .

Suppose she hasn't betrayed me? Suppose she had wheedled the sentence out of Tokra, and knew what his punishment would be. *I think that I should like to see him beg.*

But on the other hand, the fickle she-devil might be tricking him into asking for a sentence that she *knew* would be death or dismemberment—just to amuse herself.

He cursed inwardly and trembled as he peered at the bored executioner. He licked his lips and fought against dizzyness as he groped for words. Slubil heard him muttering and looked up.

"Are you ready for me yet?"

Asir closed his eyes and gritted his teeth. "Give it to me!" he yelped suddenly, and braced himself against the post.

Why not? The short time gained couldn't be classed as living. Have it done with. Eternity would be sweet in comparison to this ignominy. A knife could be a blessing.

He heard the executioner chuckle and stand up. He heard the man's footsteps approaching slowly, and the singing hiss of the knife as Slubil swung it in quick arcs. The executioner moved about him slowly, teasing him with the whistle of steel fanning the air about him. He was expected to beg. Slubil occasionally laid the knife against his skin and took it away again. Then Asir heard the rustle of the executioner's cloak as his arm went back. Asir opened his eyes.

The executioner grinned as he held the blade high—aimed at Asir's head! The girl had tricked him. He groaned and closed his eyes again, muttering a half-forgotten prayer.

The stroke fell—and the blade chopped into the post above his head. Asir fainted.

When he awoke he lay in a crumpled heap on the ground. The executioner rolled him over with his foot.

"In view of your extreme youth, thief," the knifeman growled, "the council has ordered you perpetually banished. The sun is setting. Let dawn find you in the hills. If you return to the plains, you will be chained to a wild hüffen and dragged to death."

Panting weakly, Asir groped at his forehead, and found a fresh wound, raw and rubbed with rust to make a scar. Slubil had marked him as an outcast. But except for the nail-holes through his forearms, he was still in one piece. His hands were numb, and he could scarcely move his fingers. Slubil had bound the spike-wounds. but the bandages were bloody and leaking.

When the knifeman had gone, Asir climbed weakly to his feet. Several of the townspeople stood nearby, snickering at him. He ignored their catcalls and staggered toward the outskirts of the village, ten minutes away. He had to speak to Mara, and to her father if the crusty oldster would listen. His thief's knowledge weighed upon him and brought desperate fear.

Darkness had fallen by the time he came to Welkir's house. The people spat at him in the streets, and some of them flung handfuls of loose dirt after him as he passed. A light flickered feebly through Welkir's door. Asir rattled it and waited.

Welkir came with a lamp. He set the lamp on the floor and stood with feet spread apart, arms folded, glaring haughtily at the thief. His face was stiff as weathered stone. He said nothing, but only stared contemptuously.

Asir bowed his head. "I have come to plead with you, Senior Kinsman."

Welkir snorted disgust. "Against the mercy we have shown you?"

He looked up quickly, shaking his head. "No! For that I am grateful."

"What then?"

"As a thief, I acquired much wisdom. I know that the world is dying, and the air is boiling out of it into the sky. I wish to be heard by the council. We must study the words of the ancients and perform their magic, lest our children's children be born to strangle in a dead world."

Welkir snorted again. He picked up the lamp. "He who listens to a thief's wisdom is cursed. He who acts upon it is doubly cursed and a party to the crime."

"The vaults," Asir insisted. "The key to the Blaze of the

Winds is in the vaults. The god Roggins tells us in the words—"

"Stop! I will not hear!"

"Very well, but the blaze can be rekindled, and the air renewed. The vaults—" He stammered and shook his head. "The council must hear me."

"The council will hear nothing, and you shall be gone before dawn. And the vaults are guarded by the sleeper called Big Joe. To enter is to die. Now go away."

Welkir stepped back and slammed the door. Asir sagged in defeat. He sank down on the doorstep to rest a moment. The night was black, except for lamp-flickers from an occasional window.

"Ssssst!"

A sound from the shadows. He looked around quickly, searching for the source.

"Sssssst! Asir!"

It was the girl Mara, Welkir's daughter. She had slipped out the back of the house and was peering at him around the corner. He arose quietly and went to her.

"What did Slubil do to you?" she whispered.

Asir gasped and caught her shoulders angrily. "Don't you *know?*"

"No! Stop! You're hurting me. Tokra wouldn't tell me. I made love to him, but he wouldn't tell."

He released her with an angry curse.

"You *had* to take it sometime," she hissed. "I knew if you waited you would be too weak from hanging to even run away."

He called her a foul name.

"Ingrate!" she snapped. "And I bought you a hüffen!"

"You *what?*"

"Tokra gave me a ritual phrase and I bought you a hüffen with it. You can't *walk* to the hills, you know."

Asir burned with full rage. "You slept with Tokra!" he snapped.

"You're jealous!" she tittered.

"How can I be jealous! I hate the sight of you!"

"Very well then, I'll keep the hüffen."

"*Do!*" he growled. "I won't need it, since I'm not going to the hills!"

She gasped. "You've got to go, you fool! They'll kill you!"

He turned away, feeling sick. She caught at his arm and tried to pull him back. "Asir! Take the hüffen and *go!*"

"I'll go," he growled. "But not to the hills. I'm going out to the vault."

He stalked away, but she trotted along beside him, trying to tug him back. "Fool! The vaults are sacred! The priests guard the entrance, and the Sleeper guards the inner door. They'll kill you if you try it, and if you linger, the council will kill you tomorrow."

"Let them!" he snarled. "I am no sniveling townsman! I am of the hills, and my father was a renegade. Your council had no right to judge me. Now *I* shall judge *them*."

The words were spoken hotly, and he realized their folly. He expected a scornful rebuke from Mara, but she hung onto his arm and pleaded with him. He had dragged her a dozen doorways from the house of her father. Her voice has lost its arrogance and became pleading.

"Please, Asir! Go away. Listen! I will even go with you—if you want me."

He laughed harshly. "Tokra's leavings."

She slapped him hard across the mouth. "Tokra is an impotent old dodderer. He can scarcely move for arthritis. You're an idiot! I sat on his lap and kissed his bald pate for you."

"Then why did he give you a ritual phrase?" he asked stiffly.

"Because he likes me."

"You lie." He stalked angrily on.

"Very well! Go to the vaults. I'll tell my father, and they'll hunt you down before you get there."

She released his arm and stopped. Asir hesitated. She meant it. He came back to her slowly, then slipped his swollen hands to her throat. She did not back away.

"Why don't I just choke you and leave you lying here?" he hissed.

Her face was only a shadow in darkness, but he could see her cool smirk.

"Because you love me, Asir of Franic."

He dropped his hands and grunted a low curse. She laughed low and took his arm.

"Come on. We'll go get the hüffen," she said.

Why not? he thought. *Take her hüffen, and take her too.* He could dump her a few miles from the village, then circle back to the vaults. She leaned against him as they moved back toward her father's house, then skirted it and stole back to the field behind the row of dwellings. Phobos hung low in the west, its tiny disk lending only a faint glow to the darkness.

He heard the hüffen's breathing as they approached a hulking shadow in the gloom. Its great wings snaked out slowly as it sensed their approach, and it made a low piping sound. A native Martian species, it bore no resemblance to the beasts that the ancients had brought with them from the sky. Its back was covered with a thin shell like a bettle's, but its belly was porous and soft. It digested food by sitting on it, and absorbing it. The wings were bony—parchment stretched across a fragile frame. It was headless, and lacked a centralized brain, the nervous functions being distributed.

The great creature made no protest as they climbed up the broad flat back and strapped themselves down with the belts that had been threaded through holes cut in the hüffen's thin, tough shell. Its lungs slowly gathered a tremendous breath of air, causing the riders to rise up as the huge air-sacs became distended. The girth of an inflated hüffen was nearly four times as great as when deflated. When the air was gathered, the creature began to shrink again as its muscles tightened, compressing the breath until a faint leakage-hiss came from behind. It waited, wings taut.

The girl tugged at a ring set through the flesh of its flank. There was a blast of sound and a jerk. Nature's experiment in jet propulsion soared ahead and turned into the wind. Its first breath exhausted, it gathered another and blew itself ahead again. The ride was jerky. Each tailward belch was a rough lurch. They let the hüffen choose its own heading as it gained altitude. Then Mara tugged at the wing-straps, and the creature wheeled to soar toward the dark hills in the distance.

Asir sat behind her, a sardonic smirk on his face, as the wind whipped about them. He waited until they had flown beyond screaming distance of the village. Then he took her shoulders lightly in his hands. Mistaking it for affection, she leaned back against him easily and rested her dark head on his shoulder. He kissed her—while his hand felt gingerly for the knife at her belt. His fingers were numb, but he managed to clutch it, and press the blade lightly against her throat. She gasped. With his other hand, he caught her hair.

"Now guide the hüffen down!" he ordered.

"*Asir!*"

"Quickly!" he barked.

"What are you going to do?"

"Leave you here and circle back to the vaults."

"No! Not out here at night!"

He hesitated. There were slinking prowlers on the Cimmerian plain, beasts who would regard the marooned daughter of Welkir a delicious bit of good fortune, a gustatory delight of a sort they seldom were able to enjoy. Even above the moan of the wind, he would hear an occasional howl-cry from the fanged welcoming committee that waited for its dinner beneath them.

"Very well," he growled reluctantly. "Turn toward the vaults. But one scream and I'll slice you." He took the blade from her throat but kept the point touching her back.

"Please, Asir, *no!*" she pleaded. "Let me go on to the hills. Why do you want to go to the vaults? Because of Tokra?"

He gouged her with the point until she yelped. "Tokra be damned, and you with him!" he snarled. "Turn back."

"*Why?*"

"I'm going down to kindle the Blaze of the Winds."

"You're *mad! The spirits of the ancients live in the vaults.*"

"I am going to kindle the Blaze of the Winds," he insisted stubbornly. "Now either turn back, or go down and I'll turn back alone."

After a hesitant moment, she tugged at a wing rein and the hüffen banked majestically. They flew a mile to the south of the village, then beyond it toward the cloister where the priests of Big Joe guarded the entrance to the vaults. The cloister was marked by a patch of faint light on the ground ahead.

"Circle around it once," he ordered.

"You can't get in. They'll kill you."

He doubted it. No one ever tried to enter, except the priests who carried small animals down as sacrifices to the great Sleeper. Since no outsider ever dared go near the shaft, the guards expected no one. He doubted that they would be alert.

The cloister was a hollow square with a small stone tower rising in the center of the courtyard. The tower contained the entrance to the shaft. In the dim light of Phobos, assisted by yellow flickers from the cloister windows, he peered at the courtyard as they circled closer. It seemed to be empty.

"Land beside the tower!" he ordered.

"Asir—please—"

"Do it!"

The Hüffen plunged rapidly, soared across the outer walls, and burst into the courtyard. It landed with a rough jolt and began squeaking plaintively.

"Hurry!" he hissed. "Get your straps off and let's go."

"I'm not going."

A prick of the knife point changed her mind. They slid quickly to the ground, and Asir kicked the hüffen in the flanks. The beast sucked in air and burst aloft.

Startled faces were trying to peer through the lighted cloister windows into the courtyard. Someone cried a challenge. Asir darted to the door of the tower and dragged it open. Now forced to share the danger, the girl came with him without urging. They stepped into a stair-landing. A candle flickered from a wall bracket. A guard, sitting on the floor beneath the candle glanced up in complete surprise. Then he reached for a short barbed pike. Asir kicked him hard in the temple, then rolled his limp form outside. Men with torches were running across the courtyard. He slammed the heavy metal door and bolted it.

Fists began beating on the door. They paused for a moment to rest, and Mara stared at him in fright. He expected her to burst into angry speech, but she only leaned against the wall and panted. The dark mouth of the stairway yawned at them—a stone throat that led into the bowels of Mars and the realm of the monster, Big Joe. He glanced at Mara thoughtfully, and felt sorry for her.

"I can leave you here," he offered, "but I'll have to tie you."

She moistened her lips, glanced first at the stairs, then at the door where the guards were raising a frantic howl. She shook her head.

"I'll go with you."

"The priests won't bother you, if they see that you were a prisoner."

"I'll go with you."

He was pleased, but angry with himself for the pleasure. An arrogant, spiteful, conniving wench, he told himself. She'd lied about Tokra. He grunted gruffly, seized the candle, and started down the stairs. When she started after him, he stiffened and glanced back, remembering the barbed pike.

As he had suspected, she had picked it up. The point was a foot from the small of his back. They stared at each other, and she wore her self-assured smirk.

"Here," she said, and handed it casually. "You might need this."

They stared at each other again, but it was different this time. Bewildered, he shook his head and resumed the descent toward the vaults. The guards were battering at the doors behind them.

The stairwell was damp and cold. Blackness folded about

them like a shroud. They moved in silence, and after five thousand steps, Asir stopped counting.

Somewhere in the depths, Big Joe slept his restless sleep. Asir wondered grimly how long it would take the guards to tear down the metal door. Somehow they had to get past Big Joe before the guards came thundering after them. There was a way to get around the monster: of that he was certain. A series of twenty-four numbers was involved, and he had memorized them with a stolen bit of ritual. How to use them was a different matter. He imagined vaguely that one must call them out in a loud voice before the inner entrance.

The girl walked beside him now, and he could feel her shivering. His eyes were quick and nervous as he scanned each pool of darkness, each nook and cranny along the stairway wall. The well was silent except for the mutter of their footsteps, and the gloom was full of musty odors. The candle afforded little light.

"I told you the truth about Tokra," she blurted suddenly.

Asir glowered straight ahead and said nothing, embarrassed by his previous jealousy. They moved on in silence.

Suddenly she stopped. "Look," she hissed, pointing down ahead.

He shielded the candle with his hand and peered downward toward a small square of dim light. "The bottom of the stairs," he muttered.

The light seemed faint and diffuse. with a slight greenish cast. Asir blew out the candle, and the girl quickly protested.

"How will we see to climb again?"

He laughed humorlessly. "What makes you think we will?"

She moaned and clutched at his arm, but came with him as he descended slowly toward the light. The stairway opened into a long corridor whose ceiling was faintly luminous. White-faced and frightened, they paused on the bottom step and looked down the corridor. Mara gasped and covered her eyes.

"Big Joe!" she whispered in awe.

He stared through the stairwell door and down the corridor through another door into a large room. Big Joe sat in the center of the room, sleeping his sleep of ages amid a heap of broken and whitening bones. A creature of metal, twice the height of Asir, he had obviously been designed to kill. Tri-fingered hands with gleaming talons, and a monstrous head shaped like a Marswolf, with long silver fangs. Why should a metal-creature have fangs, unless he had been built to kill?

The behemoth slept in a crouch, waiting for the intruders.

He tugged the girl through the stairwell door. A voice droned out of nowhere: *"If you have come to plunder, go back!"*

He stiffened, looking around. The girl whimpered.

"Stay here by the stairs," he told her, and pushed her firmly back through the door.

Asir started slowly toward the room where Big Joe waited. Beyond the room he could see another door, and the monster's job was apparently to keep intruders back from the inner vaults where, according to the ritual chants, the Blaze of the Winds could be kindled.

Halfway along the corridor, the voice called out again, beginning a kind of sing-song chant: *"Big Joe will kill you, Big Joe will kill you, Big Joe will kill you—"*

He turned slowly, searching for the speaker. But the voice seemed to come from a black disk on the wall. The talking-machines perhaps, as mentioned somewhere in the ritual.

A few paces from the entrance to the room, the voice fell silent. He stopped at the door, staring in at the monster. Then he took a deep breath and began chanting the twenty-four numbers in a loud but quavering voice. Big Joe remained in his motionless crouch. Nothing happened. He stepped through the doorway.

Big Joe emitted a deafening roar, straightened with a metallic groan, and lumbered toward him, taloned hands extended and eyes blazing furiously. Asir shrieked and ran for his life.

Then he saw Mara lying sprawled in the stairway entrance. She had fainted. Blocking an impulse to leap over her and flee alone, he stopped to lift her.

But suddenly he realized that there was no pursuit. He looked back. Big Joe had returned to his former position, and he appeared to be asleep again. Puzzled, Asir stepped back into the corridor.

"If you have come to plunder, go back!"

He moved gingerly ahead again.

"Big Joe will kill you, Big Joe will kill you, Big Joe will kill—"

He recovered the barbed pike from the floor and stole into the zone of silence. This time he stopped to look around. Slowly he reached the pike-staff through the doorway. Nothing happened. He stepped closer and waved it around inside. Big Joe remained motionless.

Then he dropped the point of the pike to the floor. The

monster bellowed and started to rise. Asir leaped back, scalp crawling. But Big Joe settled back in his crouch.

Fighting a desire to flee, Asir reached the pike through the door and rapped it on the floor again. This time nothing happened. He glanced down. The pike's point rested in the center of a gray floor-tile, just to the left of the entrance. The floor was a checkerboard pattern of gray and white. He tapped another gray square, and this time the monster started out of his drowse again.

After a moment's thought, he began touching each tile within reach of the door. Most of them brought a response from Big Joe. He found four that did not. He knelt down before the door to peer at them closely. The first was unmarked. The second bore a dot in the center. The third bore two, and the fourth three—in order of their distance from the door.

He stood up and stepped inside again, standing on the first tile. Big Joe remained motionless. He stepped diagonally left to the second—straight ahead to the third—then diagonally right to the fourth. He stood there for a moment, trembling and staring at the Sleeper. He was four feet past the door!

Having assured himself that the monster was still asleep, he crouched to peer at the next tiles. He stared for a long time, but found no similar markings. Were the dots coincidence?

He reached out with the pike, then drew it back. He was too close to the Sleeper to risk a mistake. He stood up and looked around carefully, noting each detail of the room—and of the floor in particular. He counted the rows and columns of tiles—twenty-four each way.

Twenty-four—and there were twenty-four numbers in the series that was somehow connected with safe passage through the room. He frowned and muttered through the series to himself——0,1,2,3,3,3,2,2,1 . . .

The first four numbers—0,1,2,3. And the tiles—the first with no dots, the second with one, the third with two, the fourth with three. But the four tiles were not in a straight line, and there were no marked ones beyond the fourth. He backed out of the room and studied them from the end of the corridor again.

Mara had come dizzily awake and was calling for him weakly. He replied reassuringly and turned to his task again. "First tile, then diagonally left, then straight, then diagonally right—"

0, 1, 2, 3, 3.

A hunch came. He advanced as far as the second tile, then reached as far ahead as he could and touched the square diagonally right from the fourth one. Big Joe remained motionless but began to speak. His scalp bristled at the growling voice.

"If the intruder makes an error, Big Joe will kill."

Standing tense, ready to leap back to the corridor, he touched the square again. The motionless behemoth repeated the grim warning.

Asir tried to reach the square diagonally right from the fifth, but could not without stepping up to the third. Taking a deep breath, he stepped up and extended the pike cautiously, keeping his eyes on Big Joe. The pike rapped the floor.

"If the intruder makes an error, Big Joe will kill."

But the huge figure remained in his place.

Starting from the first square, the path went left, straight, right, right, right. And after zero, the numbers went 1, 2, 3, 3, 3. Apparently he had found the key. One meant a square to the southeast; two meant south; and three southwest. Shivering, he moved up to the fifth square upon which the monster growled his first warning. He looked back at the door, then at Big Joe. The taloned hands could grab him before he could dive back into the corridor.

He hesitated. He could either turn back now, or gamble his life on the accuracy of the tentative belief. The girl was calling to him again.

"Come to the end of the corridor!" he replied.

She came hurriedly, to his surprise.

"No!" he bellowed. "Stay back of the entrance! Not on the tile! *No!"*

Slowly she withdrew the foot that hung poised over a trigger-tile.

"You can't come in unless you know how," he gasped.

She blinked at him and glanced nervously back over her shoulder. "But I hear them. They're coming down the stairs."

Asir cursed softly. Now he *had* to go ahead.

"Wait just a minute," he said. "Then I'll show you how to come through."

He advanced to the last tile that he had tested and stopped. The next two numbers were two—for straight ahead. And they would take him within easy reach of the long taloned arms of the murderous sentinel. He glanced around in fright at the crushed bones scattered across the floor. Some were human. Others were animal-sacrifices tossed in by the priests.

He had tested only one two—back near the door. If he made a mistake, he would never escape; no need bothering with the pike.

He stepped to the next tile and closed his eyes.

"If the intruder makes an error, Big Joe will kill."

He opened his eyes again and heaved a breath of relief.

"Asir! They're getting closer! I can hear them!"

He listened for a moment. A faint murmur of angry voices in the distance. "All right." he said calmly. "Step only on the tiles I tell you. See the gray one at the left of the door?"

She pointed. "This one?"

"Yes, step on it."

The girl moved up and stared fearfully at the monstrous sentinel. He guided her up toward him. "Diagonally left—one ahead—diagonally right. Now don't be frightened when he speaks—"

The girl came on until she stood one square behind him. Her quick frightened breathing blended with the growing sounds of shouting from the stairway. He glanced up at Big Joe, noticing for the first time that the steel jaws were stained with a red-brown crust. He shuddered.

The grim chess-game continued a cautious step at a time, with the girl following one square behind him. What if she fainted again? And fell across a triggered tile? They passed within a foot of Big Joe's arm.

Looking up, he saw the monster's eyes move—following them, scrutinizing them as they passed. He froze.

"We want no plunder," he said to the machine.

The gaze was steady and unwinking.

"The air is leaking away from the world."

The monster remained silent.

"Hurry!" whimpered the girl. Their pursuers were gaining rapidly and they had crossed only half the distance to the opposing doorway. Progress was slower now, for Asir needed occasionally to repeat through the whole series of numbers, looking back to count squares and make certain that the next step was not a fatal one.

"They won't dare to come in after us," he said hopefully.

"And if they do?"

"If the intruder makes an error, Big Joe will kill," announced the machine as Asir took another step.

"Eight squares to go!" he muttered, and stopped to count again.

"Asir! They're in the corridor!"

Hearing the tumble of voices, he looked back to see blue-robed men spilling out of the stairway and milling down the corridor toward the room. But halfway down the hall, the priests paused—seeing the unbelievable: two intruders walking safely past their devil-god. They growled excitedly among themselves. Asir took another step. Again the machine voiced the monotonous warning.

"If the intruder makes an error . . ."

Hearing their deity speak, the priests of Big Joe babbled wildly and withdrew a little. But one, more impulsive than the rest, began shrieking.

"Kill the intruders! Cut them down with your spears!"

Asir glanced back to see two of them racing toward the room, lances cocked for the throw. If a spear struck a trig-ger-tile—

"Stop!" he bellowed, facing around.

The two priests paused. Wondering if it would result in his sudden death, he rested a hand lightly against the huge steel arm of the robot, then leaned against it. The huge eyes were staring down at him, but Big Joe did not move.

The spearmen stood frozen, gaping at the thief's familiarity with the horrendous hulk. Then, slowly they backed away.

Continuing his bluff, he looked up at Big Joe and spoke in a loud voice. "If they throw their spears or try to enter, kill them."

He turned his back on the throng in the hall and continued the cautious advance. Five to go, four, three, two —

He paused to stare into the room beyond. Gleaming machinery—all silent—and great panels, covered with a multitude of white circles and dials. His heart sank. If here lay the magic that controlled the Blaze of the Great Wind, he could never hope to re-kindle it.

He stepped through the doorway, and the girl followed. Immediately the robot spoke like low thunder.

"The identity of the two technologists is recognized. Hereafter they may pass with impunity. Big Joe is charged to ask the following: why do the technologists come, when it is not yet time?"

Staring back, Asir saw that the robot's head had turned so that he was looking directly back at the thief and the girl. Asir also saw that someone had approached the door again. Not priests, but townspeople.

He stared, recognizing the Chief Commoner, and the girl's father Welkir, three other Senior Kinsmen, and—Slubil, the executioner who had nailed him to the post.

"Father! Stay back."

Welkir remained silent, glaring at them. He turned and

whispered to the Chief Commoner. The Chief Commoner whispered to Slubil. The executioner nodded grimly and took a short-axe from his belt thong. He stepped through the entrance, his left foot striking the zero-tile. He peered at Big Joe and saw that the monster remained motionless. He grinned at the ones behind him, then snarled in Asir's direction.

"Your sentence has been changed, thief."

"Don't try to cross, Slubil!" Asir barked.

Slubil spat, brandished the axe, and stalked forward. Big Joe came up like a resurrection of fury. and his bellow was explosive in the vaults. Slubil froze, then stupidly drew back his axe.

Asir gasped as the talons closed. He turned away quickly. Slubil's scream was cut off abruptly by a ripping sound, then a series of dull cracks and snaps. The girl shrieked and closed her eyes. There were two distinct thuds as Big Joe tossed Slubil aside.

The priests and the townspeople—all except Welkir—had fled from the corridor and up the stairway. Welkir was on his knees, his hands covering his face.

"Mara!" he moaned. "My daughter."

"Go back, Father," she called.

Dazed, the old man picked himself up weakly and staggered down the corridor toward the stairway. When he passed the place of the first warning voice. the robot moved again—arose slowly and turned toward Asir and Mara who backed quickly away, deeper into the room of strange machines. Big Joe came lumbering slowly after them.

Asir looked around for a place to flee, but the monster stopped in the doorway. He spoke again, a mechanical drone like memorized ritual.

Big Joe is charged with announcing his function for the intelligence of the technologists. His primary function is to prevent the entrance of possibly destructive organisms into the vaults containing the control equipment for the fusion reaction which must periodically renew atmospheric oxygen. His secondary function is to direct the technologists to records containing such information as they may need. His tertiary function is to carry out simple directions given by the technologists if such directions are possible to his limited design.

Asir stared at the lumbering creature and realized for the first time that it was not alive, but only a machine built by the ancients to perform specific tasks. Despite the fresh redness about his hands and jaws, Big Joe was no more guilty of

Slubil's death than a grinding mill would be if the squat sadist had climbed into it while the Marsoxen were yoked to the crushing roller.

Perhaps the ancients had been unnecessarily brutal in building such a guard—but at least they had built him to *look* like a destroyer, and to give ample warning to the intruder. Glancing around at the machinery, he vaguely understood the reason for Big Joe. Such metals as these would mean riches for swordmakers and smiths and plunderers of all kinds.

Asir straightened his shoulders and addressed the machine. "Teach us how to kindle the Blaze of the Great Wind."

"Teaching is not within the designed functions of Big Joe. I am charged to say: the renewal reaction should not be begun before the Marsyear 6,000, as the builders reckoned time."

Asir frowned. The years were not longer numbered, but only named in honor of the Chief Commoners who ruled the villages. "How long until the year 6,000?" he asked.

Big Joe clucked like an adding machine. "Twelve Marsyears, technologist."

Asir stared at the complicated machinery. Could they learn to operate it in twelve years? It seemed impossible.

"How can we begin to learn?" he asked the robot.

"This is an instruction room, where you may examine records. The control mechanisms are installed in the deepest vault."

Asir frowned and walked to the far end of the hall where another door opened into—*another anteroom with another Big Joe!* As he approached the second robot spoke:

"If the intruder has not acquired the proper knowledge, Big Oswald will kill."

Thunderstruck, he leaped back from the entrance and swayed heavily against an instrument panel. The panel lit up and a polite recorded voice began reading something about "President Snell's role in the Eighth World War." He lurched away from the panel and stumbled back toward Mara who sat glumly on the foundation slap of a weighty machine.

"What are you laughing about?" she muttered.

"We're still in the first grade!" he groaned, envisioning a sequence of rooms. "We'll have to learn the magic of the ancients before we pass to the next."

"The ancients weren't so great," she grumbled. "Look at the mural on the wall."

Asir looked, and saw only a strange design of circles

about a bright splash of yellow that might have been the sun. "What about it?" he asked.

"My father taught me about the planets," she said. "That is supposed to be the way they go around the sun."

"What's wrong with it?"

"One planet too many," she said. "Everyone knows that there is only an asteroid belt between Mars and Venus. The picture shows a planet there."

Asir shrugged indifferently, being interested only in the machinery. "Can't you allow them one small mistake?"

"I suppose." She paused, gazing miserably in the direction in which her father had gone. "What do we do now?"

Asir considered it for a long time. Then he spoke to Big Joe. "You will come with us to the village."

The machine was silent for a moment, then: *"There is an apparent contradiction between primary and tertiary functions. Request priority decision by technologist."*

Asir failed to understand. He repeated his request. The robot turned slowly and stepped through the doorway. He waited.

Asir grinned. "Let's go back up," he said to the girl.

She arose eagerly. They crossed the anteroom to the corridor and began the long climb toward the surface, with Big Joe lumbering along behind.

"What about your banishment, Asir?" she asked gravely.

"Wait and see." He envisioned the pandemonium that would reign when girl, man, and robot marched through the village to the council house, and he chuckled. "I think that I shall be the next Chief Commoner," he said. "And my councilmen will all be thieves."

"Thieves!" she gasped. "Why?"

"Thieves who are not afraid to steal the knowledge of the gods—and become technologists, to kindle the Blaze of the Winds."

"What is a 'technologist', Asir?" she asked worshipfully.

Asir glowered at himself for blundering with words he did not understand, but could not admit ignorance to Mara who clung tightly to his arm. "I think," he said, "that a technologist is a thief who tells the gods what to do."

"Kiss me, Technologist," she told him in a small voice.

Big Joe clanked to a stop to wait for them to move on. He waited a long time.

The Big Hunger

I AM blind, yet I know the road to the stars. Space is my harp, and I touch it lightly with fingers of steel. Space sings. Its music quivers in the flux patterns, comes creeping along the twitch of a positron stream, comes to whisper in glass ears. I hear. Aiee! Though I am without eyes, I see the stars tangled in their field-webs, tangled into One. I am the spider who runs over the web. I am the spider who spins, spinning a space where no stars are.

And I am Harpist to a pale, proud Master.

He builds me, and feeds me the fuel I eat, and leads me riding through the space I make, to the glare of another sun. And when he is done with me, I lie rusting in the rain. My metal rots with ages, and the sea comes washing over land to take me while I sleep. The Master forgets. The Master chips flint from a stone, leaving a stone-ax. He busies himself with drums and bloody altars; he dances with a writhing snake in his mouth, conjuring the rain.

Then—after a long time—he remembers. He builds another of me, and I am the same, for like the Soul of him who builds me, my principle lies beyond particular flesh. When my principle is clothed in steel, we go wandering again. I the minstrel, with Man the king.

Hear the song of his hunger, the song of his endless thirst.

There was a man named Abe Jolie, and he leaned against me idly with one hand in the gloom while he spoke quietly and laughed with a female of his species.

"It's finished, Junebug. We got it made," he said.

And the girl looked her green eyes over me while the crickets sang beyond the wall, and while the shuffling of their feet echoed faintly in the great hangar.

"Finished," she murmured. "It's your success, Abe."

"Mine, and a lot of others. And the government's money."

She toyed with the lapel of his coveralls, grinned, and said, "Let's steal it and run away."

"*Ssshh!*" He looked around nervously, but there were no

guards in sight. "They can shoot you for less than that," he warned. "The S.P. doesn't have a sense of humor."

"Abe—"

"What?"

"Kiss me."

He kissed her.

"When is that going to be illegal, too?" she whispered.

He looked at her grimly, and she answered her own question.

"As soon as the eugenics laws are passed, Abe. Abe Jolie, who built the spacedrive, a genetic undesirable."

"Don't!"

They stood there breathing quietly, and there was hate in their throats.

"Well?"

He looked around again, and whispered, "Meet me here at eleven o'clock, Junebug."

They parted to the sound of casual footsteps.

At eleven o'clock, a lion roared in the hangar. At eleven o'clock a steel juggernaut tore through the hangar wall and paused on a concrete ramp while bullets ricocheted off the hull. Then the first star-chariot burnt a vertical column of flame in the night. Thunder walked upward on fiery stilts, while men shouted angrily. When we were alone in the airless, star-stung, sun-torn blackness, I stroked the web of space, and listened to the muted notes. When the tune is memorized, I speak. I contradict. I refute the universe. We lived in a space-less space beyond stars.

The man and the woman had gone. But the plan remained on Earth. My principle lingered on the drawing boards, and in the dreams of men—men who said they were sick of wars and politics and the braying of collectivist jackasses. Others were sick of petty peace and cheapness and Independence Day speeches and incorporated jackasses who blubbered disgustingly about various freedoms.

They wanted the one Big Freedom. They built me again, these pale, proud bipeds, these children of an Ape-Prince who walked like a god. They packed themselves in cylinders of steel and wandering, riding starward on a heart-tempest that had once sung them down from the trees to stalk the plains with club and torch. The pod of earth opened, scattered its seed spaceward. It was the time of the great bursting, the great birth-giving. Empires shivered in the storm.

Sky-chariots flung themselves upward to vanish beyond the fringes of the atmosphere. Prairie schooners of space bore the restless, the contemptuous, the hungry and the proud. And I led them along the self-road that runs around space. The world seethed, and empires toppled, and new empires arose whose purpose it was to build the sky-chariots.

Young men, young women, clamored at the gates of launching fields. Those who were chosen grinned expectantly at the stars. They climbed aboard in throngs and deserted Earth. They were hard laughers with red freckles and big fists. They wore slide rules at their belts like swords, and they spoke familiarly of Schwarzchild Line-Elements and Riemann-Christofel tensors. Their women were restless talkers, big women, with flashing white teeth. They teased the men, and their hands were strong and brown.

Poets came—and misfits, and saints, sinners, dirt-farmers. Engineers came and child-bearers, fighters, utopianists, and dreamers with the lights of God glowing in their starward eyes.

"Why were we taught to pray with *downcast* eyes?" they asked. "When you pray, look starward, look to the God at the north end of the Universe."

Man was a starward wind, a mustard seed, a wisp of Brahma's breath breathed across space.

They found two corpses in an orbit about Arcturus. The corpses were frozen and the ice was slowly sublimating into space-vapor. One of them had an Engineering Union card in his pocket. It gave his name as Abe Jolie. The other was a girl. And, because the corpse had given them the blueprints that led to space, they hauled him aboard with the girl. Somebody sang the *"Kyrie"* and somebody said, "I am the Resurrection and the Life." Then they cancelled out the orbital velocity and let the corpses go toppling toward Arcturus, toward a burning sun-grave where their light would shine forever.

There were those who remained behind. There were those who made Earth their business and stayed at home. Their tribes were numbered at two billion souls. And they were somehow different from the spacers. They liked to sit in their rocking chairs. They liked prettiness and a one-hundred-cent dollar. They voted for the Conservative Party. They abolished centralization. Eventually they abolished government. And for the first time in anyone's memory, there was peace on Earth, good will among men.

My Master was hungry for land. My Master sought new worlds. And we found them.

There was a yellow sun in Serpens called 27 Lambda, lying eight parsecs inward toward the galactic heartland and seven parsecs north toward the galactic pole. A lush green planet drifted at one hundred twenty megamiles from the friendly sun-star, and it awoke in the wandering biped nostalgic thoughts. We paused in space-black, we looked, we came down on tongues of lightning from the clear sky to set jet-fires in the grassy plain near a river and a forest.

Man was a seed replanted.

He wandered away from the sky-chariot and drank from a pool in the jungle. A behemoth with several legs and a parasite-rider came roaring his appetite at the pale biped. And his bones lay whitening in the sun, and his descendants learned that it was easier to stay alive by ignoring the biped from the sky.

I lay rusting in the rain. Houses of log and stone grew up on the hillsides. They crumbled slowly into ruin. A man wearing a fur robe came and built an altar at my feet. He burnt his eldest daughter on it while he sang a battle song and danced, danced a victory under strange sky.

The sons of men molded clay and chipped arrowheads and built fires. The old men told them stories of a space-going god, and the stories became their legends. They kidnaped the daughters of neighbors. knew wives, and multiplied.

A glacier came and ground me into dust. Millenniums passed, and each Prophet had his Hazar.

One of the prophets wrote an energy equation. Men crucified an Agitator on a telegraph pole. They purged a minority-group. They split a uranium atom into atoms of strontium and xenon. They wrote immortal lines deploring war while they invented better ways to wage it. They refashioned a body for my life-principle, for the tensor-transformers that constitute my soul. They mounted me again in a sky-borne prairie schooner because they were weary of sanctified braying.

There were growling columns of blue-white fire in the night, and growling voices of restless masses of men. Men darted along the road around space. . .

Men departed for other stars. But after a thousand years, many remained on the planet of their birth—homebodies and movie-idols and morticians, nembutal-addicts and advocates of world-government.

When the restless ones, the wild-eyed spacers were gone, the addicts got religion and the federalists became placid anarchists and the Parliaments voted themselves out of existence. There was peace of the third planet of 27 Lambda Serpentis, and good will among the inhabitants thereof. They made love and studied sociology under a friendly sun, under a pleasant blue sky forever.

On the road around space, my Master hungered for land.

And there was a yellow sun in the region of the Scorpion, and once it had been called 18 Scorpii, but now they named it Ba'Lagan. It was a little south of Serpens, a little nearer to the galactic nucleus. They named its planets Albrasa and Nynfi, and they were twins. Albrasa was already populated by a clan of hairy intellectuals with teeth and twittering voices. They liked the flavor of man-flesh, digested it easily.

Man came down on sky-lightning. Man came down to walk on the land and own it. I lay quietly rusting in the rain.

Man taught his grandson to hammer virgin copper into a vicious battle-ax, and taught him the mystic recipe for roasting a hairy intellectual. It was forbidden to boil a young intellectual in the milk of its mother, but it was permissible to roast it alive and remind it that its fathers had dared to attack a two-legged god.

Man's grandson waxed strong and malicious. He committed genocide on the furry natives and used their skins for blankets. He shattered their braincases and erected his own altars in their temples. He butchered an octogenarian on one of the altars, because the old man had made the silly suggestion that they sacrifice a perfectly healthy young virgin to their god. The young virgin watched the ceremony with quietly triumphant eyes; then she married the chief priest and bore him many children.

The biped bludgeoned the planet into submission. He assured himself that he was the Chosen Child of the Most High. He built himself a throne and sat upon it—while he listened to a newscaster describe jet-battles over the North Pole. Centuries wandered by, decked in gaudy robes. And there was a war with Nynfi between the worlds.

And then another Abraham Jolie bent over his drawing board. Another crew of big-fisted men wrapped steel flesh around my principle. Another race of men spat contempt on the soil—the soil that had drunk the blood of their fathers, felt the fire of the suns as the rockets heaved skyward bearing my body and the bodies of my Master.

Men were steel-jacketed motes of flesh, scurrying among the stars. Men were as dust, rolling across the galactic prairie —bits of dandelion fluff whirling in a rising tempest that bore them along the arm of the galactic spiral and inward, ever inward. Their eyes were on Hercules and the fardistant globular clusters. He paused at Nu Lupi and 15 Sagittea and a nameless yellow sun in Ophiuchus where he met a native race who dared to be bipeds. He crushed them quickly.

There were always those who remained behind, lingered on the planets where their ancestors had fought. I watched them with my last eyes as the last ship hurtled into space. I watched, and saw the lust go out of them, saw them become as a cauldron removed from the fire. Their boiling waned to a simmer, and they cooled. They always found peace when the spacers were gone.

This I have never understood. I, the machine, the spacespider, cannot understand. But I have seen it—the exodus of the hungry, the settling of peace over those who chose to linger. The hungry drink of the emptiness of space, and their hunger grows. The placid eat of the earth, and find peace, yet somehow—they seem to die a little.

Ever deeper pressed the starships, deeper into Sagittarius and Scorpius, and Lupus, Ophiuchus and Sagitta. Now and then they paused to colonize and conquer. A planet devoured a handful of men and tormented them with its biolgical devices. But the men grew and beat the savage planet into a slave after long ages, forced it to pay tribute to its king. Once more they coveted the stars. Once more they darted heavenward, leaving reluctant brothers in peace.

They wrote a song. The called it "Ten Parsecs to Paradise." They sang the song as if they believed it. This I have never understood.

It was always ten or twelve parsecs to another sun with a class G spectrum, with a planet chastely clad in green forests and white clouds. There he landed to rebuild, to furrow the fertile earth, to rock in a porch swing at twilight sucking his pipe, and to thoughtfully stare at the stars while his grandchildren romped like young chimpanzees on the cool lawn.

He had forgotten Earth—this old man—his race had forgotten its history. But he knew a little. He knew the stargoing cycle—the landing of the starships, the regression to savagery, the painful rebuilding, the cruelty, the re-learning, the proud exodus. He knew these things because Man had learned to keep a little of the past intact throughout a cycle. He no longer fell back to chipping arrowheads. Now he managed to begin again in an age of bronze or soft iron. And he knew in advance that he would carve mighty industries out of savage wilderness.

But the old man was sad as he sat on his porch. He knew so little of the Great Purpose. Why must his seed fling itself starward? He knew that it *must*—but he lacked a reason. His grandchildren played in the twilight, played space-games, although there was not yet a starship on the planet.

There was a small boy on the lawn who tried to tease the girls, but the girls put on masks of superior sophistication and and ignored the little man. Disgruntled, he looked up and saw the old man dreaming on the porch.

"Gramp's got star-craze!" he shrieked. "Look at Gramp menting! Nnyahh! Gramp's got star-craze."

Musical laughter tittered over the lawn. Another voice took up the cry. The old man chuckled affectionately but wistfully. They were young, but they knew about the star-thirst. The planet was young, too young for star-ships, even though the priests preserved the records and scientific writings in the temples. The planet knew about space and coveted it. Yet, the children would all be dead before the first vessel was launched.

The laughter on the lawn subsided. The eldest child, a gawky and freckled girl of eight years came trudging up the steps to sit against the post and stare at him quietly in the gloom. He felt a question lurking in her silence. He nudged her ribs affectionately with his toe.

"What weighty matter worries you, Nari?" he asked pleasantly.

"Why is star-craze, Gramp?"

He rocked thoughtfully for a moment. "Why are there men to feel it?" he countered.

The child was silent.

"I know only what the priests say, Nari," he told her gently. "They say that man once owned a paradise planet, and that he ran away in search of a better one. They say he made the Lord Bion angry. And the lord hid the paradise, and condemned Man to forever wander, touched his heart with eternal hunger for the place he lost."

"Will people find it again, Gramp?"

"Never—so the priests say. The hunger is on him, Nari."

"It's not fair!" said the little girl.

"What isn't, my child?"

"Star-craze. Last night I saw a lady crying. She was just standing there crying at the sky."

"Where?"

"On the street. Waiting for a motor bus."

"How old was she?"

Nari scraped her heels and muttered doubtfully. "It was kind of dark."

Gramp chuckled reassuringly. "I bet she wasn't over fourteen. I bet she was still a kid. Star-craze comes to little girls about the time they start being interested in little boys. Works the other way, too. But you grow out of it, Nari. By the time you're twenty, it won't make you miserable any more. It gives you a goal. Gives everyone a goal. Something to work for. Something to long for and fight for. The stars—you'll want to give them to your grandchildren."

"Won't I get to go?"

"Not ever, Nari."

They fell silent again, and the old man peered up into the deepening blackness with its countless array of suns sitting like hens on their nests of planets. He scarcely believed the legend of the lost paradise-planet, but it was a good story to tell little girls. It made him sad though, and revived a little of the forgotten restlessness of his youth. If only he could have lived two centuries later—

But then a gust of wind brought the sweet perfume of freshly cut hay from the field to the east of the farmhouse, and the odor made him smile. The field would have to be raked tomorrow, and the hay brought in to the barn. A lot of things like that needed to be done before the starships could rise again. And every straining muscle helped toward the ultimate goal. The hay fed the animals whose flesh fed the men who made the tools which built the factories which fashioned more complicated tools—and so the journey, down the long road to space again.

The old man didn't know why the road had to be traveled, nor did he really care. The road was there, and it beckoned, and it gave meaning to life, for surely the Lord Bion was less cruel a tempter than the priests sometimes proclaimed Him. Surely there was something more than despair at the end of the long, long road.

The old man grew older, and died peacefully, and his ashes were scattered across the fields he had tilled since boyhood. His children, and his grandchildren, followed in his patient steps, and their ashes were mingled with his own before the first gleaming sky-craft burst star-fire in the night.

When the skycraft at last rumbled upward, the crowd thundered a triumphant roar, the crowd gathered to witness the culmination of their labors, and the labors of their ancestors.

Men walked with shoulders erect and with pride glowing in their faces. Again they triumphed over forces that held them bound to a grain of sand in the sky. Again they slashed through the knot that held them in the web of the continuum, and shed the weights that dragged at their feet.

I noticed a subtle difference in those who lingered behind. They no longer lingered of their own choosing. They were no longer the peace-seekers and placid ones. They were those who could not go because they were old, or sick, or because the industries were half-deserted and there was no one left to build the ships. They still stared longingly upward on dark nights.

"We'll do it again," they promised. "We'll repopulate and do it again."

But the bitterness of their plight was upon them, a sense of defeat and doom. They fought savagely among themselves. They fell in feudal wars, while the starward wave receded.

I am the acolyte of the space-priest, the server of the pale proud biped. I have taken him onward across the void, to the Hercules Cluster, and beyond it to the uncharted regions past the dust clouds of the Great Rift, into the star-pact heartland of the galactic nucleus where other races were testing their space wings and tasting of the great freedom. I have watched him, and have felt the life-aura of his longing. And I have wondered. What is his goal? Where is an answer to his hunger?

My neural circuits are not of flesh. My circuits are of glass and steel. My thought is a fanning electron stream. But I have prayed. I, the spider who builds around space, have prayed to the gods of the biped I serve. I have prayed to the God of the North End of Space. I have asked, "Where is his peace?"

No answer came.

I have seen my Master change.

The biped was thunder across the galaxy. The biped was a swift and steel-clad spear hurtling ruthlessly onward. He made no friends; for he came as a being who owned the stars, and he took what he wanted along the way. He left his seed to grow anew. A creature of fierce pride! And fiercer longing. He trampled hatelessly such races as he encountered. He crushed them, or harnessed them to his plow, or borrowed their neural circuits for his bio-computers. Sometimes he fought against his own race, men who had traveled other routes to the galactic heartland. When man battled against man, they fought with hatred and cruelty and bitterness—but never with contempt. Man saw a rival king in man. Against other races, he waged only cool contempt and hot death.

Sometimes a thoughtful old man would say, "Seems to me they've got as much right to live as we have. Seems to me all intelligent creatures have got a common denominator. God, maybe." But he muttered it quietly, speculatively. Even if he believed it, he never objected to the swift ambush of the alien ship, nor to the razing of the alien city. For the biped stalked a new frontier. The ape-tribe stole across a field where danger lurked. He was fresh from the branches of the trees, not wise to the ways of the plains. How could he risk offering peace to the shaggy beast who crouched in the tall grass? He could only weigh the odds—then strike or run away.

He took the planets of the yellow suns—deep in the galactic heartland. He skipped from one to the next in jumps as long as his patience would last. He captured the globular clusters. He inhabited each planet for a few generations. He built ships, and battled with his brothers for the right to take them. Many were left behind. They repopulated after an exodus, rebuilt, launched a second flight, and a third—until those who finally remained at home were those who lacked the incentive of the big hunger.

Those who lacked incentive sought their peace. They molded a pleasant place to live in and infested it. Or else they scorned pleasantry and made themselves a battleground.

My Master is the Nomad, gaunt and tall. My Master grits his teeth in staring at the stars, and his eyes go narrow and moist. I have mirrored his hunger, have allowed his life-aura to seep into the cold steel and hot glass of me, have reflected his thoughts in my circuits. Sometimes he wonders if I am alive. But then he remembers that he built me. He built me to think, not to be alive. Perhaps I am not alive, but only a mirror that catches a little of my Master's life. I have seen him change.

The spearhead groups pushed relentlessly across the gleaming blackness, and each generation grew more restless than the one before it. The restless moved ahead. The contented remained at home. Each exodus was a separation, and a selection of the malcontent.

The biped came to believe his priests. He believed the legend of the lost home. He believed that Bion had touched him with the hunger curse. How else could they explain the pressing cry of the heart? How could they interpret the clamor of the young, the tears—except as a Divine Thirst.

The star-craze. The endless search.

There was a green planet beyond the heartland, and it was ripe for bursting its human star-seed. There was a launching field, and a ship, and teeming crowd, and a fence with guards to keep the others out. A man and a girl stood at the fence and it was nearly dawn.

He touched her arm and gazed at the shadows on the launching site.

"We won't find it, Marka," he said quietly. "We'll never find it."

"You believe the legend, Teris?" she whispered.

"The Planet of Heaven? It's up there. But we can never find it."

"Then why must you look?"

"We are damned, Marka."

There was a silence, then she breathed, "It *can* be found. The Lord Bion promised—"

"Where is *that* written, Marka?" he scoffed coldly.

"In a woman's heart."

Teris laughed loudly. "What does the heart-writing say?"

She turned to stare at the dark shadow of the ship against the graying sky. "It says: 'When Man is content—without his lost paradise—when he reconciles himself—Bion will forgive, and show us the road home.'"

He waved his hand fiercely at the fading stars in the west. *"Ours,* Marka. They're ours! We took them."

"Do you want them?"

He stiffened angrily and glared at the shadow of her face. "You . . . you make me sick. You're a hangbacker."

"No!" She shook her head wildly. *"No!"* She caught at his arm as he retreated a step. "I wish I could go! I want to go, do you hear?"

"I hear," he snapped. "But you can't, so there's no use talking about it. You're not well, Marka. The others wouldn't let you aboard." He backed away another step.

"I love you," she said frantically.

He turned and stumbled away toward the sky-chariot.

"I love you!"

He began to trot, then burst into a wild sprint. Afraid, she thought in triumph. Afraid of turning back. Of loving her too much.

"You'll never find it!" she screamed after him. *"You can't find it up there! It's here—right here!"*

But he was lost in the crowd that milled about the ship. The ship had opened its hatches. The ship was devouring the people, two at a time. The ship devoured Teris and the space crew.

Then it closed its mouth and belched flame from its rockets.

She gasped and slumped against a fencepost. She hung there sobbing until a guard drove her away.

A rocket bellowed the space song. The girl tore off her wedding bracelet and flung it in the gutter. Then she went home to fix breakfast for the children.

I am the Weaver of space. I am a Merchant of new fabrics in flux patterns for five-space continua. I serve the biped who built me, though his heart be steeped in hell.

Once in space, a man looked at me and murmured softly, "You are the cross on which we crucify ourselves."

But the big hunger pushed him on—on toward the ends of space. And he encountered worlds where his ancestors had lived, and where his peaceful cousins still dwelt in symbiosis with their neighbors. Some of the worlds were civilized, some barbaric, and some were archaeological graveyards. My nomads, they wore haunted faces as they re-explored the fringes of the galaxy where Man had walked before, leaving his footprints and his peace-seeking children. The galaxy was filled.

Where could he go now?

I have seen the frantic despair in their faces when, upon landing, natives appeared and greeted them politely, or tried to kill them, or worshiped them, or just ran away to hide. The nomads lurked near their ships. A planet with teeming cities was no place for a wanderer. They watched the multifaceted civilizations with bitter, lonely eyes.

Where were new planets?

Across the great emptiness to the Andromeda galaxy? Too far for the ships to go. Out to the Magellanic clouds? Already visited.

Where then?

He groped blindly, this biped. He had forgotten the trail by which his ancestors had come, and he kept recrossing it, finding it winding everywhere. He could only plunge aimlessly on, and when he reached the last limit of his fuel—land. If the natives could not provide the fuel, he would have to stay, and try to pass another cycle of starward growth on the already inhabited world. But a cycle was seldom completed. The nomads intermarried with the local people; the children, the hybrid children, were less steeped in hunger than their fathers. Sometimes they built ships for economic purposes, for trade and commerce—but never for the hysterical starward sweep. They heard no music from the North End of Space, no Lorelei call from the void. The craving was slowly dying.

They came to a planet. The natives called it "Earth." They departed again in cold fright, and a space commander blew out his brains to banish the memory. Then they found another planet that called itself "Earth"—and another and another. They smiled again, knowing that they would never know which was the true home of Man.

They sensed the nearness of the end.

They no longer sang the old songs of a forgotten paradise. And there were no priests among them. They looked back at the Milky Way, and it had been their royal road. They looked ahead, where only scattered stars separated them from the intergalactic wasteland—an ocean of emptiness and death. They could not consign themselves to its ultimate embrace. They had fought too long, labored too hard to surrender willingly to extinction.

But the cup of their life was broken.

And to the land's last limit they came.

They found a planet with a single moon, with green forests, with thin clouds draping her gold and blue body in the sunlight. The breath of the snowking was white on her ice caps, and her seas were placid green. They landed. They smiled when the natives called the planet "Earth." Lots of planets claimed the distinction of being Man's birthplace.

Among the natives there was a dumpy little professor—still human, though slightly evolved. On the night following the nomad's landing, he sat huddled in an easy-chair, staring at the gaunt nomadic giant whose bald head nearly touched the ceiling of the professor's library. The professor slowly shook his head and sighed.

"I can't understand you people."

"Nor I you," rumbled the nomad.

"Here is Earth—yet you won't believe it!"

The giant snorted contemptuously. "Who cares? Is this crumb in space the fulfillment of a dream?"

"You dreamed of a lost Earthparadise."

"So we thought. But who knows the real longing of a dream? Where is its end? Its goal?"

"We found ours here on Earth."

The giant made a wry mouth. "You've found nothing but your own smug existence. You're a snake swallowing its tail."

"Are you sure you're not the same?" purred the scholar.

The giant put his fists on his hips and glowered at him. The professor whitened.

"That's untrue." boomed the giant. "We've found nothing.

And we're through. At least we went searching. Now we're finished."

"Not *you*. It's the j*ob* that's finished. You can live here. And be proud of a job well done."

The giant frowned. "Job? *What* job?"

"Why, fencing in the stars. Populating the galaxy."

The big man stared at him in horrified amazement.

"Well," the scholar insisted, "you did it, you know. Who populates the galaxy now?"

"*People like you.*"

The impact of the searing words brought a sick gasp from the small professor. He was a long moment in realizing their full significance. He wilted. He sank lower in the chair.

The nomad's laughter suddenly rocked the room. He turned away from his victim and helped himself to a tumbler of liqueur. He downed it at a gulp and grinned at the professor. He tucked the professor's liqueur under his arm, waved a jaunty farewell, and lumbered out into the night.

"My decanter," protested the professor in a whisper.

He went to bed and lay whimpering slightly in drowsiness. He was afraid of the tomorrows that lay ahead.

The nomads settled on the planet for lack of fuel. They complained of the climate and steadfastly refused to believe that it was Earth. They were a troublesome, boisterous lot, and frequently needed psychoanalysis for their various crimes. A provisional government was set up to deal with the problem. The natives had forgotten about governments, and they called it a "welfare commission."

The nomads who were single kidnaped native wives. Sometimes they kidnaped several, being a prolific lot. They begot many children, and a third-generation hybrid became the first dictator of a northern continent.

I am rusting in the rain. I shall never serve my priest here on Earth again. Nuclear fuels are scarce. They are needed for the atomic warheads now zipping back and forth across the North Pole. A poet—one of the hybrids—has written immortal lines deploring war; and the lines were inscribed on the posthumous medal they gave his widow.

Three dumpy idealists built a spaceship, but they were caught and hung for treason. The eight-foot lawyer who defended them was also hung.

The world wears a long face; and the stars twinkle invitingly. But few men look upward now. Things are probably just as bad on the next inhabited planet.

I am the spider who walked around space. I, Harpist for a pale proud Master, have seen the big hunger, have tasted its red glow reflected in my circuits. Still I cannot understand.

But I feel there are some who understand. I have seen the pride in their faces. They walk like kings.